## "WHAT ARE YOU TRYING TO TELL ME, CLAIRE?"

Claire hesitated. "I suppose I've always known that Lakeport isn't big enough to hold both of us, King, even for a little while."

Something flickered in King's blue eyes, an emotion that Claire couldn't identify. "I disagree. As far as I'm concerned, Lakeport is more than big enough to hold both of us. There's no need to get in each other's way, that's all."

Claire felt that King was looking down on her from a vast height. He said, "A man only needs to be left at the altar once, Claire. It's been a long time since memories of you have had the power to affect me, and that's the way I want to keep it. Does that reassure you?"

And as King walked away, a single tear rolled down Claire's cheek.

## ABOUT THE AUTHOR

This wonderfully moody love story is
Meg Hudson's thirteenth Superromance! Like the
heroine in *The Forever Promise*, Meg spent many
childhood summers in the Lake Champlain region
of New York, and the area remains one of her
favorites.

# Books by Meg Hudson

These books may be available at your local bookseller.

Don't miss any of our special offers. Write to us at the
following address for information on our newest releases.

Harlequin Reader Service
901 Fuhrmann Blvd., P.O. Box 1397, Buffalo, NY 14240
Canadian address: P.O. Box 603,
Fort Erie, Ont. L2A 5X3

**Meg Hudson**

# THE FOREVER PROMISE

*Harlequin Books*

TORONTO • NEW YORK • LONDON
AMSTERDAM • PARIS • SYDNEY • HAMBURG
STOCKHOLM • ATHENS • TOKYO • MILAN

Published November 1986

First printing September 1986

ISBN 0-373-70234-5

Printed in Canada

Kay is not Ellie . . . and
Meg is not Claire . . . but
this book is, nevertheless,
dedicated to Kay, and she
will know why.

# CHAPTER ONE

THE HOUSE LOOKED shabby. Claire winced as she noted
the sagging steps that led to the wide front porch, the
clapboard's chipped white paint and the missing slats on
the shutters that flanked the tall, elegant windows. Already reluctant, already questioning the wisdom of having come to Lakeport at all, she hesitated before opening
the door of her rented car. But it was too late to turn
back.

The rosebushes Aunt Delia had planted many years
ago still bordered the front walk. But they, too, had been
neglected. The leaves were studded with black spot and
the flowers, lacking nourishment, drooped from slender
stems. Surveying them, Claire asked herself sharply what
she had expected to find on this strange homecoming.
The old familiar perfection?

She reminded herself that she had done nothing to help
keep things up. She'd turned her back on this place. And,
in a sense, on Lakeport, a lovely old northern New York
town nestled along the shore of Lake Champlain. She'd
escaped fourteen years ago, on the day that was to have
been her wedding day. And since Aunt Delia's death—
now five years in the past—it had all been left up to Ellie.

As if thinking of Ellie was enough to conjure her into
being, she appeared. There was a moment of constraint
as the two cousins stared at each other through the screen

door. Then Ellie flung the door open and they fell into each other's arms, tears staining their cheeks as they hugged tightly.

Ellie pulled away first, pushing Claire out to arm's length. She studied her with those beautiful dark eyes that possessed the ability to see things straight through to their core.

"You're lovelier than ever!" Ellie breathed, and Claire knew that Ellie's compliment was sincere. Ellie had never been frivolous when it came to using words—or much of anything else, for that matter.

Claire surveyed her cousin and her eyes misted. Ellie had a wonderful face, as open and honest as the sun on a bright day. But the years had taken their toll. Though there was only a few months difference in their ages, Ellie looked several long years the elder. As a teenager she'd been plump, but now she was decidedly overweight, her ample figure straining at the seams of her blue cotton dress. Strands of gray mixed with her dark-brown hair, and she wasn't wearing a touch of makeup.

Claire became acutely aware of her own appearance, and the thought of the impression she must be making on her cousin made her feel uncharacteristically self-conscious. Her pale-green dress was straight from the pages of a fashion magazine, the color bringing out the coppery highlights in her shoulder-length, naturally wavy chestnut hair. Her figure was even better than it had been fourteen years ago. She weighed perhaps five pounds less now, this accentuating, rather than diminishing, the lovely proportions of her body. Her makeup, as always, was faultless. Subtle silvery shadow enhanced the clear gray of her eyes, while a touch of rose blush highlighted the contours of her cheeks. A matching rose gloss emphasized the generous fullness of her mouth. Because she usually met the public on a daily basis in the course of her work and *had* to make a good appearance, Claire had learned long ago how to use makeup to maximum advantage.

Ellie thrust a generous arm around her and drew her through the doorway. Once they were in the wide foyer she said, a catch in her voice, "Oh, Claire, it's so good to have you here. It's been so long! We have so much to catch up on."

There was unspoken volume in Ellie's words, and Claire silently conceded that they very much needed to catch up with each other. Yet she was certain Ellie would not reproach her for the omissions. The many, many omissions studding the fourteen years since they had seen each other last.

"Let's have a cup of tea before we do anything else," Ellie suggested happily.

Claire murmured agreement, following her cousin down the long hall, past the curving staircase, through the dining room and into the kitchen.

Along the way, she purposefully avoided glancing left into the Orchestra Room, which had been an integral part of the Parmeter School of Music for the better part of a century. The last time she'd seen that room it had been converted into a wonderland of white flowers and satin ribbons in preparation for her wedding. A wedding that had never taken place.

During the brief pilgrimage through the center of the house, Claire could not help but notice the water stains on the dining-room ceiling, the worn condition of the oak floors and, in places, the paper peeling off the walls.

The big kitchen she remembered so well—the source of the wonderful aromas her Aunt Delia had been forever conjuring up—looked old-fashioned and dingy to her now. But Ellie's hospitality overcame the setting as she made tea and set out a plate of freshly baked cookies.

The tea poured, Ellie adjusted her ample body to fit more comfortably on the straight-backed chair. Then she sighed with satisfaction and, smiling broadly at Claire, asked, "Well, where shall we begin?"

Claire's mind went blank. She made a business of squeezing the juice from a slice of lemon into her tea, stalling, then realized she felt empty, drained...and more than a little afraid.

This place held too many memories, and as she had feared they might, some of those memories began to rush in. Suddenly she felt as if she had become a human dam and the floodgates were about to break.

Ellie said gently, "Claire, there's no need to look like that," and Claire realized that her apprehensions, her *traumas*, must be showing. "We don't have to go back."

Something lodged in Claire's throat. A lump, a knot. She tried to swallow, but it wouldn't budge. She said uncertainly, "I'm not so sure about that."

"Well, I am," Ellie stated firmly. "Don't you think I know how hard it must be for you to come here? And you've come only to help me out. Don't you think I know that and appreciate it more than I can ever tell you?"

"Ellie..."

Ellie shook her head. "There's no need for you to feel guilty about anything. What's done is done. Believe me, I can understand why you never could bring yourself to come back...until now."

Ellie reached for a sugar cookie and took a bite. Then she said slowly, "I hated to ask you to come back at all, Claire. But besides needing you, I wanted so much to see you."

Claire felt a rush of love for this cousin who had been such an important part of her growing-up years and answered impulsively, "We should never have gone for so long without seeing each other, Ellie. We should have arranged to meet each other."

"Most of the time, I couldn't have gotten away," Ellie said frankly. "And since March, when Dad died, I've had my hands full."

Claire thought about her Uncle Ralph—Ellie's father. And about David Parmeter, their mutual grandfather. And their aunts, Delia and Charlotte. They all had been present that morning fourteen years ago when she had left. Now the house seemed so empty without them.

She asked, "What about Thomas Haskell, Ellie? Is he really out to make trouble?"

Ellie nodded. "He says he didn't want to spring this while Dad was still alive," she said. "Dad had life tenancy in this property. There really was nothing that could be done while he was living.

"I don't think Thomas expected Dad to live as long as he did," she added bitterly. "He'd had a serious kidney problem for years, and as he grew older there were complications with his heart, too. But he hung on.

"I know Dad always tended to live in a dreamworld," Ellie continued, somewhat defensively. "But he had his own special stamina, an inner strength that Thomas never expected. Anyway, Thomas claims he has this will—"

"A will?" Claire cut in, startled.

"Aunt Lottie made a new will a few days before she died. At least, that's what Thomas claims."

"And..."

"She made him executor of her estate," Ellie explained. "So he has the power to liquidate her assets. I think that's the way they put it."

"And what were her assets?" Claire asked. "She moved out of here a long time ago, when she and Thomas bought the place out on the point, right?" Claire was remembering this from what Ellie's letters over the years had told her.

"Yes." Ellie nodded. "Aunt Lottie and Thomas moved out to the point eight years ago. But legally she still owned a good share of this property. Grandfather left it equally to his three living children. Aunt Delia left her share to be divided between my father and Aunt Lottie. So Lottie still owned her own share and half of Aunt Delia's when she died."

"Two years ago?"

"Yes," Ellie said. "Two years ago."

"Didn't you tell me that as far as the things in the house are concerned, Aunt Lottie took what she rightfully owned with her when she moved?"

"She took a lot," Ellie admitted. "Furniture, paintings and most of the silver and china. She and Aunt Delia had some pretty nasty arguments about that. Aunt Delia insisted the contents of the house were all Parmeter things, and that at least some belonged to you."

Claire smiled slightly. "I never wanted any of the family treasures, Ellie," she said honestly. "For that matter, I don't deserve any of them. You should have anything there is to have. If it were enough to stock a museum, it still wouldn't repay you . . ."

Claire ran out of words. She was keenly aware that Ellie had given up some of the best years of her life for the family. Certainly, she had given up her youth. She had stayed in Lakeport to care for both her father and his older sister. And, in a sense, for Charlotte Parmeter Haskell, as well. Claire couldn't believe that Aunt Lottie ever had fully relied on the man she had married when she was in her early fifties—when he was only thirty-nine.

She remembered vividly that spring when she was almost sixteen and—soon after her parents' death—had come to live here in her grandfather's house. Thomas, who had been married to Lottie only a few months, made a pass at her. He'd been drinking and later he apologized, blaming his behavior on the liquor. But Claire had retorted that if he ever touched her again she would tell her aunt. He had not touched her again.

That was eighteen years ago. Thomas Haskell had been a big, aggressively handsome man. Today, Claire calculated, he would be in his late fifties. A widower, about to cash in on a potentially valuable legacy, from what Ellie was implying.

She said, "I hope you've retained a good attorney, Ellie."

"Yes, I have. Bill Edgerly."

Claire glanced up sharply. Ellie and Bill Edgerly had gone steady for a while when they were both in their teens. If her memory was correct, it was Ellie who had brought the relationship to an end. For a long time afterward, Bill had gone around town wearing his broken heart on his sleeve.

Ellie had never explained why she'd told Bill she didn't want to see him any longer. She'd hinted she was in love with someone else, but the identity of the mysterious "someone" had been so secret she wouldn't confide it even to Claire.

At times, Claire had suspected the object of Ellie's unrequited love might be King.

Her King.

The lump filled her throat again, and a hasty sip of tea failed to budge it. Suddenly she yearned to ask Ellie about King. She yearned to let the questions flow . . . but she knew she wasn't ready to hear the answers.

King, thank God, was undoubtedly far, far away, or Ellie would have mentioned him in her letters. Trying another sip of tea and swallowing hard, Claire warned herself that the less she learned about King the better, for her own peace of mind.

She blinked, trying to refocus her thoughts, and said, "I didn't know Bill Edgerly had become a lawyer."

"He went to the state university and then on to law school," Ellie said. "He practiced in Albany for a few years, then decided to come back here." She added slowly, "He married an Albany girl, but she died after a long bout with cancer. It was very sad."

Claire shuddered at this; she'd lost her own husband to cancer. "Did they have any children?" she asked.

"No." Ellie paused then added, "Bill's sister Stella keeps house for him. She never married."

Ellie reached for another cookie. "Anyway," she said, "Bill is going to represent both of us."

"Both of us?"

"Yes, you and me."

Claire shook her head. "I don't need a lawyer, Ellie," she protested. "I'm here only to uphold your case."

"Half of everything in this place should be yours, Claire," Ellie insisted stubbornly. "If I didn't believe that, I wouldn't have the interest in fighting Thomas that I have. Anyway, Bill wants to talk to you." Ellie smiled. "Let's not get into any arguments about family rights till we've met with him, okay?"

Claire returned her cousin's smile. "All right," she agreed reluctantly. "If you say so."

"I say so. Now, shall we get your things out of the car before it gets dark?"

It was early June, and summer was just beginning to edge into northern New York State. Still, it wouldn't be dark for a while. There was plenty of time to bring in her luggage. Nevertheless, Claire was glad to interrupt their conversation. She needed to draw a few deep breaths.

Claire took her suitcase and the couple of tote bags filled with odds and ends out of the car trunk. Then Ellie helped her lug everything up the curving staircase.

Each step Claire took became a journey back in time, sorrow and nostalgia blending to make the small safari very difficult. They had just reached the second-floor landing when the phone rang. Ellie said hastily, "I've put you in the yellow room. It used to be Aunt Delia's, remember?" She added, "I'll answer the phone, then I'll be right back."

Claire nodded and headed for the back corner room where, fourteen years ago, the beautiful wedding gown that had been her great-grandmother's had been spread out on Aunt Delia's bed.

Her memories were shaking her physically as well as emotionally as she stepped over the threshold, and it didn't help when she walked to the back window and stared out over the garden that had once been so beautiful but was now overgrown and neglected.

The dollhouse was still there.

Claire shivered. She had hoped that it had been torn down. Seeing it now was so overwhelming that she stepped back, as if retreating from a physical blow.

The dollhouse was a miniature cottage. It had been built for Ellie's and Claire's great-grandmother in an era when living was easier and far more gracious. The little house was a delight to a child. The furnishings were scaled to proportions that in some instances were just right for children and in others just right for dolls.

Gazing out at the lovely little playhouse, Claire remembered the wonderful, rainy summer afternoons when she and Ellie would join their dolls in the ritual of a solemn high tea. Later, as young girls, the dollhouse had become a place where confidences were exchanged. Away from the big house and the restricting presence of adults, it was the perfect forum for revealing delightful, delicious secrets.

It was in the dollhouse that Claire, at the age of eighteen, had first told Ellie she loved King Faraday.

She made this confidence on the Sunday afternoon following the high-school senior prom. Claire had been King's date at the prom. She'd worn a pink net dress and high-heeled satin sandals, dyed to match, and King had sent her a wrist corsage of deep pink roses. She later pressed the roses in an old novel she'd found in the back parlor. It occurred to her that very possibly they were still in the book, the petals turned brown, the flowers as withered as her love for King.

Behind her, she heard Ellie's footsteps. Ellie appeared and said somewhat breathlessly, "That was Mrs. Brinkley, over on Court Street. Nothing special." She glanced around the room and added, "I thought you'd be more comfortable in here."

In older days, Claire and Ellie had slept on the third floor of the big house. The second-floor bedrooms had been for the grown-ups, with the exception of the large front room, which had been converted into a music studio for Uncle Ralph.

Ellie said wistfully, "This room's in better shape than most of the others. I've been wanting to have some work done around the house. Everything needs painting or papering."

There was no need for Ellie to apologize. Claire didn't want her to apologize. She only wished Ellie had elected to share more with her in those letters that had spanned the years. If she had suspected there was a financial struggle going on, she could have helped. She would have been *glad* to have helped.

She said, almost curtly, "Ellie, I'd say you've never had much time to worry about interior decorating. Nor, probably, enough money, in recent years."

"Money *has* been tight ever since Grandfather died," Ellie allowed ruefully.

"How long ago did he die?" Claire asked, ashamed that she couldn't remember the exact year. But they had all died since she'd left. Grandfather, then Aunt Delia, then Aunt Lottie, then Uncle Ralph...

"Nearly twelve years ago," Ellie said. "But Grandfather was sick for a long time and in the hospital for several months. All that put a big dent in the family finances." Ellie managed a smile. "He never gave thought to anything like medical or hospital insurance."

Nor had any of the rest of the Parmeters, Claire felt sure. They had all been musicians, dreamers, living to a large extent on the family heritage of which they had such an abundance. David Parmeter had held the purse strings. And certainly, in his time, this place had been maintained to the hilt. But it was easy to understand how the decline had set in.

Ellie said thoughtfully, "It would have helped if Aunt Delia had let me sell a few things from time to time. But she never wanted to part with anything, and after she died Aunt Lottie was just as bad. And she had a lot of influence on Dad."

Ellie sighed. "I can't tell you how many times we've been approached by antique dealers who asked if we'd consider parting with some of the Sandwich glass, or the Tiffany pieces, or the Limoges. To say nothing of some of the paintings. Bill insisted that I make a start on having the things appraised. You wouldn't believe what some of those paintings in the Orchestra Room are valued at.''

"I can imagine." Claire nodded. She could imagine very well, because art was her business. Her galleries, one in New York and one in Florida, were highly successful.

She remembered each painting in the Orchestra Room vividly. Actually, she remembered the Orchestra Room *too* well. It was still painful to think about it because the vision of the room, as she'd last seen it, was such an ingrained mental picture. She couldn't fathom how she was going to garner enough courage to venture into that part of the house.

The huge square room occupied most of the left side of the ground floor. It had been named the Orchestra Room because the Lakeport Symphony Orchestra used it for their practice sessions. The actual concerts were given in the high-school auditorium.

Claire could remember going to the symphony concerts when her grandfather had been the conductor. After his death, Delia had taken over the baton. Delia had continued as the orchestra's impresario until her arthritis got so bad that her brother Ralph, Ellie's father, had been forced into service. Ralph had not enjoyed being in the limelight. Claire could remember him playing hauntingly beautiful cello solos in his studio when he thought there was no one around.

After Delia died, Ralph had persuaded Ellie to assume the conducting task.

Now Claire asked, "Does the orchestra still practice here in the house, Ellie? Are you still conducting?''

Ellie sat down on the edge of the bed and thrust her plump legs out in front of her. "Yes to both questions," she said. "We had the last concert just a week ago. It was a memorial to Dad, really. That's what he wanted. Now, well..."

"Yes?" Claire urged.

"We've never practiced in the summer," Ellie said. "The first rehearsal's always been the Wednesday after Labor Day. But this year, when September comes...I really don't want to do it, Claire."

Claire looked at her cousin, thought of her bearing the responsibility for this house and the remaining members of the Parmeter family over the years and felt a pang of sympathy mixed with guilt.

"If you don't want to keep on with the orchestra, don't!" she advised, her tone sharper than she intended.

Ellie smiled sadly. "That's easy to say."

"But not easy to do? Why not, Ellie? You have only yourself to account to now."

"No," Ellie contradicted. "I don't feel that way about it. For nearly a hundred years Parmeters have dedicated themselves to bringing music—good music—not just to Lakeport but to the whole Champlain Valley. Some of the students Dad and Aunt Delia and Aunt Lottie taught went on to Juilliard or other music schools and made names for themselves in the music world. Before that, some of Grandfather's students—"

"I know, I know," Claire interposed wearily. "But times change. There comes a point when someone else should pick up the torch. I'd say you've done enough, Ellie. It's your turn to lead your own life."

"Is it?" Ellie asked. She shook her head slightly. "I don't know. I guess I don't know what I'd do with myself if I didn't have something to cling to, some link with

the past. I'm not like you, Claire. I've never been independent. I always needed to have the family to fall back
on.''

"I'd say the family fell back on you.''

"Maybe. But I think, subconsciously, that's the way I
wanted it. I encouraged them, Claire. You and I . . . well,
when we were growing up I felt as close to you as I would
have to a sister. But I knew then, just as I know now, that
we're very different.'' Ellie forced a smile. "Look at us,''
she invited. "You're a fashion plate, modern as tomorrow. I'm an old shoe.''

Claire frowned. "I'm not going to listen to you put
yourself down,'' she threatened.

Ellie's attempt at a laugh was hollow. "I'm not putting myself down,'' she said. "I'm just telling it like it is.
You come by your spirit naturally, Claire. It was your
father who broke away in the first place. . . .''

That was true enough. Gerard Parmeter left Lakeport
for college and never returned to stay. He'd turned his
back firmly on a musical career, to his father's undying
displeasure, and instead had studied business and fi-
nance, an incomprehensible choice to the rest of his
family. After graduation, he had joined a brokerage firm
in New York and married a wealthy city girl. Lakeport
had become a place for vacations—brief vacations—on
Gerard's part.

Often, after spending a few days in Lakeport, Claire's
parents left her behind while they went off to Europe or
to the Orient or on an exotic cruise. By then her mother,
Louise, had come into a large inheritance, so there was
ample money available for those frequent trips. They always came back to reclaim Claire when it was time for her
to return to New York before going off to boarding
school in Virginia. Those had been happy occasions for

both Claire and Ellie. Gerard and Louise never failed to arrive bearing gifts, lovely works of art for the adults and enchanting surprises for the two young girls.

Claire had loved the surprises, but neither they nor anything else her parents did for her filled the empty spaces deep inside her. Gerard and Louise had loved her, she supposed, but they never really included her in their lives. Often she had felt like a stumbling block, actually in their way when the three of them had been together. So, perversely, she had become a demanding child in her bid for their attention. Spoiled, to a point...and very lonely.

It was on a helicopter flight between two islands in the South Pacific that Gerard and Louise lost their lives. Their helicopter had crashed into an extinct volcano they were exploring en route. Claire had been just two months short of her sixteenth birthday.

Uncle Ralph and Aunt Delia had come to the boarding school to get her for the memorial service in New York. Then they had driven back to Lakeport. Claire had been aware that they were worried about her. She had spoken few words and shed no tears. But that night, alone with Ellie, she'd let go. And she would always remember how Ellie had crawled into bed with her, hugged her close and promised, "You'll always have me, Claire. I'll never let you down."

Even at sixteen Claire knew that her grandfather, for a long time, had disapproved of everything his younger son had done. David Parmeter seemed to believe that Gerard had been responsible for his own death, if only because of the folly of his ways. As a consequence, though he was kind to Claire, there was a reserve in his attitude toward her that was especially chilling during those first weeks after her bereavement. Her aunts were also kind, but for a long time she found it impossible to relate closely to them. Their world and the world in which she had been brought up were simply too different. And her Uncle Ralph was something of a phantom figure. A remote, romantic presence whom everyone said had never stopped grieving for his beautiful wife who had died giving birth to Ellie. So, at that time in her life, Claire had felt that Ellie was the only person in the world entirely on her side.

Though her parents had gone through the better part of both her mother's money and her father's investment earnings, she still received a fairly large inheritance. It had been left in trust for her, her father naming a business partner the executor of both his and his wife's estates. Income from the trust had been paid to David Parmeter in the first years to take care of Claire's living expenses and her education. She had not received the bulk of her inheritance until she was twenty-five.

Thoughts about all of these things filled Claire's mind as she unpacked, aware that Ellie, still sitting on the bed behind her, must be thinking similar thoughts of her own.

She sighed as she finished hanging the last of the dresses she had brought with her in the closet. Then she turned to her cousin with a brisk, "There." Feigning a cheerfulness she was far from feeling, she said, "I want you to be my guest at dinner tonight, Ellie. Let's go to the fanciest place around."

Ellie looked horrified. "I made chicken fricassee," she managed, "just like Aunt Delia used to make. Your favorite, remember? And there are spiced currants to go with it, and hot biscuits."

Claire was tempted to protest, to suggest that the chicken fricassee could be saved for tomorrow night. But she saw she would be doing Ellie no favors by insisting they go out.

"That's too great a temptation to resist," she said warmly, and was rewarded by Ellie's smile.

The smile quickly became conspiratorial. "When Dad died," Ellie said, "people brought over all sorts of things. Among them, a couple of bottles of good sherry. How about a glass?"

"Why not?" Claire agreed.

"Why not, indeed!"

The old camaraderie bonded them as they descended the creaking wooden staircase. In the kitchen, the big oak table and the matching chairs and wall cabinets were highlighted by the golden rays of the descending sun.

"Pull the shades down a little, will you, Claire?" Ellie asked, busy with the sherry and two wineglasses. "That light hits you right in the eyes this time of day."

Claire crossed to the windows that faced west, like those of the yellow bedroom upstairs, and again looked out over the back garden. It had been June then, too, she remembered bitterly. The roses had been in bloom, as they were now. She felt bathed in the sweet scent carried to her by the gentle breezes of the early summer evening.

On that long-ago June morning, she'd also felt enveloped in the scent of roses. She'd been so happy, so much in love, wrapped in the delusion that everything was right with her world.

Claire turned quickly, not wanting to smell the roses or to think about that other June day. At that instant Ellie looked up and their eyes met, and obviously Ellie was deeply troubled.

Claire watched as Ellie drew a deep breath and noticed that her hands were trembling as she set the glasses of sherry on the oak table. But regardless of these small signs she was in no way prepared when Ellie said, "I hate to have to tell you this, but it's too risky to keep it from you. This is a small town. Maybe you won't run into each other, but I don't want to chance it."

Ellie drew another deep breath. "More than a year ago," she said, her voice shaking, "King came back to stay."

## CHAPTER TWO

KING FARADAY. Here, in Lakeport?

Claire felt her strength seep out of her.

Ellie said, "Claire, you've gone white as a ghost. I didn't know how else to tell you except to come straight out with it."

"It's all right," Claire said, her voice controlled, sanity returning. "It really *is* all right," she emphasized, to reassure herself as well as Ellie.

But again the questions, long simmering, began to churn their way to the surface of Claire's thoughts. All these years, King Faraday had been a taboo subject between Ellie and herself. When a dozen years ago Ellie had written to say, "King has left town," Claire had written in reply, "Please. I don't want to hear about him. Never mention his name to me again!" And Ellie had abided by that.

Later, much later, it no longer would have mattered. Claire had put her life together again; she had entered other spheres. Gradually, as the scope of her interests, activities and accomplishments increased, she had been able to forget about King. Nevertheless, she had maintained a definite silence with Ellie where he was concerned. Or perhaps more accurately, Ellie had maintained the silence with her.

"Claire," Ellie said, her usually smooth brow furrowed, "I decided just today that I had to tell you. No one sees much of King these days, so you probably wouldn't bump into each other around town. But there's always a chance. Anyway, I thought it would be less of a shock if you knew.''

"You're right," Claire managed, making the comment sound casual. Then she permitted herself the luxury of posing one of the churning questions. "Why did he come back, Ellie?''

"Because of his father. Dr. Faraday had a stroke the winter before last.''

Claire flinched, thinking of George Faraday. He had been a tall, fine-looking man, always so upright and, generally speaking, so unbending. But he'd made a concession to her, considering what he thought of women in general. He had been kind to her. And she had looked forward to having him as her father-in-law, sure that in time they would have achieved a good rapport.

She could imagine his subsequent bitterness toward her after she had run away. Her act must have been a confirmation of everything he felt about the opposite sex.

She asked, "Did Dr. Faraday recover from the stroke?''

"Yes—" Ellie nodded "—remarkably well. He has to use a cane, but aside from that he's fine. And his mind is as sharp as ever. King returned while his father was in the hospital. Finally, he decided to move back. He and his father live together in the old house on Elm Street.''

An extraneous memory nudged. Claire asked, "Does King's Uncle James still have the pharmacy?''

Faraday's Pharmacy had been a town landmark, located on the corner of Main and Helen streets. The pharmacy's soda fountain had played an important role in Claire's last two years of high school, spent in Lakeport. She and King, she remembered, had stopped for a cherry Coke on their first date....

"Yes," Ellie said, "Mr. Faraday still owns the pharmacy, but he's semiretired. Whenever an extra hand is needed, he goes in. And King—"

Whatever Ellie had been about to say concerning King was halted by the peal of the front doorbell.

"That must be Bill," Ellie said quickly. "He knew you were coming today, and he's anxious to talk to both of us." Ellie was walking toward the kitchen door as she spoke, but Claire stood where she was and listened to her cousin's footsteps thud down the hallway. When Ellie returned a moment later, Bill Edgerly was trailing behind her.

Bill was even thinner than Claire remembered. As a youth he'd been tall, gangling and awkward. Now, though he hadn't filled out, he'd obviously come to terms with his body. He moved easily across the kitchen, his hand outstretched.

Claire gripped it warmly. She had always liked Bill, his rugged, homely face, reddish hair, freckles and discerning green eyes.

He said with a smile, "Well, it's good to see you."

"And it's good to see you, too."

"Been a long time."

"We were about to have some before-dinner sherry," Ellie said. "Would you care for a glass?"

"Sherry would be fine."

Ellie, getting out a third wineglass, asked, "Can you stay for supper, Bill?"

"Hey," he protested, laughing as he spoke, "I didn't show up at this hour with the idea of wangling a dinner invitation."

"We'd like to have you," Ellie said. "If Stella's not expecting you, that is."

"Stella planned to catch the early show at the movies," Bill said. "I would have been ferreting for myself tonight."

The three took seats around the kitchen table. Claire wondered briefly if Bill might say something about King Faraday, then told herself he was too much of a diplomat to bring up a subject he knew would be painful. Even as a youngster, Bill had shown remarkable compassion and consideration for other people's feelings.

After they'd covered a few generalities, Bill said, "I'm sorry it was something like this situation with Thomas Haskell that brought you back to Lakeport, Claire. I wish you could have come back under happier circumstances."

"I wish so, too, Bill," Claire admitted. "I especially wish Ellie didn't have to face any unpleasantness with Thomas."

"Well, he's out to get as much as he can get," Bill stated flatly. "There's no point hedging about that. He feels he deserves it. Claims he took care of Lottie during those last months when she was so sick and couldn't do anything for herself."

"That's true," Ellie interrupted. "They were living out on the point, of course. I couldn't go out there to help with her because I had Dad to take care of. I suggested that Thomas bring her here, but he wouldn't even consider it."

"What did Aunt Lottie say?" Claire asked gently.

"We never got a chance to talk alone once she was bedridden," Ellie confessed. "Thomas was always right there. The more I think about it, it seems he wanted to make sure she didn't get the opportunity to say anything important to me. Then, toward the end, she was out of it most of the time, Claire. She would just...ramble. And before I'd been with her very long, Thomas would say, 'I think Lottie's getting tired, Ellie. Maybe you'd better leave.'"

"I can imagine," Bill Edgerly said, his voice grim. "I know damned well that Lottie never intended to cut you or Claire out of anything, and whether there's any validity to that will he's talking about, I still don't know. But even if there is, we're not going to quit without a fight, Claire."

"I'm not involved in this," Claire said quickly. "I'm here only to back up Ellie, Bill...to help her in any way I can."

"You can't get out of it that easily," Bill returned seriously. "In Ellie's opinion, and mine, too, you have a rightful legal interest in the contents of this house, if not in the property itself. It was your father's homestead also, remember. True, when your grandfather died he left this property to his three living children—Delia, Charlotte and Ralph—and neither you nor Ellie were mentioned in his will. But—"

"He wouldn't have mentioned me," Claire stated, a trace of bitterness edging her voice. "Grandfather never forgave my father for leaving Lakeport, Bill."

"I realize that. Nevertheless, your father *was* a rightful heir. As you are, being his surviving child." He smiled wryly. "Your grandfather never took the precaution of disinheriting you in his will, Claire, or of writing you off by leaving you a token dollar. Ellie, of course, inherited her father's share of everything." He paused. "But we can get into details about this at a later time."

"I don't want to get into it," Claire said unhappily.

"Claire," Ellie said, "it's just a question of our dividing up some of the family things. I want you to have them." She looked at Bill and added, "I think you know that Claire and I won't have any problems about who gets what."

"I'm sure you won't," Bill Edgerly agreed, "so let's take this a step further. When Lottie and Thomas built their place on the point, Lottie took a number of valuables with her, evidently with Delia's reluctant permission. Well, shortly after Delia's death I drew up a will for Lottie. She left her interest in this land and house to Thomas, but she said nothing about the contents of the house or the family heirlooms she took with her to the point. The problem now is that Thomas Haskell claims half of *everything* belongs to him." Bill held out his empty wineglass to Ellie and grinned. "Families drive me crazy," he admitted disarmingly.

"*This* family has been driving me crazy ever since I can remember!" Ellie blurted.

Bill cast a long and knowing glance in her direction, then winked at Claire. "So now it comes out," he observed.

Claire was trying to sort out the facts. So many people, so many things, so much confusion! "Are you saying that Ellie and Thomas own this property jointly?" she asked.

"Yes," Bill said. "There's no particular argument about that, it's the contents of the house that are in question. And when you get right down to it, my guess is they're going to turn out to be worth more than the house and grounds combined. This could be why Thomas wants everything sold at auction and the money divided between Ellie and himself," Bill continued. "Then he wants to put this place up for sale. He admits he'd like to see it converted into condominiums and," Bill concluded thoughtfully, "that's not such a bad idea. It's much too big a place for Ellie to live in alone. Certainly, she can't run an entire music school by herself. And I can't see you ever coming back to live in Lakeport on a permanent basis, Claire."

"No," Claire agreed.

"You have your galleries to run, as I understand it, in both Florida and New York."

"That's right."

Bill's implication was plain. Fourteen years ago Claire had removed herself from this scene and was now past the point of no return.

They went on to discuss Thomas Haskell, a man who had married a woman fourteen years older than himself. Whatever his reasons, it now appeared that one might have been greed.

Until he met Charlotte Parmeter, Thomas had wandered from place to place. Along the way, he had learned how to tune pianos. Delia had hired him to tune the pianos in the music school. Later, she had regretted the day she laid eyes on him. By then, she had considered Thomas a thoroughgoing opportunist. It looked as if, in the end, she was being proved right.

The evening passed, Ellie's chicken fricassee was wonderful, and the conversation moved to other things, mostly involving Lakeport. By ten o'clock Claire was so weary that she excused herself and went to bed. The will situation was troublesome, but it was the knowledge that King was here in Lakeport that had thoroughly sapped her energy and drained her emotions.

CLAIRE AWOKE to the sweet scent of roses drifting through her open bedroom window. The house was quiet. So quiet that she had the odd feeling there were invisible presences hovering, waiting and listening. The ghosts of past Parmeters? She smiled at the thought of such fantasy. Actually, she told herself, the ghosts inhabiting this old house just now were made up of memories—her memories.

Suddenly she knew she could no longer stave off going into the Orchestra Room. Or avoid roaming to the end of the garden path, opening the door of the dollhouse and letting the past confront her.

First, though, there was Ellie to face.

Claire dressed and started out the door of her Aunt Delia's bedroom, then stopped as memories flooded her. By this time of day, the house would have been resounding with a variety of musical tones that sometimes threatened to become earsplitting when heard together. There might have been the strains of a cello or a viola coming from Uncle Ralph's studio, often massacred into an effect less than pleasant by an eager beginning student. Downstairs, the echo of piano music would be emanating from the big front parlor Aunt Delia used for her teaching, unless Delia was instructing on the organ. Then the scene of activity would have been the Orchestra Room, where the huge organ dominated one wall.

Aunt Lottie taught flute, piccolo and clarinet. Her studio was a small library situated behind the Orchestra Room. From there had come sounds uniquely woodwind.

The evenings reserved for orchestra practice had produced a cacophony Claire would never forget. She smiled as she recalled listening to the orchestra tune up and remembered how she'd always wanted to play the two kettledrums that stood in the corner. As a child, she occasionally had been allowed to give them a thump, something that always made her feel great joy.

Ralph, Delia and Charlotte Parmeter had all been teaching fourteen years ago. Yet on the morning of Claire's wedding day, the house had been devoid of music. She'd gone downstairs and peeked in the Orchestra Room where the florists were at work creating a white, blossoming wonderland. Then she'd paused at the kitchen door to watch Mrs. Doherty, considered the best cook in town, decorating the three-tiered wedding cake with white roses.

Ellie and her two aunts had been busy somewhere in the house, but at that particular moment Claire had not met up with any of them. If she had, the course of her personal history might have changed drastically.

As it was, she had slipped out the back door and walked through the garden to the dollhouse. She'd felt the need of a little time to herself before she went upstairs to change into the white satin and lace gown that had been her great-grandmother's wedding dress and was now laid out on the bed in Aunt Delia's room.

The little house where she and Ellie had played as children had never seemed so precious as it did on that June morning. There was one rocking chair big enough to hold Claire and she had nestled in it, daydreaming, her thoughts in a pleasant haze.

In a few hours she would be marrying King. This would be a happy-ever-after ending to a romance that had begun when they were both juniors in high school. That had been Claire's first year at Lakeport High.

Coming out of a math class together one afternoon, King had asked her for a date. She still remembered, vividly, the thrill of that moment. King was the best-looking boy she had ever seen . . . and the nicest. He excelled in everything he did, whether academically or in sports, and was the most popular boy in school.

For all of that, though, Ellie had indicated that King had done more than his share of playing around with the girls in town—and Ellie had known King much longer than Claire had. Claire had listened to her cousin without really hearing her, because she hadn't wanted to think about what was being said. She had been much too mesmerized by King, too deeply in love with him.

By the time Claire and King were seniors, they were going steady. The fall after their graduation, Claire went away to a junior college in Massachusetts that offered an excellent art course, and King attended the state university, where he planned to major in psychology.

They decided to get married right after Claire finished with her associate degree, even though King still had two years of college ahead of him and graduate school after that. So, immediately after her graduation, Claire had come back to Lakeport to prepare for her wedding.

She and King would be going to Lake Placid for a month-long honeymoon. A friend of the family's had offered to let them use his cottage, right on the lake. Later, they could apartment hunt in the Albany area, where Claire planned to get a job to help out while King finished his schooling.

It was all so right, so perfectly planned.

Too right, Claire thought now, bitterly. As she moved toward the staircase outside Delia's room, she sadly imagined she could hear the voices again, just as she had on that long-ago morning.

Chris Talmadge, King's closest friend, would have been their best man. The Talmadges lived in the house next door. Claire, luxuriating in the dollhouse, cherishing those last blissful moments alone, had been shaken out of her reverie by the sound of voices. At first, she'd thought it was Chris's voice coming from behind the hedge at the back of the tiny house. But the tone was too familiar. Like most of the Parmeters, Claire had an excellent musical ear. Then, she recognized a cadence that could only belong to King.

Curious, she crept to the back window of the dollhouse and gently pushed it open so she could hear better.

"There's nothing I can do for you," he was saying, his tone despondent, like a sad bell tolling.

"You *have* to do something!" came a girl's voice, interrupting him. "I can't go on without you. I can't handle this!"

"You're going to have to handle it, Rosalie," King retorted.

Claire stiffened. Then, instinctively, she moved, and in doing so opened up a new scenario. Through a gap in the hedge she could see Rosalie Brenner clutching King's shoulders.

"I love you, King," the girl implored. "I've always loved you! My God, you can't go through with this marriage now!"

Claire watched King reach out, but instead of disengaging Rosalie's hands, he drew her into his embrace. Then, her shock intensifying, Claire saw Rosalie tilt her head up, saw King's mouth mesh with hers in an emotional kiss.

Stunned, Claire backed away from any further revelations. She felt as if her mind had turned into a kaleidoscope, and the whirling patterns were more than she could tolerate. Gossip travels in small towns, and in small-town schools. When she'd first started dating King, she had heard about his previous involvement with Rosalie Brenner. She had even asked him about Rosalie at one point. He had assured her that their relationship was long since over, that she, Claire, was the only girl in his life, and always would be. Still, Rosalie—a tempestuous brunette, far more knowing and sexy than most of the girls in the class—had remained a thorn, because she so obviously still wanted King, whether or not he returned her feelings.

Claire couldn't blame her. King was a prototype hero: tall, blond, handsome. Also, for all his good looks he was singularly unconceited and the kindest, gentlest person in the world.

But this scene she had just witnessed represented a lot more than simple kindness to an old girlfriend.

Claire had known she couldn't forget this, that she couldn't go back to the house and pretend nothing had happened. She had to face King immediately, had to hear his explanation. She needed an infusion of new faith from him. She turned, ready to confront him, and at that instant the door of the dollhouse opened and she found herself face-to-face with Rosalie Brenner.

Rosalie's eyes were wet with tears and wildly desperate. Her jet-black hair tumbled around her shoulders and her face was frighteningly pale. She blurted, "I saw you in the window, Claire. So...you heard!"

"Yes," Claire replied dully. "I heard."

"I'm pregnant," Rosalie stated flatly. "I'm pregnant with King's baby. He can't leave me now, don't you see? He *can't*."

Claire felt herself turning to stone. She could neither move nor speak and stood just staring at Rosalie, her world devastated. She was only dimly aware of Rosalie saying something else, then turning and leaving the dollhouse as swiftly as she had entered it.

Numb, stricken, Claire momentarily was unable to function at all. Then she crept to the door, opened it and found herself staring into King's distraught face.

"I saw Rosalie come out of here," he began, his voice as strained as an elastic band about to snap.

Claire couldn't answer him.

"You saw us." He made this sound like an accusation.

She nodded, still voiceless.

King said, helplessly, "Oh, God!"

Claire found words, but they trembled on her tongue. "You kissed her," she quavered. It was such a small indictment compared to the charge Rosalie had leveled against King. And it penetrated Claire, like a deeply thrust knife, that King did not refute that charge.

"Yes," he said, "I kissed her. I know how it must have looked to you, Claire, but I . . ."

He, too, was fumbling for words, but suddenly Claire didn't want to hear any more. When King moved toward her and touched her arm, she flinched. "No!" she exploded.

King's arm jerked back. "What do you mean, no?"

"Just that," she said tightly. "Just that. Leave me alone, King."

"Claire, for God's sake!"

"I'm going back to the house," she said dully, feeling as if both her body and mind were falling apart. "I . . . I have to be by myself for a while."

"Let me come with you," he implored.

She shook her head. "No."

"Claire, look," King pleaded. "Please don't get your aunts and the others involved in this."

*As if that mattered.*

"Go up to your room and I'll follow in a few minutes," he urged. "We've got to talk this out—by ourselves."

Claire nodded, at that instant wanting only to escape from him. At the door of the dollhouse, she heard his warning. "I'll give you fifteen minutes, Claire, but that's all!"

Claire hurried back to the house then stole around the side, hugging the hedge as if its cover made her invisible. Miraculously, the front hall was empty. She ran up the stairs, her feet given wings by the urgency that was pressing at her. Inside her bedroom, she locked the door, then stood stock-still, panting for breath.

She was sure of only one thing: that she could not possibly go through with the wedding. There had been guilt written all over King's face, and he hadn't even refuted Rosalie's terrible statement. Her King. Hers indeed! He had failed her!

That awful moment was fourteen years in the past, but as she stood now at the top of the second-floor landing, Claire felt herself reliving the agony of that morning. She remembered how physically sick she'd felt as she tried to work out a plan of action.

First, she had listened behind the closed door of her room. Then, hearing nothing, she'd opened the door a crack and peered into the empty hall. Next, she had scurried across the hall to Ellie's room, where the keys to the old car of which Ellie was so proud were in the little Limoges bowl on top of her dresser.

Ellie always kept a small cash hoard under the handkerchiefs in her top drawer, and Claire had taken both the cash and the car keys, then quickly retreated to her room. She had some money of her own and she thrust that along with Ellie's into a canvas tote bag. Then she stuffed in a nightgown and her comb and brush. She was wearing jeans and a pale pink T-shirt and decided not to bother taking any other clothes.

At the last minute, she wrenched the diamond solitaire King had given her off her finger and placed it squarely in the center of the hand-embroidered dresser scarf. Again, she canvased the hall before she moved, and when she heard footsteps on the stairs she froze, sure it must be Ellie. It was, but as if on cue someone called from below and Ellie turned back.

Reprieved, Claire sped down the hall to the rear of the house, then ran up the stairs to the attic. There was a secret passage that led from the attic right down to a shed behind the kitchen. The passage had been a source of scary delight to both Claire and Ellie when they were children, and it wasn't until they were in their teens that they'd gotten up the nerve to explore it. There were a number of family stories about why it had been built, but no one knew the true reason.

The garage was only a few short steps from the shed, but that was the most dangerous part of Claire's escape. For the brief space of time it would take to cross from one building to the other, there was a very real possibility she might be seen. Luckily she went unnoticed, and a moment later she roared onto the street in Ellie's car. She didn't know whether or not anyone had seen her go, nor did she look back to find out.

Claire had often wondered what might have happened if King had arrived in her room before she left. Could he have offered an explanation she might have believed?

Once, Ellie had innocently mentioned in a letter that Rosalie Brenner had gone into nurse's training in Burlington, Vermont, but nothing had been said about a baby. Had Rosalie really been pregnant, or had she lied, hoping that Claire would do exactly what she had done? If she had been pregnant, perhaps she'd gone off somewhere and had an abortion before anyone in town found out. And even if that was true, had the baby she had been carrying been King's?

Claire had stopped wondering about that a long time ago. On that terrible day, fifty miles from Lakeport, she'd stopped to telephone the one person in the world she felt she could turn to: Philip Bailey, her art instructor in college.

She knew Philip had a studio in the Berkshires in western Massachusetts where he spent his summers painting. She got his number from information and felt an overwhelming sense of relief when Philip answered the phone on the second ring.

A few hours later Claire was in Stockbridge, and that night she let Philip take her in his arms and comfort her. She was exhausted, physically and emotionally.

In the days that followed, she turned to Philip increasingly, relying on him for everything from the food she ate to the daily walks he insisted she take with him. She had no desire to leave the room he had given her, let alone the house.

He was sixteen years older than she was. Admittedly, a father figure in many ways. But as she gradually emerged from shock's cocoon she became ready to hear his confession that he had fallen in love with her before the end of her first semester in college. Ready to hear and to respond—not with the same kind of love, but with a deep affection.

A month later, she and Philip were married by a justice of the peace.

REFOCUSING HER THOUGHTS in the present, Claire descended the stairs and went looking for Ellie. She found a note on the kitchen table.

Thomas asked me to have lunch with him. He said he needed to talk about something. I asked Bill what I should do, and he said it might be a good idea to hear what Thomas has to say, provided I don't commit myself to anything. I may stop at Bill's office after lunch to tell him what went on, but I should be home by midafternoon. There's plenty to eat in the refrigerator.

Claire wasn't especially hungry, but she found a bowl of chicken salad, made herself a sandwich and brewed a cup of tea.

After she finished eating, she wandered around the house on a fantasy safari, a journey back in time. Everything was so familiar, so bathed in memory, yet she felt like such a stranger.

She forced herself to remain in the Orchestra Room and discovered that it was, after all, just a room. She reminded herself that years and years ago the white flowers had withered, and the satin ribbons—if they were still around—must long since have turned yellow.

Claire lingered in her Aunt Delia's studio, running her fingers over the ivory keys of the grand piano. Finally, she sat down and began to play, marveling that she could still remember at least some of the music her aunt had taught her so long ago.

Running her fingers over the keys, she thought of Delia and Charlotte and Ralph. She recalled, with a whimsical smile, how all the Parmeters had tried to inspire her to follow a musical career. Lottie had tried to

interest her in the flute. Ralph had insisted that her hands
were just right for the cello. But as much as she loved
music, Claire had felt no desire to follow in the family
footsteps. Somewhat grudgingly, she had taken occasional piano lessons from Aunt Delia, but she never
practiced as she should have, to her grandfather's displeasure.

In comparison to her present world, theirs had been
such a limited one. Claire thought of her art galleries in
New York and Florida. She and Philip had worked together to build those galleries and keep them flourish-
ing. Since his death from lung cancer four years ago after
a terrible, tragic year of illness, she had been managing
the business successfully with the help of Brent Underwood, a contemporary of Philip's. Brent had been an
invaluable assistant to Philip in earlier years, then indispensable to both Philip and Claire as the business grew.
Now he was Claire's partner in every way but on paper,
and of late she'd begun to realize that legalizing their al-
liance might be the next smart step.

Claire was thirty-four and knew she had never looked
better. She'd traveled all over the world and moved in the
most cosmopolitan circles in New York City. For ten
years she had known the love of a wonderful man, a man
who had been completely devoted to her. There was no
reason to feel a sudden lack in her life because her return
to Lakeport had forced her to think about the boy who
long ago had disillusioned her so completely.

After a time, she wandered back upstairs and stretched
out on the bed that had been Aunt Delia's. She was still
very tired, and lunch hadn't agreed with her. She hoped
that if she could drift off to sleep the discomfort might
pass, but it didn't.

Claire dozed, but was soon awakened by acute pains stabbing her abdomen. They were so excruciating they forced the breath out of her and, miserable, she began to writhe from side to side.

It wasn't long before she knew she was going to be sick, and tried to get to her feet, but the severity of the pains pushed her back on the bed. Finally, she summoned every last ounce of strength she had and staggered to the bathroom. And that was where Ellie found her, sprawled on the floor, unconscious.

# CHAPTER THREE

CLAIRE REMEMBERED being sick. Desperately sick to her stomach. All the while, she'd been engulfed by waves of agonizing pain.

The pain had subsided, leaving her feeling weak, wrung out. It took tremendous effort to open her eyes, but when she did so slowly, cautiously, she found herself staring into twin pools of angry blue fire.

She was drowning in the bluest eyes in the world, Claire thought irrationally, then told herself that wasn't possible. King Faraday had the bluest eyes in the world.

Claire's field of vision widened, and she saw the face of the man bending over her. His features—older, different somehow, yet still intensely familiar—became etched against the beige walls of the strange room she was in. A hospital room. An emergency room. More of a cubicle than a room. Gradually, these facts penetrated her hazy thoughts.

She looked up into King Faraday's face, stern and unrelenting. Only those blazing eyes revealed any emotion. Seeing the surgical cap he was wearing and the hospital green of his shirt, she knew she was in the presence of a stranger. Yet this man *was* King. He was primarily a doctor, just now, but he was also wary, hostile and as cold as steel.

This data registered slowly, since Claire lacked both the stamina and the capacity to absorb any more shocks.

Then she heard King's voice, the cadence as familiar as it had been fourteen years ago.

"Well!" he said tersely.

A wealth of emotion echoed within the simple exclamation. A wealth of suppressed ire, too, as he continued almost angrily, "Ellie thought you were in the throes of an acute appendicitis attack. However, that didn't prove to be the case. The problem was food poisoning, evidently from some old chicken salad you found in Ellie's fridge. So we were spared the need to operate."

The need? Claire had the strange feeling that King had substituted the word *need* for *pleasure*. That he actually would have enjoyed cutting her open.

She stated weakly, "You're a doctor."

"So I am," he agreed, tight-lipped and unsmiling.

"I didn't know."

"No, I don't suppose you did," he said, turning away.

Claire studied his back. His shoulders looked broader than she remembered, and he seemed even taller, though she knew this must be imagination on her part. King, after all, had been a full-grown man on that day they were to have been married.

She watched him sit down at a desk tucked against the side of the tiny room and saw his face in profile. The strong lines of his features, the determined thrust of his chin—everything about him told her how much he hated her.

Without turning to look at her, King said, "I'm admitting you for observation. I think you should stay here tonight." He added, not disguising his sarcasm, "I would hate to be mistaken in my diagnosis."

Claire tried sitting up but quickly subsided back on the examining table, her head hollowing the single flat pillow. She felt wretched, both physically and emotionally.

Seeing King's eyes, hearing the tone of his voice, were worse than the pains of the food poisoning.

He spoke again, his question expressing a curiosity he evidently couldn't stave off. But even his curiosity was cold.

"Why are you here?" he asked.

"Ellie needed me," Claire answered, her voice a whisper.

King turned toward her now, and Claire saw the thin line of his mouth, a mouth she remembered as beautifully formed, full and generous. She saw his lips twitch, his smile ironic. He said, "A little late to think about Ellie's needs, isn't it?"

Claire had no answer, nor did King wait for one.

"Ellie's in the waiting room," he informed her. "Bill Edgerly, too. Ellie called the rescue squad and they brought you in. Then she got in touch with Bill and he drove her over." King's slight smile was mirthless as he concluded, "I suppose I'd better tell her you're going to be all right."

Their eyes met as he said this and, though some of the anger had disappeared from his, there remained an iciness that made Claire shiver.

He left the room without a backward glance and, as Claire watched him go, the strength of the tug she felt toward him was both unexpected and intensely disconcerting. She actually yearned to call him back, yet knew that if she did there would be nothing further she could say.

Ellie stole into the room walking on tiptoe, afraid to make even the slightest noise. She looked pale and distraught, and blurted, "I was scared to death! But King insists you're okay. It never occurred to me you might eat some of that chicken salad. I should have thrown it out. Oh, Claire..."

"It's not your fault," Claire said gently, somehow summoning a smile. "I'm fine. Just a little weak, that's all. King wants to admit me overnight, for observation. But that's just a precaution."

"King's right," Ellie told her. "We want to be sure it really *is* food poisoning and nothing more." Ellie's eyes were scanning her cousin's face anxiously. "I'm going back to the house and get your nightgown and a robe and your toothbrush and things," she decided suddenly.

"I could last through the night in a hospital gown," Claire protested weakly.

"No, no. You'll be more comfortable with your own things. It'll only take me a little while."

Ellie was true to her word, and by the time the necessary forms had been filled out and Claire had been wheeled to a second-floor room, she was back with a small suitcase.

"The couple of times I've been in a hospital I couldn't sleep," Ellie confided, "so I brought you something to read, in case it's the same way with you."

Ellie lingered until Claire was propped up in bed, wearing a rose satin-and-lace nightgown. Even then, despite Claire's assurances that she was feeling better with every passing minute, Ellie was reluctant to leave.

"Visiting hours are until nine," she said. "Bill can go along, and I'll stay with you."

"Bill's still *here*?"

"Yes. He wants me to go out and have some supper with him."

"Go, for heaven's sake," Claire urged. "This hasn't been an easy day for you, either."

Ellie stood by the bedside, wearing a gray skirt and a loose floral-patterned blouse that did nothing at all for her. "I'm sorry you had to meet up with King like that, Claire," she said awkwardly. "Last night I started to tell you that King was a surgeon, affiliated with this hospital. Then the doorbell rang and it was Bill, and we never did get back to talking about King."

Claire nodded, not prepared to discuss King now. To placate Ellie, she said, "It's all right. I'll admit it was a rather dramatic way of encountering him again. But maybe it was better for both of us that way."

"Maybe," Ellie agreed. "Although when King came out of the emergency room he looked pretty shaken."

Shaken? King Faraday? Aside from the anger in his eyes, Claire doubted if she'd ever seen anyone as self-contained and in control—or as cold.

"King didn't know you were coming back to Lakeport," Ellie went on. "I don't run into him that often. I guess I was hoping you could come and go without having to face each other."

Ellie's voice was low. "A lot of time has passed," she conceded, "but that day, when King found out you were gone, he said if he ever saw you again he'd . . . kill you."

Shock spiraled through Claire, but she rallied quickly. "As you said, Ellie, that was a long time ago. Obviously, King's made his own life since then."

"I suppose so," Ellie mused, "but it's funny. When he left Lakeport, he said he'd never come back."

"I know," Claire said. "You wrote me that."

"I don't think he ever *would* have come back, except for his father," Ellie reported. "And, of course, he knew you were living far away from here. The first time King saw me again, when Dr. Faraday had his stroke, he asked if you ever came to visit. I told him I hadn't seen you since the day you ... left. And I said you weren't apt to return. I don't think King made up his mind to move back until then.''

*How he hated me ... how he still must hate me!* Claire realized, the thought burning inside her.

"Ellie, did King and Rosalie Brenner ever ... get together?" The question surfaced before she had time to think it out and, hearing the words, Claire wished she could have snatched them back.

"Rosalie Brenner?" Ellie looked completely puzzled. "Why would you think that?" she demanded, as if the very idea made no sense at all.

For the first time, Claire consciously realized that no one knew about that scene in the garden between Rosalie Brenner and King, to say nothing of her later encounters in the dollhouse with both of them. She had never told anyone, not even Philip. She'd told him only that at the last hour she'd discovered King had been unfaithful, and after making this discovery she couldn't go through with the marriage. But she had never named names, never gone into details.

Now, meeting Ellie's puzzled, dark eyes, she murmured, "I wondered, that's all...."

She let the words trail away and Ellie picked them up. "You're wrong," Ellie told her. "Rosalie was always after King, I admit. But once King started going with you he never had eyes for anyone else. After you ran off, he became a madman. I wouldn't have believed King could be so ... so *wild*, unless I'd seen it myself. Everyone was afraid of him, afraid he'd do something foolish. He didn't go to bed for three nights, and only then because he dropped from exhaustion. He wouldn't eat, either. I'd never seen anyone like that before, and I never want to again. Chris Talmadge and Bill and King's father and I took turns staying with him around the clock. We were afraid to leave him alone. When you left, you took everything King had in the world.''

Ellie shook her head slowly. ''I shouldn't be saying all this, especially after what you've been through today. And I'm not blaming you for anything, Claire. I never have. I've always known you must have had your reasons for what you did. Good reasons.''

Ellie stretched out a hand and clasped Claire's, and Claire realized her cousin was trembling. She was none too steady herself, and her voice shook slightly as she said, ''I *thought* I had a very good reason for doing what I did, Ellie. Now...'' She paused, then changed the subject abruptly. ''You shouldn't keep Bill waiting any longer.''

''All right,'' Ellie said on a sigh. ''I'll phone in the morning and find out what time I can come take you home,'' she promised. With a last squeeze of Claire's hand, she left.

The hospital room closed in around Claire once she was alone. But small though it was, it was a private room, and for that she was grateful. She wasn't up to sharing space with another patient tonight.

The walls were pale yellow, and bright curtains in an old-fashioned print graced the windows. An effort had been made to achieve a cheerfulness through the decor, but Claire's spirits were so heavy that nothing could have lifted them. Closing her eyes, she hoped she could doze off, while outside the shadows were lengthening as the early summer dusk yielded to darkness.

She heard the creak of a door opening and imagined a nurse was coming to check on her. To be helpful, she switched on the small lamp on the bedside table, and instantly found herself confronting King.

He had changed clothes and was wearing dark slacks and a white hospital jacket. A stethoscope dangled from his neck. His hair was thick and as blond as ever, but the bedside light revealed a glint of silver weaving through the gold. The lines in his face were grooved by time and, Claire suddenly realized, by suffering. They made him look older than he was.

He stopped short of the bed, deliberately keeping a careful distance between them. "I'm on call tonight," he said, "so making evening rounds is part of my job."

He didn't need to add, *Otherwise I wouldn't be here*.

Out of necessity, King moved close to Claire, then proceeded to take her pulse. As his strong, slender fingers pressed her wrist, Claire suddenly knew that this was too much for her to handle. Forgotten feelings and emotions suppressed for so long surged forward, and King's touch became a thermal blanket wrapping her from head to toe.

Feeling herself suffocating, Claire inadvertently gasped.

"What is it?" King asked quickly.

He had been concentrating on her pulse, but now he raised his head and their eyes met. The interval probably lasted little more than a second, yet Claire caught the pain and bitterness in those blue depths, plus a concern for her that surfaced despite himself. Crazily, she wanted to throw her arms around him and hold him close, if only to ease his hurt. Frustrated, she clenched her fists.

King, noting this, demanded, "Are you in pain?"

"No, no," she told him, shaking her head, but her words emerged like two small moans.

"This is no time to hedge."

"I'm not hedging."

"If you'd rather have me call in another physician, I will," he said stiffly. "I'm on the surgical staff here, but tonight I'm filling in for one of the residents. He had a family birthday party, but he'd get away if he had to."

"There's no need for that," Claire responded dryly. "Unless you'd rather someone else saw me."

He smiled that terrible, mirthless smile again, then said, "I'm capable of keeping my professional and personal identities separate, Claire."

"I'm sure you are."

"You shouldn't be having abdominal pains again, if that's what's bothering you. So if you are having them, it would be wise to tell me."

"My pain is not physical, King," she answered, surprising herself with the truth.

If Claire had expected a reaction from King, there wasn't any. He simply said, "I suppose many of us have that problem."

He might as well have been commenting on the weather, or on the fact that the hospital had built a new wing during the fourteen years she'd been away from Lakeport. She began to appreciate how unapproachable this man had become.

Man. The word was a penetrating arrow. Fourteen years ago, King had been a man, but such a young man. There had been an appealing boyishness about him, just one of the reasons he attracted women, women of all ages, so easily. The other reasons had encompassed his engaging personality and his striking good looks. Claire didn't think she had ever seen a man who physically measured up to King. But she silently admitted that where King was concerned, she'd always been prejudiced.

Another reason for his attractiveness had been a certain innocence about him. In an age where innocence was a quickly lost quality, King had been refreshingly different. He'd been an incurable optimist, always accenting the positive, always confident that there really was a pot of gold at the end of the rainbow. For King, though, it hadn't been a pot containing riches. Rather, it held the essence of things far more precious.

Love and understanding, compassion and tolerance. These had been built into King's nature, and Claire, young though she'd been herself, had marveled at that.

Not long before he asked her to marry him, King had finally spoken about his mother, and with a surprising lack of bitterness. He'd been eight when his mother left his father. He remembered her dimly as someone who had been very beautiful. In his memory, she floated on a lovely aroma that caressed him like her kisses each night when she'd come to tuck him into bed.

Then one day, she was gone. Other children told him she had died. So King had faced death for the first time, death coming as a black-winged, frightening thing that made him afraid to enter a dark room.

The time came when he knew his mother was alive, but far away. So far away—psychologically, if not physically—there was no chance she would ever return.

Later, he had learned about the other man, a man who had lured a mother from her husband and child. Yet when he told Claire about this, he hadn't been condemning. He'd showed an understanding of human weakness and human frailty that few people his age—or older—possessed.

In those early days after she left Lakeport, Claire had brooded over this. She had wondered if the reason King had always been so understanding about his mother was because he was cut from the same mold—a chronically unfaithful mold. An inherited malady. It had helped to think that King actually hadn't been able to control himself with Rosalie . . . because that was his nature.

Regardless, when they had been engaged, King possessed an innocence that made him very special. That innocence was lost, which was natural enough given the passage of time, she thought as she studied his face. Sadly, though, he had become an embittered man. Claire immediately thought of King's father. Much as she had come to like Dr. Faraday, there had been an impenetrable cynicism about him. In retrospect, she felt she had come closer to breaking that ice than anyone else. More the pity, as all turned out.

King was again intently considering Claire's pulse. As he released her wrist, he asked, "Have you been having any problems?"

"Problems?" she echoed, not understanding.

"Physical problems," he said impatiently. "Your pulse is very rapid."

*And you, King Faraday, a doctor, don't know why?* She was tempted to voice the question but knew she would sound as cynical as he did. Yet it didn't seem possible that King could be unaware of how he was affecting her.

"I had my annual checkup a few weeks ago. Nothing important surfaced."

He nodded, accepting this. "In view of your experience today, an accelerated pulse rate is not unusual," he conceded.

She supposed King meant the "experience" of having suffered a severe case of food poisoning. But confronting him again had been far more traumatic. Didn't he know that?

King pressed the buzzer by the bed, and a moment later a nurse appeared in the doorway. He said crisply, "I'm ordering a sedative for Mrs. Bailey, which you can give her right away. She needs to get some sleep."

He turned back to Claire. "I'm off tomorrow. Dr. Danforth will be in to see you before you're released. If you need anything in the interim, the nurse can reach me."

Again, King's meaning was implicit. He might as well have stated that he hoped she wouldn't contact him.

He was at the door when Claire called his name. She simply couldn't let him go like this.

"King!" She was uttering a plea for help, and wondered if he would realize that.

He turned, and for a brief moment his indecision showed. He asked wearily, "What is it, Claire?"

"When I told Ellie I'd come up here and help her, I didn't know you had moved back to Lakeport," she said hastily. Her voice catching, she added, "Don't you think I know how I've neglected Ellie all these years? How I let her shoulder the burden of the whole family? Maybe it's too late to make it up to her. I don't know. If you tell me that, I won't disagree. But . . . I felt I had to do what I could. And when she said she thought it would help if I faced Thomas Haskell with her—"

"You don't have to explain your actions to me, Claire," King interrupted.

"I know that," she said impatiently. "But you're not the only person with a guilt complex, King."

His mouth twisted. "What makes you think I have a guilt complex?" he queried sardonically.

Claire sidestepped this by saying, "I just wanted you to know how I feel about Ellie, that's all."

"Exactly what are you trying to tell me?" His tone was just a shade too polite. "Are you saying that if you had known I was in Lakeport you would have refused Ellie, despite her need?"

"Perhaps," Claire conceded uncomfortably.

A smile, still mirthless, curved King's lips. "Well," he offered, "if I had known you were coming, I would have arranged to have been out of town. Does that make you feel better?"

"No!" Claire answered desperately. "I'm trying to say that if I had known you were here I would have found another way to help Ellie, because..."

"Because?" he prompted.

"Because I suppose I've always known that Lakeport isn't big enough to hold both of us, even for a little while."

Something flickered in King's intensely blue eyes. An emotion Claire couldn't identify. He said evenly, "I disagree. As far as I'm concerned, Lakeport is more than big enough to hold both of us. There's no need to get in each other's way, that's all. Except for this medical emergency, I doubt we would have met."

Claire felt that King was looking down on her from a vast height. He said, "A man only needs to be left waiting at the altar once, Claire, to learn the lesson. It's been a long time since memories of you have had the power to affect me—either positively or negatively—and that's the way I want to keep it. After considerable trial and error, I've made my way. I'm content now, and I want to keep my life and my friends at exactly the present level. No additions, no subtractions. No backward glances, no trauma whatsoever. Does that reassure you?"

KING LEFT CLAIRE'S ROOM without waiting to hear her reply. He needed very much to be alone to sort out the jumble of thoughts and emotions that threatened to enmesh him.

Almost immediately, though, King was summoned to the emergency room to treat a youngster with a badly cut finger and, focusing his concentration on the intricate suturing job that was required, he was actually relieved to have something totally occupy him.

As the night passed, the hospital quieted down. The emergency room was virtually vacant, for once. King, restless, went to the doctor's lounge, poured himself a cup of coffee and tried to get interested in the latest issue of the *New England Journal of Medicine*. He might as well have been reading Sanskrit.

To his astonishment, he found himself thinking solely of Claire. He considered returning to her room, wanting to confront her again, then asked himself why, because there was no logical reason for a confrontation. Even if he'd known she'd be in town again, he wouldn't have made any moves to see her. As far as his personal world was concerned, Claire had died a long time ago. She had hurt him too badly and he had no desire to resurrect her now.

That pain had lingered for a long, long time, his outrage and resentment molding much of what he had done after her desertion. And that was the way he had always viewed it. Claire had deserted him because of a single incident, without even giving him the chance to explain. She'd accepted circumstantial evidence and had given him no opportunity to testify on his own behalf.

He was fair enough to appreciate how it must have looked to her on that long-ago day. There was no denying that he'd taken Rosalie Brenner into his arms and kissed her. But that had been the first time he had touched Rosalie since Claire captured his heart. He'd been twenty years old at the time, damn it! Rosalie had been sexy and provocative, pulling out all the stops in her desperation. Then there had been the shock of her telling him she was pregnant. Initially grateful that she could not be carrying his child, he had quickly remembered the one time years before that *could* have been a possibility. But luck had interceded, thank God.

Maybe gratitude was the reason he had kissed her. Gratitude... and Rosalie herself, staring up at him with those huge, tear-drenched jet eyes. The kiss had closed the door on something that was gone and would never return. Then Rosalie had run to the dollhouse, only to emerge a few minutes later, her face still tear-streaked, yet smiling in an oddly triumphant way.

King could still remember the fear he'd felt at that moment. The horrible premonition that Claire was in the dollhouse had gripped him, and proven true.

He'd told himself a thousand times, more than a thousand times, that he shouldn't have let Claire return to the house by herself. But she'd been so torn apart he couldn't make her see clearly. He had made the mistake of thinking she would be able to regroup, given a few minutes alone. Then they could talk things out.

Actually, less than the promised fifteen minutes elapsed before he went after her. He'd entered the house by the back door, almost tripping over Delia Parmeter. Aunt Delia had chided him for appearing there on his wedding day, asking him if he didn't know it was unlucky for the groom to see the bride before the ceremony.

King, agonizing because he *had* to get to Claire, had tried to be polite. He'd heard Delia out and tried to humor her. Then, when he realized she had no intention of letting him see her niece and actually was blocking his way, he had pushed past her and taken the stairs two at a time.

Ellie was on the second-floor threshold, and he would never forget the stricken look on her face or the tremor in her voice as she said, "Claire's gone, King." Then she had held Claire's engagement ring out to him.

He had stared at the solitaire in disbelief, choked with rage and hurt. Then he'd snarled, "You're lying!" and had brushed by Ellie. He couldn't remember climbing up the last flight of stairs, but the emptiness of Claire's room was vivid.

For months after that, King had hated Claire with frightening intensity. Hated Claire and shut himself off from everyone else. When fall came, he had refused to go back to the university and, for the next two years, stayed around Lakeport taking a series of odd jobs, drinking too much, escaping with drugs too often and indulging in a series of cheap affairs in an effort to convince himself that all women were alike—and basically worthless.

Still, time passed. And King began to realize that he was poisoning himself and not reaching Claire at all with his anger. She had gone far beyond him by then and was finally washing out of his system. But it had taken a long, long time before the catharsis was complete.

Because of what he'd been through, King became convinced he wasn't cut out to be a psychologist. He'd messed up his own life so badly that it was plain he'd never be able to help others with their emotional problems. But eventually it dawned on him that there was something valid he could do with his life.

His father was the only person in the world left for King to care about, and his father had always wanted him to be a doctor, had wanted him to one day take over his practice in Lakeport. King had no intention of doing that, certain that once he left Lakeport he would never return. Still, he decided to become a doctor and, in medical school, found that surgery was the specialty he wanted to pursue.

In medicine, King discovered a new mistress. Completely involved in his career, his relationship with women became sporadic. He never again wished to commit himself fully to a woman, and doubted he ever would. One woman, in that respect, had been enough.

Now, still restless and finding himself suddenly haunted by a past he had no wish to recall, King moved to the window of the empty doctor's lounge and stared out blankly into the June night. The moon was in the sky, the stars in their places, there was a softness to the air. Two floors below, there was a woman even more beautiful than the girl he remembered. But she was a stranger to him now, and destined to remain a stranger.

King Faraday forced himself to remember that.

## CHAPTER FOUR

IT WAS NEARLY DAWN before King drifted into an uneasy sleep. He'd stretched out on a cot in a small cubicle used mostly by residents trying to snatch a little rest during on-call hours. It offered little in the way of comfort, but then hospitals seldom provided luxury accommodations for their on-duty medical staff.

When the clatter announcing the start of the hospital day began, King was glad to let the extraneous noises wake him. He stretched and rubbed his eyes and knew he had been dreaming. The dreams hadn't been pleasant, so he was glad he couldn't remember anything in detail.

In the doctor's lounge the coffeepot had just been filled. King poured himself a cup and drank it black, needing the quick jolt of caffeine.

John Danforth, a staff physician, came on call at seven. Danforth was short and stocky and outwardly jovial. The happy mask, King knew, camouflaged an inherent worrier. Danforth had taken over King's father's practice when the elder Dr. Faraday had been forced into retirement after his stroke. He'd arrived in Lakeport from a midwestern city and George Faraday had taken an instant liking to him. King, too, liked the ebullient physician, but Danforth's physique—he was a good thirty pounds overweight—and a tendency to keep his apprehensions tightly locked inside, made King fear that his father's successor might suffer a stroke or heart attack himself before reaching the prime of his life.

Some of King's surgical patients were also Danforth's medical patients, so the two doctors reviewed a series of charts together in Danforth's office before King embarked on his day off.

Usually King was in a hurry to get this particular task over with so he would be free for twenty-four hours. But this morning he lingered, answering Danforth's questions about the various cases in far more detail than necessary.

The hospital was still quiet. No elective surgery was scheduled, and the emergency room was blessedly inactive. King and Danforth retreated to the doctor's lounge for more coffee and King surprised himself by announcing that he thought he'd check on a couple of his surgical patients before he took off.

As soon as he said this, he realized by the look on Danforth's face that he'd needlessly alarmed the man.

"Nothing to worry about," he added hastily. "They're doing fine. Just people I happen to know personally as well as professionally...."

That was not strictly true. King did know some of the patients socially, but they were merely acquaintances. This was his doing, not anyone else's. Since returning to Lakeport, he'd been careful about really getting close to anyone, and had no desire to pursue an active social life. Because of surgery his free time was limited, and he valued every minute. He couldn't afford to waste it on meaningless interchanges.

His father had taken up most of his spare moments, anyway. George Faraday hadn't driven after the stroke, so King often took his father on outings on his days off, especially when the weather was good. Sometimes they'd take the ferry across Lake Champlain and have lunch in Burlington, Vermont. Or they'd drive up into the beautiful Adirondack Mountains. In earlier years, climbing had been a hobby of George Faraday's. In fact, he was the one who'd introduced King to the exciting sport.

Thinking about this as he left the doctor's lounge and strode down the corridor toward the surgical ward, a memory flashed into King's mind, so vivid it brought him to a sudden halt.

The first summer he had known Claire, he tried to get her interested in climbing. He'd driven her out to Pocomoonshine, one of the lower Adirondacks. They'd taken a lunch and had unpacked at the large picnic ground near the foot of the mountain. King, already falling in love with Claire, had been tremendously excited about sharing one of his favorite hobbies with her. But it hadn't turned out as he'd hoped.

Claire hadn't been too bad on the ascent. He remembered now, with a wry smile, how he'd thoroughly enjoyed helping her along. He'd had many chances to touch her, using the ruse of assisting her, and he still keenly remembered her warmth and softness. Even her sweet scent, a provocative, feminine aroma made up of soap and eau de cologne and just Claire herself, had wafted back to his nostrils as he'd followed her, more than ready to catch her should she slip.

It was only when they had reached the top that King realized how shaken she was—and not by his proximity. She was terrified of heights, and when he suggested they climb the lookout tower where the view would be even more spectacular, Claire actually froze.

"I can't, King," she murmured, her voice laced with desperation.

King had stood there dumbfounded and later cursed himself for not realizing that all the time they had been climbing, all the time he had been enjoying touching Claire with every helping hand he could find an excuse for, she had been scared to death. Much too scared to be aware of his mounting feelings, feelings that had worked themselves up into a strong desire.

Not yet eighteen, King hadn't been very adept at hiding evidences of desire. He'd known that his maleness was showing, he recalled now, his wry smile deepening, and had hoped rather frantically that Claire wouldn't lower her eyes and notice.

She hadn't. As he remembered, her skin had turned many shades lighter than usual, and her lips had a bluish hue that would have worried him if he'd known what he knew now about stress reaction. Her eyes had been huge and eloquent as she'd confessed, on the verge of tears, "I'm so *sorry*, King."

He had been so awkward, he thought now. "There's nothing to be sorry about, Claire," he'd said. "It doesn't matter if we climb the tower or not. I've been up before with my Dad. I thought you'd enjoy the view, that's all."

"I'm sure . . . I'd enjoy the view." Claire's voice was trembling and she started to sway. King reached out and grabbed her, then held her tightly, knowing forever after it was at that precise moment he had fallen totally in love with Claire Parmeter. Maybe her helplessness had propelled an emotion sure to crystallize sooner or later anyway. Her helplessness, there on top of the mountain, had been undeniably appealing. Her gutsiness had been equally irresistible. Claire had forced herself to stand on her own, had gently disengaged her arms and managed the faintest of smiles. "I'm okay," she'd insisted, even though it was quite apparent she wasn't really okay at all.

King had said uncertainly, "I think we'd better start down." Noting Claire's shudder, he'd wondered how he was going to handle her. Suddenly, she looked so fragile.

He did his damnedest, though, leading the way down the trail, and wished he could admonish Claire not to look down, but that was impossible. She had to look down to keep her footing, even if it terrified her. It wasn't so bad when they were surrounded by thick wooded areas, but every so often they would break into the open, practically on the edge of the mountain. Then King would stop and gaze back at Claire anxiously. He wouldn't have believed that someone could be so parchment white and still breathe.

They were about two-thirds of the way down when they came to a rather difficult part of the path. There were no real obstacles on Pocomoonshine for anyone with even the slightest climbing experience, but for Claire the whole trip was a challenge, that spot especially. She stumbled and, though King grabbed her before she'd taken a nasty fall, their moment of truth was at hand.

"I . . . I think I wrenched my ankle," Claire said anxiously.

She tried to keep walking but she couldn't. King saw her biting back the pain, and the only immediate solution was to carry her the rest of the way.

That wasn't easy, certainly not a performance he would have wanted to repeat, despite having the pleasure of holding Claire in his arms. It was a cool day for summer, and Claire was slender—light as a feather, King told himself assuredly—but by the time they reached the picnic grove at the base of the mountain he was sweating profusely.

Claire's ankle had started to swell, so King cooled it with icy water from a nearby stream. Then he gallantly tore his shirt into strips and bound her ankle, having observed his father doing this on a variety of occasions. Claire gritted her teeth and pretended everything was fine, and even made a stab at having their picnic. But after one bite of a cream-cheese-and-olive sandwich, King saw by the expression on her face that if she ate any more she was going to be sick. Quickly, then, they packed up and he drove her home.

He never suggested to Claire that they try mountain climbing again. There were other things to do on a lazy summer holiday that would be infinitely more pleasurable—like falling in love.

Falling in love. Fighting back the odd feeling that phrase gave him, King stopped in front of a patient's door. Somewhat absently, he ran an exploratory hand over his chin, felt the stubble and decided that before he presented himself to anyone he had better shave. He retreated to the lounge again and used the small bathroom reserved for the staff.

He stopped in to see three of his patients, even though the visits were totally unnecessary. John Danforth was more than capable of handling these cases and, admitting this, King finally faced the fact that he was stalling about leaving the hospital, and asked himself why.

Did he want to see Claire again? She'd probably been released already, but even if she hadn't been there was absolutely no point in provoking another encounter. Naturally, seeing her had stirred up a past he'd long since put behind him. He shouldn't have expected otherwise, but...

As he strolled toward the cafeteria, deciding to have a late breakfast before he headed home, King conceded that one reason he was stalling was that he wasn't looking forward to facing his father this morning. George Faraday was an extremely discerning man—*he* could have been a psychologist, King had often thought—and had the ability to read his son like a book.

Still, because he felt restless and out of sorts after hardly any sleep, King also admitted that he wasn't relishing taking his father on an outing. But it was a beautiful June day, and it wasn't fair to expect his father to sit at home, which was exactly what he would do if King didn't suggest some sort of diversion for both of them.

Usually King could think of many things he and his father would enjoy doing, but today nothing beckoned. Shelving the decision about how to spend the balance of the day, he moved down the cafeteria line, opting for scrambled eggs and bacon, a croissant and more coffee. He was paying at the checkout counter when he saw Ellie sitting alone in a corner, lingering over coffee and a croissant.

At that moment Ellie glanced up and their eyes met. She looked so forlorn King found it impossible not to acknowledge her with a brief nod. Then, carrying his tray in one hand, he walked over to her table. "Mind if I join you?"

The thought raced through his mind that Ellie's presence must mean Claire still hadn't been discharged, and he wondered why. Had she been lying to him last night when she'd insisted she had no more pain? Could her problem have been an acute appendicitis attack, after all? Common sense as well as medical acumen told King this was highly unlikely. Nevertheless, he wondered what was happening. And his tone of voice almost revealed his concern, though he'd learned to camouflage his feelings too well to give them away so easily.

"What are you doing here?" he asked casually.

By then he was placing the contents of his tray on Ellie's table, so it was too late to retreat when she said, "I'm waiting for Claire."

"What's the holdup?" King queried politely, hiding his shock. He was still wondering and, he had to admit, worrying.

"Dr. Danforth wanted to give her a final check over, that's all," Ellie told him.

That made sense. King recalled an older physician once confiding that doctors tended to fall into three categories. There were those who pushed the panic button and became true alarmists. Others swept everything under the rug, ignoring things they should have been dealing with largely because they had missed the boat in keeping up with their profession. Lastly, there were those who did manage to keep up with the exhausting supply of new literature and information while still maintaining a practice. This group followed a middle course, neither ignoring nor alarming.

King wouldn't go so far as calling Danforth a downright alarmist. But the man was overly conscientious, and that usually meant he took more time than really necessary with most of his cases. If Claire had continued improving at the rate she'd been last night, there seemed no reason she shouldn't haven't been discharged after the briefest of examinations.

Even as he thought this, King glanced up and saw her standing in the cafeteria doorway.

He'd just lifted his coffee cup to his lips and, to his astonishment, his hand actually shook during that telltale moment. He didn't like the feeling and resented thinking that after fourteen years Claire could affect him this way—or any other way.

He told himself he was suffering from a sudden confrontation with a past he'd thought was long buried, so his reaction was natural enough. But even though his hand steadied, he returned the cup to its saucer without taking a sip.

Claire hesitated and, despite himself, King sympathized with her. She obviously didn't want to face him any more than he wanted to face her... and that was to the good. The sooner they went their separate ways again, the better.

She paused in the doorway, and as their eyes met King wondered, his irritation mounting, what the hell he was supposed to do. Stand up and beckon a welcome to her? She looked as if she didn't known whether to move forward or turn around and flee.

Ellie took charge of the situation. "Claire," she called, waving. "Over here."

King could see that Claire felt trapped. Looking down at the untouched breakfast in front of him, he knew it would be much too transparent a ploy to get up suddenly and say he had to leave.

For once in his life, King wished that the beeper he always carried on his belt would go off, but for once in his life, it didn't.

He stood as Claire neared their table.

"Sit down, please," she said quickly.

Ellie asked, "What would you like, Claire?"

Claire looked at her cousin uncomprehendingly. "Like?" she echoed.

"Coffee? Maybe a breakfast roll or something?" Ellie suggested.

"No, nothing."

"Did you eat breakfast?" It was the physician in King speaking, as if he'd been programmed with two voices.

Claire shook her head. "I wasn't hungry," she told him. "Anyway, my throat is still rather sore."

"You *should* eat something," King insisted firmly. He rose again. "I'll get you some tea and toast."

The interval away from the table was welcome, and King took advantage of it by reminding himself that in a very short while Claire would again be out of his life. There was no reason to be any more than polite, as he would to any ex-patient, until that short while was over.

As he returned to the table with Claire's tea and toast, King saw Ellie talking earnestly to her cousin, as if trying to convince her of something. Then Ellie glanced up and, obviously deciding that he was nearly within hearing range, abruptly stopped talking.

This small bit of byplay gave King the ridiculous feeling that he was intruding, especially when Claire murmured thanks as he placed the tea and toast in front of her. Feeling awkward, he resumed his place and stared down at his breakfast. The eggs were cold, damn it, the bacon limp and soggy. And when he took a bite of croissant he found it had lost its crispness and had the consistency of malleable rubber. Nonetheless, King was determined to eat something, as if this action might prove his imperturbability.

Annoyed at himself, he wondered why he should care whether or not he appeared imperturbable, especially to Claire. He owed her nothing. Absolutely nothing. The shoe, if anything, was very much on the other foot.

Claire pushed away her toast, having barely touched a corner of one wedge. "I'm sorry, King," she said. "I really can't eat it."

"If your throat is *that* sore," he began, "I could—"

She shook her head. "It isn't that. It's..." Her words halted, her mouth twisted slightly. "I guess I'm just tired," she allowed.

"I should think you would be," Ellie said staunchly. "You had a miserable experience. Didn't she have a miserable experience, King?"

King was briefly amused that Ellie would turn to him for affirmation about anything concerning Claire. Still he nodded. "Yes," he said, knowing he was making a mockery of sounding grave. "Yes, she did."

Claire's eyes met his and King registered her suspicion, laced with some rightful resentment. Despite himself he smiled. She had a right to feel provoked, he conceded. He was behaving like a jerk.

Favoring her with the edge of his smile he said sincerely, "You *have* had a rotten experience, Claire. Food poisoning is no joke. I'm glad we got you when we did, thanks to Ellie, or the situation could have been considerably more serious."

King refrained from any medical analysis of his statement. Seeing the glow that spread across Ellie's face was reward enough for having perhaps perjured himself just slightly. Certainly it was true that a person could become extremely ill from food poisoning. And with pains like the ones she'd been having, Claire would have wound up in the emergency room sooner or later.

King gave up on his cold breakfast and glanced at his watch. "Well, I really have to be going," he announced.

"This is your day off?" Ellie queried.

He nodded. And at that precise instant, his beeper came to life.

He groaned and Ellie asked anxiously, "That doesn't mean you have to go back to work, does it, King?"

He grimaced. "I really don't know," he replied. Suddenly his time off became extremely valuable, even though a short while earlier he had been wondering what to do with the balance of the day.

Excusing himself, he went to the nearest phone and answered the page. There was an emergency that required a surgeon, he was told, and the surgeon who was supposed to be covering for him today wasn't available.

As he headed toward the ER, King looked out the windows and again noticed how nice the weather was. From now on, he chided himself, on his day off he'd arrange to take his father fishing. Out in the middle of the lake he couldn't be reached, beeper or no beeper.

"HE LOOKS TIRED," Ellie commented, but Claire's mind was far away.

She'd been contrasting the King she had known so long ago with the man who had just been sitting next to her, and it hurt to accept how much of a stranger this older, wiser King was. If there weren't so many memories to cloud the issue, and if his wasn't such a familiar face, he could well be someone she'd just met for the first time.

Suppose she had met King for the first time last night? Claire turned the thought over and knew that had that been the case, she definitely would have been attracted to him. For one thing, she would not have immediately encountered that blazing hostility in his eyes.

That hostility and the bitterness implicit in the statement he'd later made about how being left at the altar once was more than enough in any man's life were the only real proof Claire had that King felt any emotion toward her at all. But if last night had been their first meeting, the emotions King experienced would have been quite different.

It was tantalizing to speculate about how they might have reacted to each other. Would the chemistry between them—once such a potent factor—have been there if they'd faced each other as two strangers? Or would they simply have played out the roles of an emergency-room surgeon and a transient patient meeting, literally, in passing? Would King have tried to prolong their meeting or suggested they see each other while she was in Lakeport? And where might such a date have led?

Claire suddenly realized Ellie was tugging at her sleeve.

"Are you all right?" Ellie queried.

"Yes. Why?"

"I've mentioned twice that King looks tired, and I don't think you even heard me."

Claire forced a smile. "Sorry," she said. She took a sip of the tea, but it was cold. Pushing it aside, she suggested, "Shall we go?"

Ellie nodded. "Yes."

Claire looked around for her possessions, then reminded herself that Ellie had already stashed everything in the car. She shook her head in self-reproof and couldn't blame her cousin for thinking she was behaving oddly.

It was such a glorious day outside. Remembering past summers, Claire asked impulsively, "Ellie, has Baskin's Beach been all built up, or can you still go swimming there?"

Ellie, concentrating on driving out of the hospital parking lot, replied, "The lake's still too cold for swimming, Claire."

"I know. I wondered if the beach is still a beach, that's all."

Ellie glanced sideways, surprised. "What else would it be?" she asked reasonably.

Claire chuckled. This was a brand of logic typical of Ellie. At times, when they were younger, her rationality had been annoying. Now, though, Claire could have hugged Ellie simply for being Ellie.

"Places change," she explained simply. "I thought maybe the Baskins had sold their farm and maybe the land had been subdivided and..." She shook her head. "Ellie, is the beach still open to the public?"

"It's never been open to the public," Ellie pointed out. "We knew the Baskins, remember? The children used to take lessons from Dad and Aunt Delia. So they told us we could use their beach whenever we wanted."

"It seems to me a lot of people used their beach," Claire recalled.

"And probably still do," Ellie agreed. "The Baskin family still owns the land and operates the farm. The gate on the beach road is open to friends and, I guess, friends of friends."

"Do you go swimming there?"

Ellie shook her head. "Matter of fact," she said, "I haven't been swimming in years."

Claire leaned back, not wanting to delve into why Ellie didn't go swimming anymore. Instead, she felt herself whirling into memory's vortex once again. Years ago, she and King had spent wonderful hours together at Baskin's Beach, swimming and sunning and planning for that spun-gold future—their future—so dazzling to even think about.

Claire suppressed a sigh. *Who ever said that gold could not tarnish?* she asked herself sadly.

## CHAPTER FIVE

"YOU SHOULD get some rest," Ellie stated firmly.

"I've *been* resting," Claire protested.

"That's not what I'd call resting," Ellie retorted. "No one ever gets any rest in a hospital."

They were pulling up in front of the old Parmeter house as Ellie spoke. Looking out the car window, Claire again was struck by the shabbiness of the place. She remembered that when she was living here, people in town always referred to the house as the Parmeter mansion. She wondered if there was anyone around who still called it a mansion. Somehow, it was sadder to see a mansion fall into disrepair than an ordinary house. Like watching a famous screen beauty age ungracefully.

She followed Ellie up the walk and decided that tomorrow, when she felt stronger, she'd do something about Aunt Delia's roses. Certainly the hardware store would have something for black spot, or at least something to keep the plants from getting any worse.

Ellie paused at the big mailbox that, for as long as Claire could remember, had been affixed to the railing at the top of the porch steps. Even the mailbox, Claire observed, needed a coat of paint.

"Postman's been," Ellie announced, withdrawing an assortment of newspapers, magazines and envelopes. She sifted through the mail, then held one of the envelopes out to Claire. "Something from your art gallery in New York."

Claire recognized Brent Underwood's stylish handwriting and knew this must be a personal note. Tucking the envelope into her handbag for later reading, she reminded herself to call Brent. When she'd left New York, the gallery had been negotiating with a private collector for the purchase of two Monets. Claire smiled. If they were lucky enough to acquire the paintings, it would be hard to put them up for sale because she knew she was going to covet them for herself. She loved Monet's work, with the exception of some of his Venetian scenes and one rather lurid sunset. Those aside, he was her favorite Impressionist.

Ellie was watching her closely and Claire knew her cousin was probably curious about the contents of the unopened letter.

Suddenly, Ellie asked, "Something funny?"

"No," Claire answered quickly, slightly taken aback by the question. Then she realized she'd been smiling. "A letter from my associate," she said, "which reminded me of an important art purchase we're on the verge of making."

Ellie nodded then turned to unlock the front door with a large old-fashioned key. Watching her, Claire remembered that in earlier days people in Lakeport never thought about things like locking their houses.

Walking down the hall toward the kitchen, Ellie asked over her shoulder, "Is your associate that man you've written about now and then? Brent, isn't it?"

"That's right," Claire answered. She hesitated to say more because she knew how quick Ellie was to latch on to information and often inadvertently magnify it. The fact was that Brent was not only her closest business associate, literally her right-hand man in the Bailey Galleries, he was also her dearest friend. But only her friend. There was a special love between Brent and herself, but there would never be any romance for the simple reason that Brent was gay. Gay and very discreet. His private life was entirely his own and never infringed upon either his business or personal relationship with Claire.

Brent, she mused now, was the one person in the world who had appreciated how difficult it was for her to make this trip back to Lakeport. Still, he had urged her to do it.

"You can't run away forever, Claire," he'd told her as they lingered over demitasses in their favorite French restaurant, a small place in the West Fifties in Manhattan.

"I stopped running a long time ago," Claire assured him, then knew immediately how defensive she had sounded.

Brent smiled and said gently, "It's a matter of definition, my dear. Call it running, call it whatever you want to call it, but the fact remains that it's time you went back and faced up to your *escape*. Only when you do that will you really be able to view your past objectively. You have to confront your ghosts and exorcise the bad ones, Claire. It's difficult but not impossible, believe me."

She did believe him. Brent had many years of experience on Claire, though exactly how many she didn't know. He laughingly refused to reveal his age—probably within a year or two of Philip's, Claire guessed—preferring to remain, as he put it, "Thirty-nine, forever!"

As she followed Ellie into the kitchen, Claire wondered if Brent would consider King a ghost that needed exorcism.

Ellie filled the teakettle with water and set it on the stove. Then she opened the freezer above the fridge, peered in and withdrew a package of frozen Danish. "I'll heat these up so we can have a little snack," she said. "Then I want you to go upstairs and lie down for a while."

Ellie had always turned to food when she was puzzled or discouraged or in any sort of emotional state about anything, Claire remembered. It was, perhaps, the main reason for her weight problem. Food represented consolation, not entirely bad except for the effect on one's figure.

Claire wished ruefully that she'd had something she could turn to the many times in her life when she'd needed solace. But chocolate cake and buttery pastries had never done anything for her in that respect.

She was tempted to snap at Ellie, "I don't want anything to eat and you don't need anything." But she knew she would only hurt her cousin by doing so. She temporized by saying, "My stomach's still a bit upset, Ellie. I'd rather give it a chance to settle down before I eat something."

Ellie nodded, and after a moment of hesitation put the pastries back in the freezer. "I'll make some soup for lunch," she decided. "That'll be soothing."

First, though, she pulled out a chair at the kitchen table, sat down and thumbed through her mail. After a moment she pushed everything aside. "Nothing but bills and junk," she said. The teakettle whistled and she added, "You will have a cup of tea, at least, won't you, Claire?"

"That will be fine." Claire nodded, sitting down at the kitchen table while Ellie busied herself at the counter.

She loved Ellie, but now that they were together again she remembered how dependent Ellie could be. Dependent in the sense that Ellie really didn't like to be alone. On the other hand, there were many times when Claire enjoyed being alone—actually needed solitude. It had always been that way, and now Claire recalled those long-ago years when she'd lived in this house, always feeling guilty—subconsciously, at least—for stealing so much of Delia's and Lottie's and Ralph's attention away from Ellie.

Ellie never gave even the slightest indication of resenting this. Rather, she had been generous to a fault, sharing absolutely everything with Claire, from her favorite possessions to her most intimate confidences. But there had been moments when Claire had yearned to escape from her cousin, feeling that she would suffocate if she didn't breathe for herself, just once in a while. At those times, Claire had taken refuge in her favorite hideaway, the dollhouse.

The dollhouse had never meant to Ellie quite what it meant to Claire. Ellie enjoyed the tea ceremonies with the dolls, to be sure, and the make-believe. But as a teenager she would never have thought of the dollhouse as a place of sanctuary, as Claire did. By then Ellie had put dolls, magic and fantasy behind her and was already helping Delia with the cooking for the family. Once she got her driver's license she did a major part of the marketing, and perhaps because of this it was always something of a struggle for her to keep up in school, especially in Latin and math.

Claire wondered now why she'd never been motivated to share in the cooking and housework. Her only answer emphasized something she'd just dimly understood all these years. She'd moved into the Parmeter house after her parents' death, but she'd never felt like a real part of the family, as Ellie obviously did. In the eyes of her aunts and uncle, Claire had deemed herself a visitor, a guest. And, she suspected, in her grandfather's eyes she had forever been an intruder who reminded him too vividly of the son he'd never been able to conquer. She looked like her father and, in many ways, was like her father. She'd not been born to be cast in a mold by an irascible old man who took out his frustrations on his family. Claire thought sadly how he'd only succeeded in magnifying those frustrations when his daughters and one remaining son had become good musicians, but not the kind of great musician he'd always yearned to be himself.

"Whew!" The expression, involuntary and as audible as this truth she'd never fully appreciated, swept Claire in a moment of surprising revelation.

Ellie, having brewed the tea in a lovely old porcelain pot, paused in her pouring and asked, "What is it?"

"I was just thinking about . . . a lot of things," Claire answered lamely, knowing that to say "nothing," would only precipitate another question from her cousin.

Ellie nodded sympathetically and, carrying the brimming teacups over to the table, said, "I guess there's a lot for you to think about right now. It must have been enough to really start the wheels turning, seeing King again like that."

"Yes, it was," Claire admitted quietly.

"The way he looked when he recognized you," Ellie mused, stirring sugar into her tea. "It never occurred to me that he's still been carrying a torch for you all these years."

"Ellie, please . . . don't leap to conclusions!" Claire urged. "I can assure you, King Faraday hasn't been carrying a torch for me, as you put it. He's had much too busy and full a life to stoke flames that ran out of fuel years ago.''

"It seems to me that King leads a lonely life,'' Ellie said. "At least, since he's been back in Lakeport. For those first couple of years after you went away..."

"Yes?" Claire prodded, tensely.

"Well, King went pretty wild. He got in with the wrong crowd and some of the things I heard he was doing—''

"Please, Ellie," Claire said swiftly. "I don't want to hear about it. I honestly don't want to. Whatever King did after I left, what he does now, for that matter, is none of my business.'' She forced herself to sip the hot tea, even though her throat still hurt and swallowing was painful.

"All right, Claire. I know that look on your face. I'm not trying to stir anything up, you know. And chances are you won't see King again anyway. Like I told you, he keeps pretty much to himself.''

Ellie's statement had the effect of making Claire's throat hurt all the more. Did she want to see King Faraday again? she asked herself. If so, she should be woman enough to seek him out and suggest they have dinner together for old times' sake. For new times' sake. For whatever.

She managed to finish her tea and a glance at the kitchen clock told her it was still an hour short of noon. She said, "I think I'm going to take your advice and get a little rest."

"Good," Ellie approved.

At the kitchen door memory struck again and Claire turned. "Ellie, you haven't said a word about your lunch yesterday with Thomas Haskell.''

"I know," Ellie said, smiling. "There hasn't been much chance to get into *that*. I guess I was so worried about you I put Thomas right out of my mind. Anyway, Bill said he'd like to come over tonight, if you feel up to talking about things. I thought I'd fill you in then."

"Of course I'll be up to it," Claire said quickly. "I'm fine. Just a little tired, that's all."

She was tired. But far more emotionally than physically, despite yesterday's ordeal. Back in her room, she soon discovered she wasn't going to be able to take a nap after all. Nor could she rest, with so many thoughts spinning around inside her head, with echoes of the past sounding their own kind of muted thunder.

She opened Brent's letter and smiled. He'd sent her a humorous card just perfect for the moment, and had added a brief message of encouragement in her endeavors.

Before long, though, Claire became so restless she could no longer tolerate trying to relax on the bed that once had been Aunt Delia's. She got up, splashed her face with cold water, brushed her hair, and with her purse and car keys in hand went downstairs, prepared to break the news to Ellie that she was going to drive around for a while just to get a breath of air and maybe a glimpse of the lake.

Ellie's feelings might be hurt. Even more likely, Ellie might quickly, innocently, include herself in the plan. Claire warned herself she must be prepared to say, "Ellie, I love you. But I honestly need to be alone for a little while."

This rehearsal was unnecessary. Ellie had left a note on the kitchen table.

Needed to stock up on some staples so I've gone over
to the Champlain Mall while you get some rest.
Thought I'd get the grill out and buy some charcoal
and we can barbecue steaks for dinner. I'll stop at
Bill's office and see if he can join us.

The errands would undoubtedly keep Ellie busy for a
while and, though she felt guilty for thinking of it like
that, Claire nevertheless seized the opportunity to get out
by herself. Still, she didn't do what she'd intended.

Forcing her spine to stiffen, she walked out the back
door and down the path to the dollhouse. All the way she
was thinking of Brent Underwood, of his saying that
ghosts had to be exorcised because they were practically
impossible to bury. Claire's ghosts were not actually *in*
the dollhouse, but surely they were floating around
nearby. For it was in this charming Victorian miniature
cottage that her world had ended and her dreams had
died.

She tugged at the door, its once bright blue paint now
faded, and for a moment thought it must be locked. But
after she twisted the knob and tugged again, the door
creaked open.

With the dusty windows shut against the infusion of
fresh air, the musty smell of a place abandoned wafted
around Claire and she grimaced. It was a smell she associated with old trunks packed with papers and clothing that had once belonged to people now long dead, and
she hated it. In the attic of the Parmeter house there were
many such trunks, she remembered, stacked atop one
another like discarded memories.

She crossed the floor of the tiny parlor and, after a bit
of wrestling, managed to open first one window, then the
others. The June sunshine spilled into the room, golden

and inviting, spattering the furniture exactly as it had done so many years before.

The dolls' tea set was on the small sideboard and their chairs were grouped around the little maple table. The dolls themselves were sitting in a prim row on the scaled-down velvet-covered settee by the far wall. Six of them, the six who had been the permanent residents of the dollhouse. Other dolls were transient, visitors coming for tea who later returned to the big house.

Seeing the sextet with their lovely old wide-eyed china faces, Claire didn't know whether to laugh or cry. Then, in the corner rocking chair that had been just big enough for her to sit in that last terrible morning when she'd come here, she saw a seventh doll.

Jewel. Her favorite doll. A doll given to her by her parents when she was six and cherished for years thereafter.

Jewel sat alone, wearing the bright-yellow pinafore Claire remembered so vividly. A flower-embroidered sash of pale ecru circled her waist, and beneath the pinafore she wore a checkered yellow and white blouse trimmed with white lace. Her hair was as red as autumn's rust chrysanthemums, waist-long and twisted into two yellow ribbon-tied braids. Her features were embroidered, her eyes cocoa-colored, her mouth a scarlet line tilted upward to give Jewel the engaging appearance of forever awaiting a wonderful surprise.

Longing and nostalgia blended in such a poignant mixture that tears stung Claire's eyes as she reached for Jewel. She cuddled the doll against her just as she used to, especially right after her parents' death, when she'd been a very young and very lost sixteen. Alone and feeling unwanted, despite the kindnesses of her aunts and uncle, she'd been especially vulnerable to the moods of her grandfather, whose dislike had the power to sting even today. Remembering, a chilled blanket from the past wrapped around her, its edges frayed.

She had no recollection of Jewel's presence on that long-ago morning. Rather, she had the distinct feeling that Jewel couldn't have been here at the time, for she would have clutched the doll desperately, Claire was sure of that, which meant that at some point Ellie must have brought Jewel to the dollhouse and left her in the rocking chair to maintain a mute vigil.

Claire could only imagine why Ellie would have done such a thing. Perhaps, at this point, Ellie wouldn't remember herself. Yet her gesture indicated vividly to Claire how much her desertion had hurt her cousin, and how lonely Ellie, who couldn't bear to be alone, must have felt.

Ellie never knew why she'd left, never knew the reasons that her cousin in effect stole her car and money, then sped off.

Later, Claire had mailed back the money. And two friends of Philip's had obligingly dropped Ellie's car off in Lakeport on their way to Montreal. But that, of course, had not compensated for Ellie's immensely hurt feelings.

No one had understood Claire's actions. Not Ellie or anyone else in the Parmeter family.

Nor King Faraday.

Placing Jewel carefully back in the rocking chair, Claire thought about how she had flung angry words at King during that brief, bitter moment...then had left him to reach his own conclusions. In every sense of the phrase she'd left him waiting at the altar; she'd totally deserted him.

A bee droning outside the window screen caught Claire's attention, and the scent of roses began to displace the mustiness of the little room. As the golden warmth of the June sunshine caressed her face, a sense of terrible helplessness gripped her. The past was the past, she knew. And whether she'd been right or wrong in what she had done, there was no going back.

Suddenly Claire sensed the dollhouse beginning to close in on her and she had the horrible feeling that at any moment Rosalie Brenner was going to loom in the doorway, her hair disheveled, her eyes wild, her face streaked with tears.

Had Rosalie lied?

The question came involuntarily. Claire tried brushing it away because she didn't want to know the answer but it hung suspended in her mind, pointing an accusing finger at her.

Other questions rushed in. Was Rosalie in Lakeport? Had she given birth to King's child? Or had she been persuaded to have an abortion?

*Had Rosalie actually been pregnant with King's child?*

Questions that had plagued her so long ago, questions she had suppressed, even buried, with Philip's understanding and help, began to resurface. Claire wanted only to avoid them now, and turning her back on the room she hurried through the door and out into the sunshine. She was halfway down the garden path when she was startled by someone saying, "Claire Parmeter! It is you, isn't it?"

The voice, she realized after a second, was coming from the other side of the hedge that separated the Parmeter property from the house next door. Unconsciously, she looked for the same gap through which she had witnessed that never-to-be-forgotten kiss between

King and Rosalie. The gap had grown over and the hedge was the verdant green of early summer and higher than ever. So high that the man who had just spoken to her had to walk around it and into the open before she realized who he was.

"Chris!" she sputtered. "Christopher Talmadge." Strange, how totally she had forgotten about Chris, King's closest friend who was to have been the best man at their wedding. As he grinned down at her and she took his outstretched hand, Claire remembered how much she had always liked Chris Talmadge. He was tall and sandy-haired, with handsome features, an easy manner and an engaging personality.

"Ellie told me you were coming back," he said. "I've been in New York on business. Just flew in this morning."

"You still live here, Chris?"

He nodded. "Now I do, most of the time," he said. "I spent a few years away, in the New York City area. Then...I decided Lakeport was where I wanted to be. My business is here. I own Champlain Plastics." Noting Claire's puzzled look, he elaborated, "Our plant is up on the north edge of town. It was built five years ago as the branch of an outfit in Albany, but I bought them out, so now we're purely a local industry. We make plastic containers for pills, mostly...we do a lot of work with pharmaceutical companies. Right now I'm happy to say we employ about fifty people, and hope to keep expanding."

"That's wonderful," Claire said, and she meant that sincerely. Her eyes flickered toward the hedge and the glimpse of a roof beyond it. "So you live in the family house."

"Yes. My father retired a few years back and the parents took the route south. They live in the St. Petersburg area. Get up here for a couple of weeks late in the summer, but for the most part they've become real Floridians."

Claire heard this but skipped ahead. "Are you married, Chris?" she asked.

"No." His smile was rueful. "I tried it, but it didn't work." He sobered suddenly. "I was sorry to hear about your husband, Claire."

She nodded, still finding it difficult to cope with expressions of sympathy though Philip had been dead four years now.

"Any children?" Chris asked softly. "Ellie never said, but—"

"No," Claire answered, her voice equally soft. "No, Philip and I never had any children. Did you?"

Chris shook his head. "No," he said. "Which, under the circumstances, was just as well. It wasn't a very pleasant divorce... not that divorces are usually pleasant. But there was a lot of bitterness between Sarah and me by the time we decided to call it quits. It would have been hard on kids."

He shrugged and Claire realized that he was striving for a change of subject. She wanted to help, but her own mind was blank.

After a rather heavy moment, Chris asked, "Going to be around long?"

"I don't really know," Claire admitted. "I'm here to help Ellie. You've probably heard about that."

"About Haskell and the will he claims Charlotte Parmeter made just before she died?" Chris asked, referring to Lottie by her maiden name, probably the way most people who had known her would, Claire realized.

"Yes, and it seems wrong. Ellie should get much more than it appears she will, should Thomas have his way," Claire said.

"Ellie deserves a hell of a lot, that's for sure," Chris agreed. "She gave some of the best years of her life to her family. Not that she's the kind of person who'd ever expect to be paid back, but it's a cinch Haskell doesn't deserve to inherit much of anything. I can tell you honestly, Claire, I've never cared for the man. But then he'd be an unlikely candidate to win a popularity contest around Lakeport. He comes on as a bully and a braggart." Chris smiled reminiscently. "My mother used to say she could never understand what Lottie Parmeter saw in him," he confided.

Claire returned his smile. "I imagine your mother was actually voicing public opinion."

"Yes, I'd say so." Chris glanced at the heavy gold wristwatch he was wearing and added, "Claire, I have a luncheon engagement. It's business, so I have to run along. But I hope you'll be free for dinner one of these nights?"

"I'd like that, Chris."

"I'll be in touch then," he said, and ambled off.

Claire started back toward the house, thankful that Chris hadn't brought up the subject of King yet strangely wishing that he had.

She wondered if King and Chris were still close friends, or if they'd lost touch with each other during their years away from Lakeport and had never gotten back on the same track. That often happened with friendships formed in youth.

Even if they weren't close anymore, Chris would still know the answer to many of her questions, Claire thought as she slowly walked back to the house.

For one, he would probably know the answer to the riddle of Rosalie Brenner. And whether or not there was somewhere—perhaps right in Lakeport—a teenage girl or boy who had been fathered by King.

# CHAPTER SIX

ELLIE'S REPORT of her luncheon with Thomas Haskell was not very satisfactory. She'd set up the charcoal grill on the flat grassy lawn beside the kitchen door and had unearthed three canvas-backed folding chairs and an old picnic table. Bill brought over a bottle of rum and mixed rum and tonics decorated with slices of lime. While they were sipping the drinks, he and Claire listened.

Ellie said that Thomas had taken her to a drive-in restaurant on the outskirts of town and that the so-called luncheon had consisted of cheeseburgers and milk shakes consumed while seated in his car.

"He seemed to be in a hurry," Ellie said. "I couldn't help wondering why he'd asked me to have lunch with him in the first place. To tell you the truth, I think he was interested in what you plan to do, Claire."

Claire had been sipping her drink through a thin green-plastic straw, wondering if perhaps Christopher Talmadge also made plastic straws at his plant. Ellie's comment startled her. "Me?" she echoed.

"Yes, you." Ellie paused then added, a note of resignation in her voice, "I have the idea he thinks he can handle me without any trouble. But he's not so sure about you, Claire."

"And he shouldn't be sure about you, either, Ellie," Bill growled.

Ellie turned and shrugged. "Bill, I haven't told Thomas that you're representing me," she confessed.

"Oh?"

"Don't look like that! You don't know how thankful I am to have you on my side. It's just that I thought..."

Bill sighed. "Okay. What did you think, Ellie?"

"I suppose I thought it might be a good idea to seem as helpless as possible. That way I'd find out what Thomas really has up his sleeve. I guess that sounds silly, but—"

"It's not the wisest thing to do," Bill stated bluntly. "If Haskell believes you're helpless he'll only take advantage of you all the more, I can assure you of that. You're going to have to face the man in a court of law whether you like it or not, Ellie."

"I don't like it, you know that. I don't want to go to court and have our family linen washed in public," Ellie said, looking so miserable that Claire felt sorry for her, yet wanted to shake her at the same time.

"Haskell won't hesitate to do your laundry right in the middle of Main Street if it means getting what he's after," Bill warned. "You know damned well the way your family wills were originally drawn up, Ellie. Your grandfather left everything to his three living children," Bill added, glancing at Claire. "Right or wrong."

"I never expected my grandfather to leave *me* anything," Claire assured him.

"I know that," Bill said patiently. "Ellie and I have been over it, and I understand your position. Insofar as the property itself is concerned, you'd have to go to court and try to break the will yourself if you want what both Ellie and I consider your fair share. The contents of this place are something else again. Ellie feels, and I agree, that your father was entitled to inherit many of the family heirlooms. So it stands to reason they should go to you. We're not talking about dime-store china and stainless steel, Claire. There are some very valuable antiques under consideration here.''

"I know that,'' Claire said, determined to remain calm. "And I very much appreciate how Ellie feels. A lot of people, especially when they're related, wouldn't feel that way. But let's face it. I turned my back on Lakeport—on my family, that is—a long time ago. Ellie was the one who stayed with the ship, even when it looked like a sinking ship. She's the person who deserves to be rewarded.''

"Stuff and nonsense!'' Ellie expostulated.

It was a phrase Ellie had used for as long as Claire could remember. And Ellie could be very intense when she uttered it. Watching her cousin, flushed of face and righteously indignant, Claire smiled fondly. Damn it, she did love Ellie! And, seeing the look on Bill Edgerly's face as he watched her cousin, it was plain she wasn't the only person who loved Ellie. Even a casual eye would note that Bill was wearing a very transparent heart on the thin sleeve of his summer shirt.

The lawyer in Bill surfaced quickly, though. "Let's take this a step at a time,'' he cautioned. "No more lunchtime meetings with Haskell or private meetings with him at any other time, Ellie. If you want to meet with him at all, or if he wants to see you, Claire, I want to be present. The first of next week I'll call his lawyer and we can start our own ball rolling. If he really has a valid will, he's going to have to prove it!''

With that, Bill turned his attention to fixing another round of drinks. Then he presided at the charcoal grill as if this were the most natural milieu in the world.

Watching him, Claire had a vision of Bill and Ellie sharing the rest of their lives together. Ellie still wasn't too old to have a child, maybe even more than one—if she came to her senses and realized that a chance for happiness was being offered her, a chance to which she seemed annoyingly oblivious.

Didn't Ellie *realize* that Bill Edgerly was still as crazy about her as he'd been when they were teenagers? Now, though, his devotion had the added dimensions of maturity and experience.

Claire conceded that very probably Ellie wasn't aware of Bill's yearnings at all. There was an odd little stubborn streak in Ellie, not exactly an inferiority complex. Ellie didn't really suffer from an inferiority complex. But she'd been a behind-the-scenes personality for so long in the Parmeter family that she'd relegated herself to a secondary role and had made it impossible to put herself first. At least, that's the way Claire analyzed it, and despite their years of separation she suspected she still knew Ellie better than anyone else.

Bill cooked the steaks perfectly and Ellie produced hot rolls and a tossed green salad. Afterward, for dessert, they had homemade strawberry shortcake. Like a lot of naturally thin people, Bill had an enormous appetite and did full justice to everything set before him. Ellie beamed with pleasure at his compliments, and observing this Claire wondered if perhaps the way Bill could reach her cousin was through her cooking.

After a discreet interval following dinner, Claire said she had to make a couple of phone calls to New York, and excused herself. The calls were valid, or at least one of them was, she thought, smiling at her little conspiracy. She phoned Brent Underwood and learned it was virtually certain they were going to get the Monets for the galleries.

Brent chuckled at her reaction and teased, "Suppose I tell you I have an immediate buyer."

"Please!" Claire protested.

"I know you want them, Claire, so why don't you just buy one for yourself? You have it coming, darling."

Claire asked excitedly, "Which one, Brent? You know I couldn't possibly make a choice!"

"Greedy," he accused laughingly, because they both knew Claire was anything but greedy. She and Philip had started the gallery a couple of years into their marriage, and though the money and expertise had been Philip's, Claire had worked very hard under his tutelage. By the time Philip died, the Bailey Galleries—one on New York's East Fifty-Seventh Street, the other on the Florida Gulf Coast's Siesta Key—had achieved an international reputation. And Philip and Claire Bailey and their assistant, Brent Underwood, were highly respected in the art world.

Philip had always referred to Brent as their associate and, at times, Claire had wondered why he'd never made Brent an official partner. Brent's share of the profits had been rightfully excellent, and the title of partner would have been frosting on his cake. She had edged into the subject with Philip on several occasions, but Philip had always hedged. This puzzled her because the two men had been friends for years, and Claire knew that Philip's trust in Brent was absolute. It wasn't until after his death, when the contents of his will were revealed that Claire discovered what her husband's rationale had been. He left her sole ownership of the galleries, thus insuring her financially and professionally for the rest of her life.

Philip had been sixteen years older than Claire, and no man could have been more appreciative of his wife's beauty or her youth. He'd wanted her to live the balance of her life free of worry, financial worry at least. Like most wise people, Philip had realized that complete freedom from worry was as uncertain as death itself was a fact.

Alone at the helm, Claire often thought of offering a full partnership to Brent. He'd voluntarily shouldered many extra responsibilities during the four years since Philip's death and really deserved an official voice in the affairs of the firm. Speaking to him on the phone now, Claire filed a memo in the back of her mind to explore the partnership situation as soon as possible after her return to New York.

Meantime, there were details to discuss concerning the acquisition of the Monets and a number of other matters involving the New York gallery. The Siesta Key gallery, in essence, was hibernating, kept open during the off-season summer months but not expected to flourish again until late fall. There was a skeleton staff and, admittedly, the gallery was on view more for the sake of voyeurs than for purchasers. Some, come the season, would become purchasers, but in the interim, the gallery mainly promoted goodwill and served as a colorful advertisement for its sister in New York.

When they finished with the business details, Brent asked softly, "Has it been very bad up there, Claire?"

She hesitated. Brent was not easily fooled by anyone, and he knew her so well she doubted she could fool him now.

She said honestly, "In some ways, it's been traumatic. In other ways, easier than I expected. At first I thought this old house would be full of ghosts for me. So many people gone, since I left. But after the initial shock of the...the emptiness, I adjusted. Maybe because of Ellie. She's still so much like the Ellie I've always known. A little older, a little plumper. But still so lovable in some ways, so irritating in others.''

''No other ghosts, Claire?''

A couple of months after Philip's death, Brent had come to Claire's apartment for dinner one night. Afterward they'd sat for a long time in her small private sitting room sipping sherry and talking. Brent hadn't asked any personal questions, but something about him, his quiet empathetic interest in others perhaps, had sparked a flow of words from Claire unlike anything she'd uttered in almost a decade.

That night she'd told Brent more about King Faraday than even Philip had known. She talked about the terrible, terrible hurt, and about her escape. And about the refuge she had found in Philip's arms and heart.

Brent had listened with only an occasional comment. And when Claire had purged herself of all that had been pent up for so long, when she had apologized for involving him, he had said, ''Some day you'll have to go back and face him, Claire. Even now, after Philip's death, you haven't gotten over King.''

She had protested this. She had been loyal to Philip, devoted, she had never so much as glanced at another man. Had she loved him? Yes, and deeply, too. In an entirely different way than she had loved King, but that had been the ecstatic, impetuous love of youth. Passion unrestrained by either caution or experience. Love, God, yes, it had been love. But love not to be trusted, unreliable, as dangerous as thin winter ice.

''Claire, are you still there?'' Brent asked, snapping her back.

"He's here in Lakeport, Brent. King. He's a doctor, a surgeon. Last night, Ellie had to take me to the emergency room at the hospital—"

Brent's horrified *"What?"* cut across her words.

"Ellie thought I had appendicitis, but it was food poisoning," Claire said. "I'm fine now," she added hastily. "King was the physician on duty. It was...quite a reunion. A shocker for both of us. You can imagine."

"Yes," Brent said dryly. "I can imagine."

"It's unlikely I'll see him again. He's very busy professionally, and I understand he lives an intensely private life."

"You *should* see him again, Claire."

Claire hedged. "Are you saying I should confront him...about our past?"

"Perhaps," Brent told her. "Yes, that's exactly what you should do."

CLAIRE HAD NO INTENTION of confronting King Faraday. Instead, her conversation with Brent made her resolve to get on with her business in Lakeport then return to New York as quickly as possible. She told herself she wanted to be at the gallery when the Monets arrived, and tantalized herself with the thought of buying one for the personal collection that Philip had started long ago. Among the Impressionists, Claire owned a Renoir, a Degas and a Pissarro. But Monet was her favorite and the thought of actually living with one of his works was exhilarating.

Philip, artist and art lover though he was, had started his collection primarily as an investment. Claire had never been able to consider paintings in that light. She loved being surrounded by them because she loved looking at beautiful things. Nor was she just a devotee of

French Impressionist art. Her tastes were wide-ranging, her likes and dislikes motivated almost entirely by her own sense of beauty. She'd never felt a strong sense of possession about things, and even now she would have said that all the art they had still belonged to Philip.

Claire shied away from true material "possessiveness" because she'd seen too much of it as a very young woman. The Parmeters had clung to everything they owned, often endowing inanimate objects like the family heirlooms with more attention than they gave the living, breathing members of their family. From an early age, Claire had never wanted to feel that way about anything.

Yet there had been one person in her life about whom she had felt possessive. She had wanted King entirely for herself. She'd wanted his attention, his devotion. Wanted him to acknowledge her as her parents, her grandfather and most of the rest of the Parmeters never had.

But King had never been hers. In a single moment on a June day, she had learned that truth for all time.

THE NEXT MORNING, Claire went down to breakfast determined to level with her cousin.

Over coffee, she said, "I don't know how much longer I'm going to be able to stay here, Ellie."

Ellie was spreading an English muffin with a thick coating of jam and looked up, appalled. "You just got here, Claire!" she scolded.

*Had* she just gotten here? For a moment, Claire felt as if she'd been back in Lakeport forever. Yet it was only three and a half days since she'd arrived, and a large chunk of that time had been devoted to recovering from food poisoning.

"I called Brent last night," she said hastily.

"And he suggested you get back to New York?"

Claire shook her head. "No, but there are some purchases coming up in the near future that I'm very much interested in. I should be there. Really, I want to be there, Ellie. But no, please don't worry. I definitely won't go until we have things straightened out here. I'd just like to expedite this will business, that's all."

"Bill said he's going to talk to Thomas's lawyer next week," Ellie reminded her.

"I know." Claire saw that Ellie had donned her stubborn look, so she proceeded cautiously. "I don't want to rush anyone," she said. "But I think it might be an idea for me to talk to Bill myself. Professionally, I mean. In his office."

Ellie wasn't one to mince words when the occasion called for forthrightness. "Why?" she demanded bluntly.

"When the three of us talk, sentiment tends to edge in," Claire said, equally frank. "Even Bill refers to the contents of this house as 'the family heirlooms.' To me a family heirloom has a value that far surpasses, emotionally, the dollar value of a piano or a painting or a chest of drawers. Do you understand what I mean?"

"I think," Ellie said, "you're trying to tell me you don't want anything in this house."

"I've already said that, Ellie," Claire replied patiently.

"Then you're telling me you don't want anything *from* this house," Ellie corrected herself. "You don't want any Parmeter memories, because everything concerned with this house and...and with Lakeport must seem like a bad dream to you."

Ellie stood and got the coffeepot from the counter, then poured refills for both of them. She resumed her seat, plopping down heavily on the wooden kitchen chair and, looking at her, Claire had the impression that everything about Ellie was sagging right now. Not just physically, but emotionally and mentally, as well.

She said slowly, "You're misreading me, Ellie. You're inferring that Lakeport and this house hold nothing but miserable memories for me. That isn't true. Some of the happiest times of my life were spent right here, playing with you. When I was a child and came here summers—"

"And later, after you came here to live?" Ellie challenged.

"It was difficult to adjust, but you helped me. You and Aunt Delia, your father... and even Aunt Lottie. They were all very kind to me, Ellie, and as time went by I came to care more and more about them."

"You never even came back for their funerals," Ellie accused.

A sharp current of shock jolted through Claire. Looking at Ellie, she saw that her cousin's face was closed to all emotion, as if she had shut herself behind a door.

Yet for all the shock, there was relief, too. Finally it was out. Finally Ellie had said what she must have wanted to say for a long time. Finally she was uttering the irrefutable truth that Claire had fallen far short in her obligations to the Parmeter family.

It was impossible not to feel defensive, but Claire told herself how important it was not to sound that way. She said, determined to make Ellie understand, "I admit that when Grandfather died I didn't come back because I... didn't want to." She tried again. "That's not right, either. I couldn't face it, Ellie. I couldn't cope. Try and understand that, will you? I was terrified that I'd run into King... and even the thought of that was something I couldn't handle."

Ellie nodded gravely. "King was still around town when Grandfather died," she conceded. "He left not long after that, but he didn't come to the funeral, either. Not that anyone expected him to. King had changed a lot by then. He stayed out of sight, as far as we were concerned. Anyway..."

Claire realized Ellie was waiting for further explanations. She said, "When Aunt Delia died, Philip was already gravely ill. We went to Mexico on what proved to be a wild-goose chase in the hope of finding a cure for him. Instead, he came home to die nearly a year later. There was no chance of my getting back here or, believe me, I would have come." Claire thought for a moment, then continued, "When Aunt Lottie died I was in Paris on business for the gallery. By the time I got your letter... it was too late."

"I know," Ellie admitted. "I tried to reach you in New York, but Brent said you were overseas." Plainly, it never would have occurred to Ellie to place a phone call to France.

"When your father died," Claire went on, feeling as if she were being choked by this depressing recital of her omissions, "I was in the Orient, again on business for the gallery. My secretary called me in Hong Kong to relay your message, but I'd already left. Anyway, it would have been too late, but I did phone you as soon as I got back to New York..."

"I know." Ellie nodded, visibly more relaxed, evidently satisfied by what Claire had told her. "All those times," Ellie confessed, "I...I missed having you around, that's all."

It was a simple remark, all the more poignant because of its simplicity. Tears stung Claire's eyes and she tried to blink them away. But one escaped, trailing a salty pearl down her cheek.

"Ellie . . ." she began.

Ellie smiled. "Don't say any more, Claire," she said. "It's all right, really. And if you want to talk to Bill by yourself, go ahead."

That should have been good enough, yet Claire had the uneasy feeling she would be playing the traitor were she to make a private business appointment with Bill.

*I'll let this go till next week,* she decided, *and we'll see what Bill comes up with on his own.*

THE CHAMPLAIN MALL had been built since Claire had lived in Lakeport. With the breakfast dishes washed and put away, Ellie decided to take Claire there and suggested they could go to lunch afterward at the Iroquois Inn, a lovely old place along the Lakeshore drive.

Claire, eager to please, did her best to act enthusiastic about the mall. But it was the usual composite of discount stores, cut-rate pharmacies and fast-food restaurants that under other circumstances she would have breezed through without making so much as a single purchase. Primarily to please Ellie, she bought a cotton-knit sweater in soft yellow, then stopped in a jewelry stall where she bought Ellie a pink-pearl pendant with matching earrings. Ellie was as enchanted with her gift as if it had come from Tiffany's. And her pleasure was sincere, Claire reflected—another of the wonderful things about Ellie.

The next day was Saturday and, on the spur of the moment, the two cousins decided to take the ferry over to Burlington just for the fun of it. The weather was glorious and Lake Champlain seemed more than ever like a great landlocked sea framed by mountains to the east and the west. Since she had left Lakeport, Claire had done a lot of traveling, but as she gazed out over this region that had been the home of her ancestors, she reminded herself that she'd never seen more beautiful scenery anywhere.

It wasn't until Saturday night that Ellie revealed she was still playing the organ for the Sunday services at the Episcopal Church. She had taken on the task several years before when Delia's arthritis had forced her to step down from a job she'd held and loved since she was a young girl.

"You'll come, won't you?" she asked Claire as they started upstairs to bed.

"To church?"

"Yes, to church."

"No, Ellie," Claire said firmly. "I can't. I really can't."

"Don't you go to church anymore?"

"It isn't that. It has nothing to do with church in general. It's just that...well, my being here in Lakeport. You know small towns. Everyone in the congregation would be staring at me. Later, I'd meet up with so many people..." She shook her head. "I'm not ready for that."

"A lot of people do know you, Claire," Ellie said. "And a lot of them want to see you. I know. Every time I've run into someone who'd heard you were coming back, they've asked me to bring you over for lunch or dinner or tea or whatever. These people were all your friends, after all."

"Acquaintances," Claire amended.

"All right, acquaintances."

"I know. But please don't ask this of me. Maybe next Sunday."

They let it go at that. And in the morning, Claire watched Ellie head off for church with the guilty feeling that, come next Sunday, it was doubtful she'd still be in Lakeport.

With Ellie gone and church bells pealing in the distance, the house at once became both too empty and too full for comfort. Confronted by this emotional dichotomy, Claire knew she had to get away for a while and, as she gazed out the parlor windows, she again noticed the rosebushes flanking the front walk.

She'd intended to get some first-aid treatment for them, but most of the downtown stores would be closed on Sundays. Then she remembered seeing a garden center about five miles out of town when she and Ellie had been out driving around together the other day.

There were dark clouds in the west, she noted as she climbed into her car. The weather was worsening. It looked like June's perfection was going to yield to a rainy spell. Nevertheless, the air was wonderfully fresh, the warm summer breeze conveying the intimacy of a caress as it brushed Claire's cheeks.

As she had expected, the garden center was open. Claire browsed for a time, feasting her eyes on the fantastic splashes of colors blended in the flats of annuals. Pansies and marigolds, zinnias and daisies surrounded her, all lovely. Years ago, Aunt Delia would have planted her annuals by this time of year, and they would have thrived under her tender loving care.

Claire herself had not been blessed with a green thumb. But then, at least for the past fourteen years of her life, there had been no time, place or real motivation for her to garden.

There were rosebushes for sale, too, and time left for planting them in the upstate New York climate. Perhaps, Claire mused, it might be wise to replace the sick-liest roses with entirely new stock.

She picked up one of the bushes, its base wrapped in thick green foil, and was studying the information printed on the sticker when someone said, right at her shoulder, "I thought the Parmeter mansion was overgrown with roses."

Claire glanced up suddenly into King Faraday's face and was so unprepared for the sight of him, so shocked, she instinctively clutched the rosebush too tightly. In an instant, a thorn pierced her finger, drawing from her both a gasp and a shining globule of bright-red blood.

## CHAPTER SEVEN

KING'S LIPS QUIRKED into a near smile. "Will you be requiring medical attention again?" he asked politely.

Claire translated the near smile into a smirk and felt a healthy surge of anger. It would be a pleasure to wipe that smug expression right off his handsome face.

She put the rosebush down and started to reach in her handbag for a tissue, but King was quicker. Producing a snowy handkerchief, he took her hand in his and carefully blotted the drop of blood.

Claire flinched, but not because he was hurting her. Rather, his touch sparked a feeling she found impossible to define. There was an intense familiarity to having King hold her hand, while at the same time it was so totally alien. She shivered, this echo of the past like being brushed by a warm breeze, only to find its core ice cold.

King scrutinized the spot the thorn had pierced with a seriousness that was amusing under the circumstances. Watching him, Claire began to relax.

He said, "The thorn didn't break off, which is good. You can get nasty infections when rose thorns become imbedded." As he spoke, he squeezed Claire's finger until it began to bleed again.

"Hey, wait a minute!" she protested, wincing.

"It's good to let a puncture wound bleed as freely as possible," King advised. "There, that'll do it. Do you have a Band-Aid in your car?"

"No, I don't," Claire snapped. "You're the doctor. Shouldn't you be the one carrying Band-Aids around?"

"Most of what I do requires a hell of a lot more than a Band-Aid," King informed her evenly. He looked around. "They probably have a first-aid kit around here somewhere," he decided.

"I'm really fine, King."

"If you say so." The agreement came more readily than Claire expected. Then King glanced down at the rosebush she'd been admiring. "Still going to buy it?" he queried.

"I don't know."

"The Parmeter mansion is somewhat overgrown with roses, isn't it? At least, that's my recollection."

"Aunt Delia must have planted hundreds of roses in her time," Claire conceded. "Most of the ramblers are still in good shape. But some of the bushes—hybrid teas, I think—are diseased. I don't know whether to try treating them or just replace them."

King laughed. "You make it sound like a medical problem."

"Oh? Have they come to the point of replacing people these days?"

The near smile faded from King's face. "No," he said, somewhat shortly. "People can't be replaced. Done without, perhaps, but not replaced."

He turned and surveyed the colorful assembly of annuals Claire had been admiring a few minutes earlier. With a quick change of subject he said, "I think I'm going to buy some marigolds. Those pale yellow ones are kind of pretty."

With his profile toward her as he spoke, Claire was given a brief opportunity to study his face. The boyishness was gone, and it saddened her to see this. King, in every way, was a fully matured man, his features honed and refined. Fourteen years ago there had been an appealing softness to his face, but now the late-morning sunlight highlighted threads of silver running through his blond hair and etched the shadows under his eyes. He looked tired and strained and could plainly use more of the warm June sun.

Claire felt an unexpected urge to touch the silver at his temples and smooth away the lines grooved around his mouth. She wanted to see him smile again and hear his laughter ring out as it had when they were young. These desires, though Claire wasn't immediately aware of this, became translated into an expression on her face that mirrored its own brand of anguish. And King saw this before she realized she was showing him too much.

He instinctively backed off, taking a step in reverse before he realized what he was doing and halted in his tracks. He had forgotten how expressive Claire's face could be, how eloquent her eyes were. And he didn't want to remember.

"Well," he said, suddenly wanting to end their encounter.

He was concentrating on the marigolds but heard the small hiss of Claire's indrawn breath. A small, awkward moment passed and a thought edged in. He found himself thinking, *She needs time to regroup, too.*

She said, too casually, "Well, I think I'll try to find one of the employees here who can advise me about roses."

King nodded and said, "Good luck."

"Thanks." Claire smiled, moving away. "I'm probably going to need it."

King surveyed the marigolds again but found it impossible to keep his eyes entirely off Claire's retreating figure. Out of the corner of his eye, he watched her ad-

vance toward a man wearing a gray smock with a garden-center insignia on it, and a moment later saw they
were deep in conversation. Then they moved into the
covered shed where the fertilizers and insecticides were
kept. Probably, King surmised, Claire had been told to
try treating the ailing Parmeter roses rather than dispense with them needlessly.

The medical parallel was inevitable. Healing was the
route preferably tried before anything more drastic was
undertaken. Healing, thank God, usually worked in the
majority of cases. But King had learned a long time ago
that physical healing, for all its inherent perils and
complexities, was often a hell of a lot easier to effect than
emotional healing. Injury to the psyche could leave scars
so fragile that weak places might easily become open
wounds again.

King pondered this as he selected several flats of marigolds and zinnias, then impulsively added some sweet-
smelling white stuff advertised for planting around rock
gardens. Actually, he was buying the flowers for his father. He had neither the time nor inclination to get into
gardening. But last summer George Faraday had evinced
an interest in growing flowers, with the help and encouragement of old Joe Landry, his part-time gardener for
years. King had quickly latched on to the gardening impulse as a good source of therapy. He only hoped his father would again welcome getting out into the sun and
working with the soil as he had last year.

AS SHE LEFT the garden center with her bottles of prescription rose treatment, Claire knew she couldn't drive
straight back to Lakeport. Ellie was probably back from
church by now, or would be soon. And she wouldn't be

ready to face Ellie until she'd done some soul-searching and come up with a few answers on her own.

Seeing King today had rocked her in quite a different way than their initial traumatic encounter at the hospital. She'd felt a sense of caring toward him just now that was very difficult to understand.

Viewing King as the mature man and obviously dedicated doctor he'd become made it impossible to continue casting him in the villain role she had assigned him. Worse, she had made King the *only* villain of their drama fourteen years ago. There was no doubt about that.

*But he broke my heart, damn it!* Claire reminded herself fiercely.

Only occasionally during the intervening years had any real doubts about what she'd done entered Claire's mind. She had deliberately locked the door on the past and had concentrated on living very fully in the present. There had been months when she'd not thought once of King Faraday. Primarily he had come to mind whenever she'd received a letter from Ellie, and communication between the two cousins had been sporadic, at best.

Ellie never mentioned King after the time she reported he had left town, and Claire had warned her that she never wanted to hear his name again. But Ellie always represented Lakeport to Claire, and it was impossible to think of Lakeport without thinking of King.

There had been a few hazy moments when she'd allowed herself to wonder what might have happened if she had waited for King that day, as he had asked. Mostly, though, she had wondered what would have happened had she not had Philip to turn to. She'd had very little money, no place else to go. Would she have returned to Lakeport out of necessity?

There were no ready answers to any of these questions and it was a waste of time to even consider them, Claire told herself angrily as she drove out of the garden-center parking lot and turned north, taking a road that followed the edge of Lake Champlain. She bypassed Plattsburg a few miles later and kept driving with no particular destination in mind until, to her surprise, she realized she'd come all the way to the Canadian border.

The drive back to Lakeport took the better part of an hour. By then, Claire had relaxed to the point where she could enjoy the beautiful scenery. Just beyond Plattsburg, she pulled into a small roadside cafè and had a sandwich and a milk shake. As she ate, she hoped Ellie wasn't in the process of fixing an enormous Sunday dinner. She should have said, in the note she'd left, that she might be late getting back.

Nearing Lakeport, she yielded to impulse and turned down the road to the point. The small peninsula ended in a beautiful beach that had been developed for public use by the state some years before. Along the way, the twisting road hugged the lake on one side and was bordered with beautiful homes on the other.

Claire wondered which of these houses was the one Lottie had built with Thomas Haskell.

It was still very cold swimming in Lake Champlain, so there weren't many people on the public beach. Claire got out of the car and, strolling to the water's edge, gazed across at Vermont's Green Mountains in the distance. When she turned, she was facing the Adirondacks. She could identify Whiteface and Mount Marcy, and wondered if one of the others might be Pocomoonshine. Then, for the first time in years, she recalled the day she'd climbed that mountain with King. Her first and last attempt at mountain climbing, she thought wryly.

She'd tried her damnedest that day because she had wanted so much to please King. But she had failed.

On the way back to her car, it occurred to Claire that possibly that wasn't the only time she had failed King.

THE BEGINNING of the new week brought with it an appointment for Claire and Ellie with Bill Edgerly in his Lakeport office. Thomas Haskell had promised to attend this meeting, too, and by the time the two cousins were ready to leave the Parmeter house, Ellie's nervousness was much too visible.

Claire decided that they'd use her car today, as Ellie was in no state to drive. As they started out, she cast an admonishing glance at Ellie and said, "Look, you've got to calm down. You're going to give Thomas a big advantage if he sees you like this."

"I don't like it," Ellie said, her eyes fixed on the road ahead as if she were afraid disaster would overtake them at any second. "I don't like any part of it."

"Ellie," Claire said patiently, "It's just a preliminary meeting. Don't say too much, that's all. Follow Bill's guidance."

Ellie sidestepped this advice. "If we have to go to court, the whole town's going to know our personal business," she lamented.

"Is that so bad?" Claire queried reasonably. "Do we really have so much to hide?"

"That's easy for you to say," Ellie said, her resentment surprising Claire. "You'll just pack up and leave when this is over. I'll have to live with it."

"On the contrary," Claire pointed out, "you don't have to live with it at all."

Ellie swung around sharply and out of the corner of her eye Claire could see the suspicion in her cousin's

brown-velvet stare. "What's that supposed to mean?"
Ellie demanded.

"Has it ever occurred to you that once you and
Thomas settle the estate you could leave Lakeport if you
wanted to?"

The silence was absolute. Out of it, Ellie finally said,
"No, it's never occurred to me. I've spent my whole life
here, Claire. There'd be nowhere else for me to go."

"That's not true," Claire contradicted gently. She
waved her hand toward the car window. "There's a whole
world out there, Ellie. A pretty interesting world, for the
most part. I think you owe it to yourself to see some of it
once you get your affairs straightened out."

"No!" Ellie said, making a small explosion of the
negative. "I'm not like you, Claire, I've told you that
before. I don't want to travel all over the place. That kind
of life isn't for me. I belong here, and I want to stay here
until I die!" she concluded defiantly.

Listening to this, Claire felt sure that Ellie wasn't revealing her true feelings, but rather her fears. Deep-
rooted fears that needed to be dealt with.

Claire never fancied playing amateur psychologist. She
felt that fooling around with other people's psyches could
become a very dangerous hobby. Part of this feeling went
back to when King was in college and had begun studying psychology in depth.

Now she wished that King had continued in that field
because he would have been the perfect person for Ellie
to consult. If there was anyone in the world Ellie might
be expected to have faith in, it was King.

Memories crowded in. Claire recalled the details involved in Ellie's long-ago rejection of Bill Edgerly. At the
time, Ellie had said only that she loved someone else.
Stealing a glance at her cousin, whose face was again

stony, her eyes riveted on the road, Claire was more sure than ever that someone had to have been King.

It must have hurt Ellie deeply when King had turned his attention not toward her, but toward her cousin.

Bill Edgerly's office was in a new building next to the courthouse. Claire had expected Bill to be practicing in a Spartan setting, but this did not prove to be the case. His suite of offices, while not luxurious, was decorated in an understated yet surprisingly sophisticated way. The furniture was Scandinavian in design and several interesting paintings graced the off-white walls. Claire wished she might have a chance to look at them without being too obvious.

Bill's secretary was a pleasant, attractive blonde named Melinda who, at Bill's request, brought coffee for them to his inner office.

Seated behind his desk, wearing gold-framed glasses, Bill presented an entirely different image than he had at the Parmeter house. Claire admitted silently that she'd expected him to project a "country-lawyer" image, but this was not so at all. In his handsome tan suit with his conservative brown-striped tie knotted precisely, Bill could have served as role model for an astute, competent young attorney practicing anywhere.

Ellie, by contrast, looked dowdy—there was no kinder word for the flower-printed gray dress she was wearing—and she was plainly flustered and ill at ease in this sector of Bill's world. Glancing at her, Claire had to fight a rising sense of impatience. Ellie, damn it, could do more with her appearance, overweight or not. She had a naturally lovely face but did nothing at all to enhance her potential beauty.

Another memory interrupted Claire's thoughts: the night of their high-school senior prom. Ellie, she remembered, had stoutly maintained she wasn't going. By then she had broken with Bill, and whomever it was she had fallen in love with remained completely offstage, as he always would.

Claire, suspecting that no one had asked her cousin to the prom—and knowing that Ellie was far too shy to issue an invitation to a boy herself—had consulted with King. Chris Talmadge had been seeing Angela Beaudreau, another classmate, but he and Angela had quarreled the week before. Claire had urged King to persuade Chris to invite Ellie to the prom, and when this was accomplished she'd virtually browbeat Ellie into accepting.

She had been possessed by a fierce determination to make the night a memorable one for her cousin. Ellie had been plump in those days, too, though not nearly as overweight as she was now. Perhaps because she was conscious of the drawbacks of her figure, her choice of clothes had been almost as disastrous as it was currently. Further, Grandfather Parmeter had been a miser when it came to doling out an allowance to Ellie. Claire had contemplated telling him herself that Ellie really had to have a new dress for the dance, but she had realized this would be the worst possible course of action. David Parmeter almost certainly would have refused her.

As the day of the dance neared, Claire was in a panic about her cousin's wardrobe. Ellie, on the other hand, was totally indifferent and even wished aloud that she could conveniently sprain her ankle or do just about anything that would prevent her from going to the prom.

Finally, on the very morning of the fateful day, a Friday, Claire cut her Latin class, went downtown to Crenshaw's Department Store and picked out a pretty dress she was certain would not only fit Ellie, but look good on her. The dress was a froth of chiffon and net and would emphasize Ellie's reasonably small waistline. The bodice was snug-fitting, then flared into a wide skirt. And the color was a luscious tone of peach that complemented Ellie's complexion and hair.

Claire paid for the dress with her own money. She had a limited income from the trust she would be inheriting under the terms of her father's will. When she got back to the Parmeter mansion with the dress, however, Ellie was far more horrified than pleased.

"I can't afford this, Claire!" she protested.

"No one said anything about your paying for it," Claire told her.

"I'll have to pay you back."

"No. No, you don't," Claire insisted. She didn't realize then that Ellie almost never spent a cent of her meager allowance, but carefully hoarded it away. Later, it was because of her cousin's frugality that Claire had managed to surreptitiously "borrow" everything Ellie saved, thus financing her escape from Lakeport.

When Ellie finally tried on the dress, Claire remembered, her lips curving into a smile as she thought about this, her attitude changed. She'd been awestruck by her reflection in the full-length mirror behind the door in Aunt Lottie's room. Claire had taken advantage of Ellie's rare preoccupation with her physical self and had persuaded her to let her shampoo and set her hair. Later, when she'd feathered bangs across Ellie's forehead and brushed the rest into soft waves around her shoulders, she even persuaded Ellie to experiment with a little makeup.

That night, for the first time—for one of the only times in her life, Claire thought wryly—Ellie Parmeter had shown the world what can happen when a dormant lily is adroitly gilded. Claire had brought out the beauty of her cousin's eyes with a gold-tone shadow and mascara, then added exactly the right touch of eyebrow pencil and eyeliner. Finally, she had touched peach-colored gloss to Ellie's cheeks, used a matching lipstick and brushed her face ever so lightly with powder. And even she had been surprised at the results.

King and Chris Talmadge had both been staggered when they arrived at the house bearing wrist corsages for the girls. King had brought a daisy corsage for Claire, while Ellie's was fashioned of sweet peas in shades of pink that perfectly complemented her dress.

The evening had started out with promise, but it hadn't ended that way. Angela had been at the dance, and when she saw Chris with Ellie, she swiftly mended her ways. Ellie had been totally unable to cope with feminine competition, and long before the last dance Claire noticed that her cousin was nowhere to be seen. The dance had been held in the school gym, but King and Claire scoured virtually all the darkened classrooms looking for Ellie . . . to no avail.

Claire had been frantic and even King, always very calm about most things, was getting anxious. With the orchestra still playing, they'd left the school and driven slowly around the adjacent neighborhood in King's old Dodge, peering into the night for a glimpse of a girl in a peach-chiffon dress until their eyes hurt from squinting.

At the Parmeter house, King had waited in the car while Claire slipped around to the back door and went upstairs via the secret passageway she would use for such a different purpose two years later. She'd found Ellie in bed, sound asleep. The peach dress had been tossed into a heap on the floor, never to be worn again.

Claire remembered switching on the bedside lamp, furious with her cousin. Then, in the pale-yellow glow, she glimpsed Ellie's tearstained face, saw that her eyelids were puffy from crying, and compassion dissolved her anger.

Remembering all this, Claire glanced toward Ellie now and marveled that she still so often felt the same blend of emotions toward her. There were times when she wanted to protect Ellie from everything cruel in the world. And times when she wanted to shake her into an awareness about herself and what she rightfully had coming. She wondered if Bill Edgerly ever felt the same way.

At the moment, he was studying some papers on his desk, then he glanced at his wristwatch.

"Thomas is late," he observed.

"He's probably not coming," Ellie said quickly.

Bill frowned. "That wouldn't be very wise of him."

Claire glanced impatiently at her cousin. Damn it, this was something Ellie *had* to face up to! She asked, "Is he bringing his attorney with him, Bill?"

"He hadn't made up his mind when I last talked to him," Bill said. "Maury Fletcher is his attorney. I've already spoken with him enough to convince myself that Thomas really does have a will with Lottie's signature on it, written later than the one I drew up for her," Bill added grimly.

"Do you think it's valid?"

"I don't know," Bill admitted. "That's one of the things we're going to have to find out."

The buzzer on his desk sounded. Bill pushed a button and said, "Yes?" The single word conveyed both impatience and irritation.

"Mr. Haskell is here, Mr. Edgerly," Melinda announced.

Bill's lips tightened. "Send him in, please," he directed.

Claire was curious to see Thomas Haskell. She had come to despise him at age fifteen, after he'd made that single, ill-chosen pass at her. During the next four years she had avoided him as much as possible when they were in the house together. This, she knew, had amused more than nettled him. Thomas Haskell had been very sure of himself. Lottie had been besotted by him. Now, from the vantage point of experience, Claire had to conclude that he must have been very good in bed. She could think of no other hold he could have had over her aunt.

She remembered him as a big man, strong, muscular and undeniably handsome. There had been the sort of roguishness about him that many women found appealing, an outgoing charm. He had even been able to beat down Delia's usually unshakable reserve upon occasion, Claire remembered, though she had been convinced then, and still was, that basically Delia disliked Thomas just as much as she did.

His hair had been thick, dark brown and naturally curly. Now, when he entered Bill's office, the first thing Claire noticed was that his hair had turned snow-white, though it was still as thick and curly as ever. Also, the years had taken their toll. The muscles had turned to fat. Thomas had quite a paunch and the whites of his blue eyes were yellowish. He looked, in short, as if he drank too much.

But the roguish charm was still there. It registered instantly as he greeted Claire, managing to give her the impression he was undressing her visually, just as he always had. She shook hands with him politely and forced herself not to show her resentment at the suggestive bit of squeezing he managed, his hand lingering in her palm.

His greeting to Ellie was equally friendly, though he omitted the handshake. But, whereas Claire had made herself return his smile, Ellie's face was expressionless. Someone, a long time ago, should have taught Ellie just a tad about the art of diplomacy, Claire thought, again wishing that her silent message, to the effect that what she was doing was not playing the game, would reach her cousin.

They suffered through a few generalities about the weather and Lakeport, then Bill came to the point with a suavity that surprised Claire. Before she quite knew what was happening, the issue of the will was out in the open.

Thomas, she saw, obviously hadn't expected to get down to basics so quickly, either. His laugh rang false as he said to Bill, "I don't know, Edgerly. Maybe I should have brought Maury along with me at that."

"We're not in a court of law, Thomas," Bill reminded him with a frost-touched smile. "We're merely exploring the issues here, trying to get some concept of our respective positions."

"Yeah, I see," Thomas said vaguely. "All right, look. The issue, as you put it, is pretty clear. Lottie wanted me to have half of her share of the Parmeter property, including the contents of the house. A couple of days before she died, she realized that wouldn't happen the way she'd written her will."

"The will I executed?" Bill queried.

"I guess that's the one she was talking about. I never saw it, myself. If you drew it up, you'd know what the terms are."

"I drew it up," Bill said quietly. "I drew up wills for Delia and Ralph Parmeter, as well. They were all relatively simple documents. And they all expressed essentially the same wishes."

Thomas's gaze shifted from the edge of Bill's desk, upon which he had been focusing, to the floor at his feet. He said uncomfortably, "I wouldn't know about that, either." He shrugged. "Okay," he said, "what were the wishes you're talking about?"

"When David Parmeter died," Bill answered, "his will instructed that his property be left equally to his three living children. His property was defined as the house occupied by the Parmeter School of Music and the adjacent grounds. He left no wishes in regard to the contents of the house, but he did speak about them to Delia, who was the executor of his estate. When I drew up her will six years ago, about a year before she died, Delia told me that her father instructed her to dispose of the articles in the house as she saw fit. He felt, insofar as value was concerned, that the contents should be divided between Delia, Lottie, Ralph and—" Bill's eyes swerved to Claire "—you, Claire."

Claire was so surprised she nearly jumped out of her chair. A rush of conflicting emotions assaulted her; she'd been so certain her grandfather wanted to disinherit her totally. She had lived with that certainty for twelve years. Now...

Bill continued, "Delia told me she had been intending for years to have everything appraised. Then she planned to draw up a list concerning exactly what should go to whom. She said she felt that Lottie had already taken more than her share when she moved to the point," Bill finished, his eyes fixed on Thomas Haskell's face.

"That was Delia," Thomas said, his tone turned sullen. "She and I never did see eye to eye."

"Yes, I got that impression," Bill agreed. "In any event, Delia never got around to the appraisal or to putting anything about the contents in writing. However, I do know what her wishes were. The will I drew up for Lottie, and Ralph's will, too, confirmed them. They instructed that the property we're talking about—the house and the grounds—be left either to their surviving siblings or to their surviving spouses or issue."

Thomas flushed. "Just what the hell is that supposed to mean?" he demanded.

"I think you know exactly what it means," Bill stated firmly. "If the property is sold, it must be because Ellie wants to sell it. Under the terms of the Parmeter wills, you are now joint owners. As far as the contents of the house are concerned, you're not entitled to a thing. If we abide with Delia's wishes as she expressed them to me, half the contents belong to Ellie and the other half to Claire.

"As to this alleged later will you're talking about, Thomas," Bill concluded, "it would be interesting to know why it took you two years to decide to bring it into the light of day."

## CHAPTER EIGHT

BY THE TIME THEY GOT HOME after their meeting with Thomas Haskell, both Claire and Ellie were emotionally exhausted.

Thomas had become volubly indignant after hearing Bill's question. He tossed out a few scathing insults aimed at the Parmeter family in general and one or two at Ellie and Claire specifically. Then he stormed out of the office raging that he should have brought his lawyer with him in the first place.

"As he probably should have," Bill commented, once Thomas had slammed the door behind him.

They all exhaled sighs of relief, then Bill took the initiative.

"This didn't turn out the way I'd hoped it might," he confessed. "But I'm glad we went through with it anyway. I told Maury Fletcher that I felt it's late in the day for Haskell to suddenly produce a will, and I asked him why it hadn't been offered for probate earlier. He said he'd deliberately arranged a delay at Haskell's request."

Bill grimaced. "Your uncle would have us believe that he delayed having the will filed because he wanted to spare your father, Ellie. He says he realized Ralph Parmeter's days were numbered and he wanted him to die in peace. Altruistic of him, wasn't it?"

Claire was seeing a cynical side of Bill Edgerly that was as foreign to her as Bill in his professional role. But his caustic comment only made her more glad that he was on Ellie's side. Ellie, she thought grimly, was going to need all the help she could get.

At that moment, Ellie could not have looked more miserable. She slumped in the beige armchair adjacent to Bill's desk, already a study in defeat when the battle had yet to be fought.

"Bill," she said, "if Aunt Lottie really made a later will, we should stand by it."

"I'm not about to go along with that until I know more about the circumstances under which she made the will," Bill stated sternly.

"But you saw Thomas's face," Ellie protested. "He's furious at all of us."

Bill picked up a smooth silver pen and tapped it against the desk surface. "Frankly, Ellie," he said levelly, "I don't give a damn whether Haskell is furious or not. He'll cool down once we get him in court."

"I don't want to go to court," Ellie wailed. "How often do I have to tell you that?"

Bill's desk phone rang as if on cue and, feigning impatience, he picked up the receiver. Claire was sure he actually welcomed the interruption as much as she did. They needed to call a halt to the entire matter for now. Later, hopefully, Ellie could be persuaded to look at the situation more objectively.

Claire stood up the moment Bill finished his conversation and suggested it was time she and Ellie let him attend to some of his other work. She was afraid her cousin was going to burst into tears, but somehow Ellie managed to contain herself. Still, she was stiff-lipped and silent on the way home, and once in the house, fled to the kitchen, sat down at the big oak table, buried her head in her arms and cried.

Claire put on the teakettle and foraged in the cupboard for the box of "homemade" cookies Ellie had bought at a church bake sale the day before. She knew Ellie usually found solace in food and Claire hoped the formula would work again.

This time, though, Ellie had no appetite for the cookies and scarcely touched the tea.

The balance of the afternoon and evening stretched ahead. Then tomorrow and the next day, and as long as it might take until they met with Thomas Haskell again, undoubtedly in court.

Claire seriously considered going back to New York and returning to Lakeport only for the court appearance. This would be the logical thing, as she did, after all, have a business to run.

Then honesty compelled her to admit that Brent Underwood was doing very well handling the galleries by himself. He would soon be acquiring the Monets, and Claire knew she couldn't have done better herself, if as well.

The bottom line was she couldn't desert Ellie until the whole sorry matter with Thomas Haskell was finalized. Short of an actual crisis rearing its ugly head at the Bailey Galleries, a crisis Brent came right out and told her he couldn't handle, her concern for her cousin would keep her here.

She was stuck in Lakeport for God knew how long! A bearable predicament, she conceded, if not for the fact that King was here, too. Knowing this was like developing an itch that was just out of reach for scratching. He was living and sleeping in a house just four scant blocks from her, and this was not only tantalizing Claire, it was beginning to torment her.

*Damn it!* she thought. There was no logical reason she shouldn't be able to shut King out of her mind. Maybe she'd never entirely get over the trauma of that one terrible day. That had left a very deep-rooted scar. But she'd gotten over King himself. She had gone way beyond him, grown way beyond him, and could say the same for King. They were strangers now, a man and woman walking entirely different paths. It shouldn't even bother her if King were living right here in the Parmeter house. But would it ever! Claire confessed silently, honesty forcing the admission.

She sighed, and hearing the sigh Ellie matched it with one of her own, then said surprisingly, "Bill is right. This whole mess should never have been allowed to happen. Thomas should have come out right after Aunt Lottie died and said he had a later will than the one Bill had drawn up."

*Amen,* Claire thought. Ellie's statement was a step in the right direction. The job now would be to keep Ellie moving in the right direction.

An idea struck. An idea so obvious Claire couldn't fathom why she hadn't thought of it before.

"Ellie," she began, "what about doing that inventory Aunt Delia intended to start years ago? No matter what happens with Thomas, we need to know exactly what there is in this house, what it's all worth. Don't you agree?"

"Yes, I suppose so." Ellie nodded, not evincing any real interest. After a moment she said more decisively, "Yes, we should inventory everything, Claire. It's been my intention all along, but I just never got started. With both of us working on it, though . . ." Ellie's face brightened. "It could actually be fun," she decided.

Fun? Claire doubted it would be fun. To inventory the family heirlooms would be embarking on a nostalgia trip that might be painful for both Ellie and herself. Ellie didn't seem to realize this. Still, it was a job that needed doing, and even more important, would serve to fill up a major share of Ellie's somewhat empty hours.

THE PARMETER MANSION WAS FILLED with a multitude of valuable objects, most more aesthetically pleasing than functional, Claire discovered the next morning. When it came to finding something as practical as a notepad and pen to work with, there was not merely a lack but a near-total void.

"This is ridiculous," she proclaimed, when all Ellie could produce was a chewed-on ballpoint pen near the end of its ink supply and a stub of a pencil sans eraser. To this her cousin added a few sheets of scrap paper, some of which had already been written on. "I'll dash down-town and get us some things to work with," Claire offered. "I need a new lipstick, anyway."

It was the lipstick that made Claire decide on Faraday's Pharmacy for her purchases. Otherwise, for stationery supplies, she could have gone to Dawson's Hardware. But she knew that Faraday's had always carried a good line of cosmetics and enough in the way of notepads and the like to fill in her list of necessaries.

It wasn't until she was at the door of the pharmacy that she realized this small safari would unleash yet another flood of memories. Pushing the door open, she glanced instinctively to the left. That's where the soda fountain had been, a rendezvous place for King and herself after school. She wondered how many cherry Cokes she'd sipped at that fountain.

Only...the soda fountain wasn't there anymore. In fact, the entire floor plan of the pharmacy had been changed. Now it had a modern look, geared for self-service. The walls were the same soft pastels, but the aisles had been narrowed and the rows of shelving increased, stacked with a myriad supplies.

Fighting back her disappointment—had she actually been thinking of sitting down at the soda fountain and ordering a cherry Coke, thus permitting herself a maudlin excursion back to her adolescence?—Claire found the stationery section and chose the notepads, pens and pencils she needed.

Then she moved on to the cosmetics area, passing the glassed-in enclosure from which prescriptions were dispensed. She stole a glance at the pharmacist on duty and was relieved to see it wasn't James Faraday, King's uncle. A scholarly looking young man, blond and wearing glasses, was carefully measuring pills into a vial.

Claire found a lipstick shade that suited her, chose some pale-green eye shadow and indulged in a bottle of her favorite after-bath splash. She carried her purchases to the checkout counter and had just paid the clerk when, looking up, she found herself face-to-face with Dr. George Faraday.

He looked much older. Thinner and drawn. But he was still a very handsome man—King had certainly inherited his masculine good looks from his father.

His eyes, like King's, were blue, though not as deeply blue. Just now they looked as cold as the lake water in winter, and Claire flinched, seeing in his expression everything he would forever be too polite to say.

She'd always known that he'd take King's side, and it stood to reason. George Faraday had lost faith in women almost thirty years ago, the day his wife deserted him. It

hurt Claire to know this, especially in the beginning, because she had come to be very fond of King's father.
Right after she left Lakeport, she'd almost written him a
letter telling him what had happened. She really wanted
him to understand what she had done, and why. Then she
had accepted the futility of doing that and, over the
years, had shut Dr. Faraday out of her mind just as she
had shut so many things out of her mind.

Now, seeing him, all the visions of the past were con-
jured up and she felt foolishly young and tongue-tied.

He was using a cane, leaning heavily on it as he surveyed her. "Claire. King told me you were in town."

She nodded, trying to control herself, but her voice
quavered as she said, "How are you, Dr. Faraday?"

"Well, thank you." It was an answer Claire knew he
would have given her if he were dying.

A strange desperation clutched her and she found herself wanting to blurt out-of-context statements to this
man. She wanted, though she couldn't have explained
why, to tell him she was sorry.

Sorry about what? Sorry that she'd walked out on King
because, on their wedding day, she'd discovered he had
gotten another girl pregnant. A girl with whom he'd once
had an affair, and had obviously never entirely re-
nounced.

Claire faced these bare facts and was suddenly assaulted by a powerful wedge of doubt. As if the words
had been spoken aloud, she heard the voice of her con-
science say sternly, "You never gave King a chance to
explain." And for a moment she almost believed it was
George Faraday who was saying this.

She couldn't imagine what her face must be revealing.
King's father was still leaning on his cane, gazing down
at her politely. Years from now King was going to look

even more like his father, Claire realized. He, too, would have that same grave, polite, almost courtly manner.

Thinking this, something twisted inside Claire and she yearned for King so much she physically hurt. She swallowed hard and George Faraday, watching her, asked, "What is it, Claire? You're not ill, are you? King said something about your being brought into the emergency room."

"No," she said hastily. "I . . . it's just good to see you again, that's all."

Her words, she thought dismally, could not have sounded more inept. What an idiot this man must think her! At least he didn't comment, he didn't mouth a false, "It's good to see you again too, Claire." He only nodded with that gravity that managed to tear at her heartstrings and, using the cane, slowly, carefully moved on.

Claire walked out onto Main Street, tears stinging her eyes. By the time she reached her car, the tears were blinding her. Annoyed at herself, her composure shot, the veneer that she'd so carefully applied beginning to chip, she wished she could scream in frustration.

Her ensuing anger at herself enabled her to yank a handkerchief out of her handbag, mop away the tears and start the car. But as she drove back to the Parmeter house, Claire knew she was going to have to get a firm grip on herself before she faced Ellie. There'd already been too much backtracking and an obsessive dwelling on the past by both Ellie and herself that was threatening to become maudlin.

As she pulled up in front of the house, Claire also knew she had to see King again. She would have to gather up the courage to talk to him. She needed to open the door just one more time and hear his side of the story.

BY THE MIDDLE of the afternoon, Claire knew avoiding
the past was especially impossible under the circumstances. As she and Ellie began their inventory with the
contents of the dining-room cupboard, everything they
touched evoked nostalgia.

Ellie was a fountain of knowledge about almost every
piece. As she handled the different objects, each assumed an identity of its own.

"Aunt Delia always loved this Limoges pitcher," Ellie
said. "The flowers were hand painted by her great-
grandmother. In those days, painting china was a popular hobby. The undecorated pieces—blanks, they called
them—were ordered from France. Then the ladies would
paint them and have their designs fired. Someplace
there's a teapot Aunt Delia covered with pink roses. You
know Aunt Delia and roses. She was such a love, Claire.
It's a shame she never married. She would have, except
for Grandfather. When she was young, she went to Boston for a year to study piano. She told me once she met a
young man there and..."

This recital of Ellie's was one of many, and they'd only
been at the task a couple of hours, Claire thought wryly.
She was relieved when the story of Aunt Delia's unrequited love was cut short by the telephone ringing.

Ellie went to answer the summons and was frowning
slightly when she came back. "It's Chris Talmadge. He
wants to speak to you."

"That's a surprise," Claire said, pleased. She'd been
removing old platters and pitchers from the bottom shelf
of the cupboard. Now she stood carefully, avoiding the
objects she'd placed on the floor around her, and wiped
her hands on the apron she was wearing. "Be right
back," she promised.

"Did I get you away from something?" Chris asked, once she'd picked up the receiver. "Ellie sounded a bit flustered."

"We've decided to inventory the Parmeter possessions," Claire said dryly. "I'm beginning to think it's going to take half a lifetime to complete the job, so thank you for getting me off the hook, temporarily at least."

Chris laughed. "This is last minute," he said then, "but I was wondering if you'd be free for dinner tonight."

"Why, thank you, Chris," Claire replied promptly. "That would be very nice."

"Shall I pick you up at seven, then?"

"Seven would be fine."

Claire hung up, pleased that Chris had followed up on their encounter of the other day. He couldn't have chosen a better time to have issued a dinner invitation. She needed out for a while, needed to talk to someone other than Ellie or Bill Edgerly. She needed to get both the actual and the symbolic dust in the old Parmeter house out of her system.

Ellie was sitting at the dining-room table making notations on a yellow legal pad about several pieces of glass and china lined up next to her. She glanced up at Claire and, to Claire's surprise, frowned again.

"What did Chris want?" she demanded abruptly.

Briefly, Claire was taken aback. She wasn't used to being questioned like that, nor did she like it. She was tempted to tell Ellie that it had been a personal call, but knew that would only hurt Ellie's feelings needlessly. So she said, pleasantly, "Chris and I met down in the garden the other day. He suggested that we have dinner together, and was just calling to ask if it could be tonight."

Ellie's mouth became set in a familiar stubborn line. "We've got leftover beef stew to eat up," she said. "And anyway, I really don't want to go out tonight."

This wasn't easy. "I'm sure Chris didn't intend to exclude you," Claire said lightly, "and I'm sure he'd be happy to have you join us. But it was *me* he was inviting."

"I see," Ellie said stiffly. "Well, then . . ."

"Ellie . . . don't you like Chris?"

"*Like* Chris?" Ellie looked genuinely puzzled. "What's that got to do with it?"

"You've been scowling ever since you answered the phone," Claire accused. "Why?"

"I . . . don't know," Ellie said vaguely. "I suppose it's just that Chris has always been King's best friend. Used to be, anyway. I don't know how close they are nowadays."

Claire was puzzled. "I can't see what that has to do with anything," she said frankly.

"Well, Chris was King's friend and . . ." Ellie stalled.

Claire stared at her cousin in disbelief. "Are you saying that I shouldn't go out to dinner with Chris Talmadge because fourteen years ago I was engaged to King Faraday? Is that what you're saying?"

"I suppose maybe it is," Ellie mumbled.

Claire shook her head. "I don't believe this."

"Lakeport's a small town, Claire."

"What does *that* have to do with it? I don't care if it's the world's smallest village. Everything came to an end between King and myself fourteen years ago! You better than anyone should know that, Ellie. So if you're thinking that King's feelings might be hurt if he learned I went out with Chris, spare yourself. Believe me, King Faraday washed me out his life a long, long time ago."

"I'm not so sure about that," Ellie said stubbornly.

"Well, I am," Claire snapped, knowing privately that perhaps the worst part of all was the truth in this.

CHRIS TALMADGE WAS PROMPT. Claire was watching from the parlor window and when she saw him pull out of his driveway she slipped out the front door and met him at the curb.

"Nothing like living next door to each other to ensure punctuality." He grinned as she slid onto the seat beside him.

"No red lights or traffic jams," Claire agreed.

He was looking at her approvingly and she was glad she'd made the effort to look nice. She was wearing a pale-pink dress that had a becoming bateau neckline and she had agreed with Ellie—who had mellowed and proffered them at the last minute—that Aunt Delia's pink pearls and matching earrings would complement her outfit perfectly. She had twisted her hair into a chignon and took more pains with her makeup than she'd been doing since coming back to Lakeport. Perhaps because Ellie never bothered with makeup, Claire had been settling for little more than a touch of lipstick.

Chris took her to a new place outside of town, new since her time, anyway. He'd reserved a table for two overlooking Lake Champlain and they were in time to see the afterglow from the Adirondacks sunset paint the lake with an incredible palette of color.

Later, as the light faded, candles were lit at each table. In an adjacent room, an orchestra began playing soft background music. Claire sipped the daiquiri Chris had ordered for her and felt herself relaxing. It was a long time since she'd been out with an attractive man, except when there had been business involved.

They kept the conversation on an impersonal level all through a delicious dinner and Claire found herself having a surprisingly pleasant time. Chris talked about Champlain Plastics and asked her questions about the galleries. She told him about life in New York and commented on the changes she'd discovered in Lakeport. And when the orchestra switched to dance music, it was entirely natural to move to the parquet floor. Yet, as much as she was enjoying herself, Claire had the feeling there was something hanging in the air between them, an invisible presence. And she was sure Chris felt it, too.

As she savored small spoonfuls of a delicious apricot mousse, Claire came to the reluctant conclusion that unless she captured this something and caused it to materialize, she and Chris would never feel entirely free with each other. Perhaps, she conceded whimsically, Ellie had not been so wrong after all! She wouldn't go so far as to say that she and Chris were dining with King's ghost, but more than King's name was there between them, there was no doubting that.

Finally she found a question she could pose. "Do you see much of King these days?" she asked, managing to stumble only slightly over his name.

Chris smiled. "I was wondering when we were going to get to that."

Claire suddenly remembered Ellie's vivid description of the way King had behaved once he discovered she'd run away. Chris had been among those who had taken turns staying with King until he'd begun to return to his senses . . . and he'd been totally out of them, unless Ellie was exaggerating.

Chris, though, was looking at her openly. Claire sensed no judgment, no vibes of disapproval or anything stronger than mere concern coming from him. He had exhibited only friendliness toward her from the moment they'd met again, and that wasn't changing now.

She said carefully, feeling she could be completely honest with this man, "It was very difficult to come back to Lakeport, Chris. But . . . that wasn't because I felt I'd been wrong to leave in the first place. I had my reasons for doing what I did. Reasons that were totally valid to me at the time. In fact, leaving was the only thing I *could* do," Claire told him, faltering slightly.

Chris said quietly, "I know that. I've always known it. I knew you weren't the kind of person who would wreck someone else's life if there was any kind of choice involved."

Surprised at his way of putting it and stung slightly by his bluntness, Claire reacted before thinking the question through. "Do you really feel I wrecked King's life, Chris?" she asked.

"The way I feel about King . . ." Chris started. "Well, his life was in a shambles for a long time after you left. Then, almost miraculously, he was . . . reincarnated. I'd say that from about age twenty to twenty-two, King was on the skids in every sense of the word, Claire. No one would have given you dust for his chances. At that point he left Lakeport and rarely came back for visits—until his father had the stroke.

"Dr. Faraday used to meet King in Albany or New York. They went on a couple of Caribbean cruises together, went skiing in Idaho, things like that. This was while King was in college, then med school. The two of them were always close, Claire. Today more so than ever. That's the only reason King decided to come back to Lakeport and join the staff at Lakeport General. To be with his father."

Claire nodded. "I had a feeling that was why."

"King and I are still very good friends," Chris said. "But not the way we were before...well, before you left. I tried to stick with King, but I couldn't follow his route. I didn't like the crowd he was hanging around with, the things he was doing. Then I went away myself, later I got married and had my own fiasco to deal with." Chris shrugged reflectively, then said, "Since King's come back, we've mended a lot of fences. But you can never totally repeat anything in life, if you know what I mean. Places change, people change, circumstances change. It's like going back to a resort where you had a wonderful vacation as a kid and expecting it to be exactly the same. That just doesn't happen. I'd say King and I have been building a new friendship on a new foundation. Sure, the past is there. But those bricks would only crumble, so we've started anew."

Chris finished his chocolate ice cream and set the dish aside. "Coffee?" he asked.

"Please."

He signaled the waitress and ordered for both of them, and Claire sensed that this small interlude offered Chris a welcome diversion. As if verifying this, once the waitress had left them alone again, he looked up and smiled. "Confession times are hard for me," he admitted.

"Chris, please! I wasn't trying to wring any confessions out of you," Claire protested.

"I know. Maybe that's a poor choice of words, but I think you know what I mean. In this life, there's no way to go but forward, Claire."

She returned the smile. "I think I learned that lesson a long time ago."

"You must have. Look at you! You're more beautiful than ever, a sophisticated and self-assured woman who has the world exactly where she wants it, I'd say," Chris told her. "You're a successful business executive—"

"Please!" Claire held up her hand. "You sound like a talk-show host trying to build up a guest."

"That's not the way I meant it."

"I know, Chris. Just remember, no one's life is entirely the way it seems."

"True."

"My life . . . well, it's full and wonderful, as you suggest. But . . ."

"But?"

"There are a few things lacking," she admitted. "I agree that we can only go forward, yet sometimes the past tugs us backward until we're forced to confront it."

Claire created her own diversion by spooning sugar into her coffee. She knew Chris was watching her closely and was not too surprised when he asked, "Is the whole thing with King still tugging at you, Claire?"

"I'm not sure I know the answer to that," she said cautiously. "Naturally, coming back to Lakeport has opened up all sorts of things. I didn't even know King was here until Ellie told me. Then I came face-to-face with him in the emergency room, and we ran into each other at the garden center on Sunday. He . . . he's a stranger, Chris," she concluded, feeling a weird little emptiness saying this.

"Wouldn't it be better to let him remain a stranger?" Chris queried gently. "I imagine you're not going to stay around town any longer than you have to for Ellie's sake."

"True."

"Then don't you think it would be better to leave things as they are?"

Claire toyed with her spoon then raised her eyes to Chris's and said slowly, "I'm not sure I can. I don't think I'll have peace of mind unless I resolve the past with King. I'd forced myself to suppress so many things. But as soon as I saw the house again and faced the garden and the dollhouse, I began to realize that I can't leave without clearing this up."

"Why you left?"

"Yes. Maybe I'm getting my impressions from Ellie, but it's seems to me increasingly that King never understood why I left."

"King never did understand why you left," Chris confirmed.

"Well, you'd think he would have realized..."

"Yes?"

"Damn it!" Claire said suddenly. "We shouldn't have gotten into this. It's been such a lovely evening and I've put a damper on it."

Chris smiled. "You've only said what had to be said," he told her. "I wish I could help, but I can't. It's something strictly between you and King. I have the gut feeling things would be better if you just let them lie. But I could be wrong."

Claire considered this then said, "I know you can't help, Chris, and I don't expect you to. But there's one question you could answer for me."

"Fire away," Chris said cheerfully.

"Do you remember Rosalie Brenner?"

Chris's eyes narrowed and he couldn't have looked more puzzled. "Rosalie Brenner?" he echoed.

"She was in school with us, a dark-haired, dark-eyed, rather tempestuous-looking girl. She and King...well, they went around together before he met me." After all these years, Claire thought dismally, it shouldn't be so difficult to say that.

"I know," Chris said, his face wary. "I remember Rosalie, but what I don't understand is why you're even asking about her."

"She told me something," Claire said. "I don't want to go into what it was, but . . ." She drew a long breath, then asked, "Do you know whatever happened to her?"

"She moved to Vermont not long after you left," Chris said. "She went into a nursing program at a hospital in Burlington and became a nurse. Later she married an Air Force pilot who was stationed at the SAC base up in Plattsburg. Last I heard, she's still married and has three kids."

All by her husband? Claire wondered. Or was one of those children the result of an affair with King? That was the question she yearned to pose, but couldn't.

# CHAPTER NINE

THEY WERE DRIVING BACK to Lakeport when Chris said, "King called just before I met you and said tomorrow is his day off. He wants me to meet him out at Baskin's Beach and go Windsurfing, but I'm afraid I'm not going to be able to make it."

Claire had been trying, unsuccessfully, to force King out of her thoughts. She was reaching the conclusion that Chris was right: she wasn't going to be in Lakeport long enough to afford stirring up the past. She and King had both learned to live with their separate memories. Why let loose angry ghosts that might be difficult to lay to rest later?

She latched on to two words. Baskin's Beach. "I was asking Ellie about the beach a while ago," she said. "We used to go swimming there all the time." As a child Claire had gone to Baskin's with her aunts Delia and Lottie, and with Ellie and Uncle Ralph. Even with her mother and father a few times, she remembered dimly. The beach wasn't solely associated with King.

She added, "I wondered if it was still there."

"Still there?" Chris asked quizzically. "Beaches don't usually disappear, do they?"

"Some places become obliterated by development," Claire said. "You know, condos, shopping centers . . ."

"We haven't exactly had a population explosion around here," Chris pointed out. "One new mall since you left, a couple of professional buildings and restaurants. Lakeport is progressing. At least I certainly hope so, or I picked the wrong place to set up my business. But I doubt if there'll be a rush to build condos, not in the foreseeable future, anyway. We're too far from any really big city to become a bedroom community. For which I am duly thankful.''

He smiled at Claire. ''Baskin's is still the same,'' he said. ''Same family owns the farm and the beach hasn't changed at all.''

''That's what Ellie said.''

''You haven't investigated for yourself?''

''Not yet.''

''Well, you should. It's a great place for Windsurfing. Gives you the illusion of having Lake Champlain entirely to yourself. There usually aren't many people around and maybe one or two other Windsurfers at the most. The water's still cool enough so that King and I have had the place entirely to ourselves last couple of times we went. Matter of fact, we were using wet suits until last week. And even then the water temperature was borderline.''

''Too bad you can't make it tomorrow,'' Claire murmured. ''It must be a great escape.''

''The best,'' Chris concurred. ''Ever tried it?''

''No,'' Claire said, laughing. ''Volleyball and field hockey were the great highlights of my sports career, and I wasn't very good at them.''

''You were a good swimmer, I remember. And I learned tonight that you're a very good dancer. I think tonight's the first time we ever danced together. I don't recall King ever giving me the chance to cut in at the high-school proms.''

Chris said this easily, and there was a sweet sadness in remembering the proms if she didn't recall them in depth. Maybe that was the best way to handle the past, Claire thought. Hold on to the good times and let the bad times fade into obscurity.

They drove the rest of the way in a companionable silence and when Chris stopped the car in front of the Parmeter house, Claire protested, "You could have pulled into your own driveway. It's not a long walk, you know."

"I could have," Chris agreed. Then he grinned. "Claire, I really enjoyed tonight."

She smiled back. "So have I."

"Maybe we could do this again before you leave?"

"I'd like that."

And she would, Claire told herself as she entered the house. Chris was a good companion, charming and fun to be with. He was exactly what she needed to break up the heaviness of dealing with Ellie and Bill and the whole mess surrounding Lottie's will.

A single light had been left on in the downstairs hall and another light shone at the head of the stairs. Claire ascended slowly, knowing it was late enough for Ellie to have gone to bed yet also knowing this was one of Ellie's favorite television nights, so she might still be watching her programs.

As she passed the door to Ellie's bedroom, she noticed the room was dark. But Ellie called out, "That you, Claire?"

"Yes," she answered softly, pausing in the hall.

"Did you have a good time?"

"Yes, I did," she said honestly. "It was very pleasant."

"Where did Chris take you?"

"To Borracini's."

"I've never been there," Ellie informed her.

"Then we'll go one night. It's a very attractive place."

Ellie didn't answer this. After a moment of silence she said, "See you in the morning."

Claire was tempted to say something, but Ellie was just being Ellie, she decided, and retired to her room.

Morning came and Claire awakened with the awareness that she had been dreaming, but couldn't remember what the dreams were about.

She slipped on a robe and went downstairs. Ellie had already made coffee and was sitting at the kitchen table perusing an antique guide. She smiled sweetly at Claire then held up the book. "This might give us an idea of what some of the things are worth," she said.

Claire poured herself a cup of coffee and sat down at the table but didn't take the book Ellie was proffering. She said tentatively, "I think we'll be getting in awfully deep if we try to price things. If we just give an accurate description of each piece, we can get an expert to do the appraisals." When Ellie didn't say anything she added, "I know I wouldn't think of pricing a painting based solely on my own research, even though that's an area where I'm fairly knowledgeable. For so many things, there's a fluctuating market. It depends on how popular Tiffany glass is at the moment, let's say, or Pierpoint silver or cut crystal."

"I thought we might be able to trust an appraisal more if we had some basic ideas ourselves," Ellie said.

"I don't know," Claire hedged, not wanting to disagree outright with Ellie yet dreading the thought of adding another time-consuming chore to the inventory. "When it comes right down to it, the value of most of this stuff really depends on its worth to us. There's the sentimental value to be considered over and above the monetary value.''

"Well, maybe I'll just dabble around with the price lists myself," Ellie decided.

Claire let it go at that. As she sipped her coffee, she watched the sunlight stream in through the kitchen windows, and the glory of the outdoors beckoned her. There was no longer any doubt in her mind that she had to see King, that she had to talk to him. There was also little doubt that to do this would mean staging an encounter. Certainly, he wasn't going to come to her!

Baskin's Beach would be an ideal place for such a rendezvous, she realized. Her problem was how to break away from Ellie for the day. She couldn't tell Ellie what her plan was or where she was going without getting into a dialogue about it, and she didn't want that. She was unsure of herself as it was.

Ellie unexpectedly solved the problem. "One day a week, usually, I volunteer in the hospital thrift shop from ten to four," she said out of the blue. "I started, oh, right after Dad died. I . . . well, I just had to do something that would make me get out of the house." She added lamely, "Today's supposed to be my day, but I thought I'd call them and say I couldn't make it."

Claire, riding on a surge of relief, said hastily, "Don't be silly, Ellie. If you're worried about leaving me, don't be. It won't hurt if we miss a day here."

"Well, I don't know," Ellie said doubtfully. "You could come with me, Claire. They can always use an extra pair of hands."

"I'm sure they can. But to be honest, I'd rather do something else," Claire responded gently. "Look, it'll do you good to get me out of your hair for a day."

"How can you say that?" Ellie countered. "The best thing that's happened to me in years is having you come back."

Claire was startled by her cousin's vehemence. Then Ellie smiled, having heard the sound of her own voice. She said mildly, "Well, it's true."

"I'm flattered you should say that," Claire managed. "But . . . I'm not going to be around forever." Seeing Ellie's expression sink, she added, "Please don't look so stricken! We're never again going to go so long without seeing each other, I promise you. After we get everything settled here there'll be no reason you can't come to New York to visit me. Or to Siesta Key, for that matter."

She held her breath, fearing that Ellie was going to ask if she'd also come back to Lakeport from time to time. She didn't want to fib, but knew there was no way she could make that commitment. The way she felt now, she doubted she'd ever set foot here again, once she left this time. She only hoped she could truly burn all her bridges and dispense with the ashes. This wound between King and herself would hopefully be healed, and that done, there would be no reason to return. Also, it would be much healthier for Ellie to get away once in a while—from this house, from Lakeport, from an environment so suffocatingly familiar.

Fortunately, Ellie had turned her thoughts to her day at the thrift shop. Claire persuaded her to go ahead and get ready while she washed their breakfast dishes. She felt like a truant child eager to skip school as she waited for Ellie to dress and leave the house.

Only when Ellie was finally driving up the street was Claire able to relax. Then she sped up the stairs, changed into jeans and a pink T-shirt, threw a sweater over her shoulders, grabbed an old blanket and took off.

Along the way, she pulled into the Champlain Mall and patronized a deli she'd spotted the other day with Ellie. She bought two pastrami sandwiches on rye, two corned beef on pumpernickel, some potato salad, some cole-slaw, pickles and almond macaroons for dessert. Then she picked up a six-pack of cold beer and, stashing the food on the back seat of the car, had to smile at what she'd done. It was obvious she'd gotten more than enough food for two, but Claire really didn't care at the moment.

It was a five-mile drive out to Baskin's Beach. A dirt road wound off the state highway, meandered through the woods for several hundred yards then ended in a cir-cular clearing. On the far side of the clearing a barbed-wire fence was centered by a sagging gate, just like al-ways. As if she'd done this only yesterday, Claire opened the gate and, picnic materials and paperback novel in hand, started down the path to the lake.

The beach was pebbly and viewing it again reminded Claire of how the stones had hurt her winter-tender feet the first few visits each summer. But there were hard-packed areas of darkish sand, too, and grassy patches sloping up toward the nearby farmland.

Claire settled for a place on the grass, laid out the blanket and sat down. She was aware that her pulse was beating faster than normal—pounding, in fact—and knew she needed to get a grip on herself. Determined to get calm and stay calm, she donned a pair of purple-rimmed sunglasses and began to read, but the words blurred before her eyes. It was impossible to concen-trate. She was becoming intensely aware of the passage of time and of the possibility that, since Chris hadn't been able to make it, King didn't plan to Windsurf to-day, after all.

Claire was so hopeful of seeing King it was terrible to think he might not appear. She'd actually expected he might be out on the water when she first arrived, and not seeing a sail had been the initial disappointment. Maybe he'd had to stop by the hospital, she rationalized. Maybe something had held him up.

When the hands on her watch pointed to noon Claire just about made up her mind that King wasn't coming. She'd been an idiot to take it for granted that he would, she realized soberly, and decided she should either wade in the water a little and eat her lunch or simply go home right now.

She started for the water, finding the going every bit as rough as she remembered. The pebbles were murder, but she had to admit that her feet had been completely pampered for years. Hobbling awkwardly to the lake's edge, she shrieked aloud as she tested Champlain's temperature with her big toe. Even in the shallows, the water was icy.

Her shriek was overheard. King had just reached the end of the path and stepped onto the open beach, and now he stared in disbelief at the sight of Claire hopping up and down as if she were being stung by a swarm of underwater bees. Despite himself, he laughed. Claire had always reacted to the water like that in early summer, he remembered. Inevitably, he would stride right in ahead of her, as if his feet weren't freezing and about to drop off, then would turn and splash her while she shrieked louder. She would become sufficiently furious and splash him back. Then they'd chase each other until they were standing in water up to his waist, her chest, at which point they would tumble into each other's arms and a slow warmth would begin to seep through them, igniting their veins with passion's fire until they were no longer aware of the cold water, or much of anything else.

Briefly, King was tempted to let history repeat itself. But he was fully clothed and so was Claire. He saw that she was wearing jeans rolled up above her ankles.

Suddenly, wearily, King closed his eyes and wondered if he'd imagined hearing the shriek. Perhaps he'd seen a memory mirage, not Claire in the flesh. But when he looked again she was still there.

He watched as she turned and started out of the water then looked up to discover his presence. The shock caused her to lose her balance, and stumbling over a round gray stone she nearly twisted her ankle. That, Claire thought wryly, would *really* have lent the perfect touch to this occasion. The last thing King needed was to be called upon, yet again, to administer first aid.

She regained her balance and proceeded more cautiously, and King met her halfway. Glancing down at her, he asked, "What are you doing out here?" There was a natural curiosity to the question but nothing more.

"The house was getting to me," Claire told him truthfully. "I wanted to get out in the fresh air for a while, and I've wanted to come here. I brought a picnic lunch along and, well . . . there's more than enough for two." She felt like a tongue-tied schoolgirl as she asked, "Have you eaten yet?"

"No," King said. "As a matter of fact, I haven't."

He was gazing out across the lake as he spoke and, catching the weariness in his voice, Claire looked at him more closely. There were shadows of fatigue etching his face and the dark outline of a beard.

"Are you all right?" she asked.

He smiled. "That's usually my question."

"Seriously, King . . ."

He ran a hand over his chin. "I should have shaved before I left the hospital," he said. "I always look run-down when I let myself go."

"You don't look run-down," Claire corrected. "You look exhausted. Anyway, wasn't this supposed to be your day off?"

If King wondered how she had known that, he didn't show it. He merely nodded and said, "Yes, but I had to go in."

"An emergency?"

"It was more of a . . . crisis," he said hesitantly. He turned, glancing back to the grassy slope where she'd spread the blanket and left the food. "Those your things?" he asked.

"Yes."

He seemed to be deliberating over something. Then he said slowly, his voice low, "I lost a patient this morning, a young woman I operated on last week. She seemed to be doing well, considering how dangerous the surgery was. There was a sixty-percent mortality risk, but she wouldn't have lived more than a few months without it, so there was no great choice."

As if the words were being torn from him, King added, "She is, or was, a very brave person. She looked me right in the eye when I told her what the odds were, and said simply, 'Go ahead, doctor. I trust you.' Her husband went along with her decision. I give him great credit for that. He was as gutsy as she was, and was right there this morning." King drew a deep breath. "Watching him was hell," he confessed. "That, and knowing, once I'd sized up the situation, there was no way we could hold on to her. She knew she was going, too. She . . ."

King's last words were strangled. "Hell," he choked. "She *smiled* at me."

It was impossible not to reach out and touch his arm. Claire said softly, "King..."

"She left a three-year-old daughter," King told her. "Maybe that's good, I don't know. At least her husband has someone to live for."

Claire saw his shudder, slight though it was. He forced a smile, but it was the kind of smile that made her want to cry. "I shouldn't be loading this on you," he said simply.

She said what she felt. "You need to talk."

"It's rare that I'm able to," he admitted. They had reached the blanket and Claire knelt down on it. She had placed the deli bag and the six-pack in the center of the blanket, and as King took his place across from her it was as if they were on opposite sides of a table.

Claire opened a bottle of beer and handed it to him. He accepted it wordlessly and took a long draft. She peered at the sandwiches and hoped her voice didn't sound as tense as she felt as she asked, "Corned beef or pastrami?"

"Either," King said, then managed a grin. "Or both."

Claire gave him a sandwich then opened a bottle of beer for herself. She wasn't much of a beer drinker, but the cool, golden liquid tasted good to her now.

She tried a corned-beef sandwich and, surprisingly, that tasted good, too. She'd thought she wouldn't be able to eat until she calmed down a little. It was the fresh air, she told herself. The air was so wonderfully free of pollution.

They enjoyed the beauty of Lake Champlain and ate without speaking. When Claire noticed that King had finished his sandwich, she gave him another. He took it with a murmured thank-you and she began to feel that her crazy impulse to come out here and bring lunch with her was a good one. Being with him like this seemed so normal, so ordinary...and there were no echoes of the past. She could almost believe that they *had* met for the first time in the hospital emergency room, then had bumped into each other at the garden center as innocent strangers.

Innocent or not, though, she realized that King's traumatic experience this morning had lowered his guard where she was concerned. He'd been emotionally drained when he'd arrived at the beach. He'd needed someone to talk to. A sympathetic ear, someone who would simply listen and not ask any questions.

He finished the second sandwich, but shook his head when Claire offered him a macaroon. "I'm fine," he told her.

"How about another beer?" she suggested nonetheless.

"I wouldn't mind."

King sipped the beer and leaned back on his elbows, but then a silence dropped between them, a silence Claire was all too aware of. She forced herself to sit still and tried to analyze things. Maybe it was all her problem, she admitted. But she was so conscious of King's nearness that maintaining her composure was becoming more difficult every second.

He still looked fatigued, but evidently the food had helped. There was more color in his face now and his eyes were brighter. As Claire watched, King nestled the beer in a hollow by his side, then stretched out on the blanket, folding his arms and pillowing his head in his hands.

Claire felt herself stiffen and was unable to stop her eyes from traveling the length of his body. It was a sensual safari and made her tremble inside, because King still had the most beautiful body she had ever seen. Fourteen years had done nothing to alter that conclusion.

She and King had never been lovers. They had come close, but had never fully consummated the powerful physical attraction that had drawn them together from the first moment they met. This seemed incredible, Claire thought now, but credit for their restraint could be given to King . . . if credit was required. In the beginning, after she'd left, Claire felt a profound sense of loss because she and King had never yielded fully to the passion that more than once had threatened to burn them up. He held back on those occasions when it might have been possible to make love, telling Claire he wanted to wait until they were married, that he wanted things "right" with her, in every way. She knew she wouldn't have been his first, but that hadn't mattered. What mattered was he wanted her to be special, entirely different from anyone else in his experience. So, even when every fiber of her being had cried out for surrender, she had followed his lead.

Of course, there really hadn't been very many occasions when they could have made love. There were few private corners around Lakeport where they could retreat without fear of discovery. The Parmeter house was absolutely out-of-bounds, as was Dr. Faraday's house. The only place left was the vast outdoors itself, special spots like this grassy slope at Baskin's Beach. Perhaps that's what had caused King to exercise such caution, Claire thought. Perhaps he had felt it would cheapen their love.

Still, Claire had been fully aware of King's body then. And God knows she was fully aware of him now. In the intervening years, she had learned a great deal about the expression of physical love. Her husband had been gentle and considerate, a very experienced lover. Since Philip's death, she'd had one other lover, equally considerate and experienced. So she knew what it was to respond fully to a man, to let passion take its course. But she also instinctively sensed that were she to make love with King, it would be very different for her than it had ever been before.

Claire realized something else, too. Her attraction to King now was on a different level than when, long ago, she had been so deliriously in love with him. Maturity put this new attraction into another perspective entirely. Her response to King Faraday today was more real, more complete. Claire knew that even if she and King had met for the first time in the hospital emergency room she would be experiencing this same new response, a response with such potent possibilities that she was at once intrigued and frightened.

There was a chemistry between King and herself that could not be negated. A chemistry, a current—there were all sorts of names for this primitive force. It was as old as man, something that spanned the millennia of human existence and would always survive.

Glancing at King, Claire saw that his eyes were closed. She noted the regular rising and falling of his chest. He had fallen asleep, and as she watched him her lips curved into a smile. Actually, this was a compliment. He had confided in her the agony of losing his patient that morning, then he had been able to relax in her company, finally giving way to his own inner needs. That, she suspected, was something he seldom did.

Claire stretched out and gazed up at the intensely blue sky. *Perhaps I've been his catalyst,* she thought, rather enjoying the idea of that role. Still, she had no idea what King would think of her analysis . . . and wasn't sure she wanted to find out.

## CHAPTER TEN

KING AWAKENED SLOWLY, letting himself enjoy the rare experience of not having to hurry, not having to answer an imperative summons. He lingered along the hazy borderline between drowsiness and being alert, savoring the pleasure of giving in to this kind of laziness. Finally he stretched, a long, body-satisfying stretch.

He turned his head from side to side, flexing his neck, and that felt good, too. But then he stiffened. Claire was sitting not five feet away, her legs akimbo, her chin propped on her hands as she stared out at the lake.

The sharp sense of déjà vu King experienced was uncanny. He had imagined Claire in exactly that pose so many times before, in precisely this location. But he had no illusions about the reality of the present situation. Claire was not a mirage. She was flesh and blood.

He permitted himself the luxury of appraising her inch by inch while she was obviously deep in thought, her focus elsewhere.

The appraisal became a heady trip, yet King had to admit it was enjoyable. Claire was lovely to look at, even lovelier than he remembered. Her hair was a glorious color, full of hidden chestnut fire, and swept back from her forehead, touching her shoulders in gentle waves.

Her delicate features and enchanting profile made him want to touch her chin and turn her face toward him. She had a smooth forehead, a nose that tilted slightly and a generous mouth. Her eyebrows arched over eyes that could only be fully appreciated by gazing directly into their clear gray beauty. The resolute thrust of her chin was still there and she still held her head erectly. King noticed slight lines at the corners of her eyes now, and lines at the edges of her mouth. Marks of maturity, and not at all unattractive.

Claire was thinner than she'd been years ago and her body was more gently curved. She was full-busted for a person her size, with a narrow waist, slim hips and long, shapely legs. He remembered her playing volleyball and field hockey in high school, and she'd always been a good swimmer and an excellent dancer. Evidently she still exercised regularly, for she appeared in great shape.

King's mouth twisted involuntarily. Claire had become an extremely attractive woman, provocative and sophisticated in her mature beauty, youth's innocence replaced by a blend of wisdom and slight melancholy that was very alluring. He wondered how they would have reacted to each other if they had met for the first time just recently. If he had run into Ellie downtown, for instance, and Ellie had said, "This is Claire Bailey, my cousin from New York. I don't think the two of you have ever met." *And they hadn't.*

King played the scene out in his mind and knew he would have been attracted to Claire Bailey at first sight. Especially if there had never been a Claire Parmeter in his life. He was attracted to Claire Bailey anyway, damn it! She was a person he would like to know better. He wished it was possible to know her in a casual and pleasant way while she stayed in Lakeport. But he recognized the impossibility of his wish. What chance could there be of keeping things innocent and carefree, as if there had never been anything between them?

He stirred restlessly. Claire must have caught the movement out of the corner of her eye because she turned. "So, you've decided to join the world again," she said lightly.

The full impact of her unusual eyes hit him. Then he saw her smile, heard the laughter in her voice and responded instinctively. Wryly, he told himself he would have to be made of iron or stone *not* to have responded to her.

He laughed. "I owe you one," he confessed. "That wasn't very polite of me, falling asleep on you."

She shook her head. "You needed the rest," she reminded him.

"I can't deny that," he said, sitting up.

Suddenly, the possible reasons for her presence here began to nag him. How had she happened to come out to Baskin's Beach, today of all days? How had she known he'd be here?

King again noticed Claire's jeans. They looked new—deep blue and crisp—and somehow vaguely suspicious. "By chance," he asked, "would you have a bathing suit on under those?"

"No," she said. "Do you have a bathing suit on under yours?"

"As a matter of fact, I do."

"You're going Windsurfing, then?"

Only Chris could have told her he'd intended to go Windsurfing today! "No," he said. "I didn't bring the board."

Claire laughed. "Your eyes are full of questions, King," she teased. "Yes, to answer a couple of them, I know that you like to go Windsurfing on your day off when you can, and that this is your day off. Chris Tal-

# HARLEQUIN GIVES YOU SIX REASONS TO CELEBRATE!

MAIL THE BALLOON TODAY!

*INCLUDING*

**1.
4 FREE
BOOKS**

**2.
AN ELEGANT
MANICURE SET**

**3.
A SURPRISE
BONUS**

**AND MORE!**

*TAKE A LOOK . . .*

# Yes, become a Harlequin home subscriber and the celebration goes on forever.
## To begin with we'll send you:

- **4 new Harlequin Superromance novels – Free**

- **an elegant, purse-size manicure set – Free**

- **and an exciting mystery bonus – Free**

### And that's not all! Special extras – Three more reasons to celebrate

**4. Money-Saving Home Delivery** That's right! When you become a Harlequin home subscriber the excitement, romance and far-away adventures of Harlequin Superromance novels can be yours for previewing in the convenience of your own home **at less than retail prices.** Here's how it works. Every month we'll deliver four new books right to your door. If you decide to keep them, they'll be yours for only $2.50! That's 25¢ less per book than what you pay in stores. And there is **no charge for shipping and handling.**

**5. Free Monthly Newsletter** – It's "Heart to Heart" – **the** indispensable insider's look at our most popular writers and their up-coming novels. Now you can have a behind-the-scenes look at the fascinating world of Harlequin! It's an added bonus you'll look forward to every month!

**6. More Surprise Gifts** – Because our home subscribers are our most valued readers, we'll be sending you additional free gifts from time to time – as a token of our appreciation.

*This beautiful manicure set will be a useful and elegant item to carry in your handbag. Its rich burgundy case is a perfect expression of your style and good taste. And it's yours free in this amazing Harlequin celebration!*

# HARLEQUIN READER SERVICE
# FREE OFFER CARD

**4 FREE BOOKS**

**ELEGANT MANICURE SET – FREE**

**FREE MYSTERY BONUS**

PLACE YOUR BALLOON STICKER HERE!

**MONEY SAVING HOME DELIVERY**

**FREE FACT-FILLED NEWSLETTER**

**MORE SURPRISE GIFTS THROUGHOUT THE YEAR – FREE**

☐ **YES!** Please send me my four Harlequin Superromance novels **Free,** along with my manicure set and my **free mystery gift.** Then send me four new Harlequin Superromance novels every month and bill me just $2.50 per book ( 25¢ less than retail), with no extra charges for shipping and handling. If I am not completely satisfied, I may return a shipment and cancel at any time. **The free books, manicure set and mystery gift remain mine to keep.**

134 CIS KAZP

FIRST NAME            LAST NAME

(PLEASE PRINT)

ADDRESS            APT.

CITY            PROV./STATE

POSTAL CODE / ZIP

## HARLEQUIN "NO RISK GUARANTEE"
- There is no obligation to buy – the free books and gifts remain yours to keep.
- You pay the lowest price possible – and receive books before they're available in stores.
- You may end your subscription anytime–just let us know.

PRINTED IN U.S.A

madge told me, as I imagine you suspect. We had dinner together last night—''

''You and Chris?'' he interrupted. He didn't know why this should surprise him so much.

Claire nodded. ''We ran into each other the other day,'' she said. ''Yesterday he called and asked me out to dinner. Frankly, I was yearning to escape.''

''Oh?''

''Ellie and I are doing an inventory of the contents of the house,'' she explained. ''We decided it would be a sensible thing to do while we're waiting out this business with Thomas Haskell and the second will he alleges Aunt Lottie wrote.''

''Haskell really intends to follow through?'' King asked. Lakeport was still a small town. He'd heard a number of stories about Thomas Haskell's intentions.

''I'm afraid so,'' Claire said. ''Bill Edgerly feels we'll be going to court, and Ellie dreads that. Anyway, it was my idea that we start an inventory and get things in some sort of order for a professional appraisal. It hasn't been very easy.''

''In what way?''

Claire shrugged. ''Too much nostalgia,'' she confessed. ''Too much going back. Too many reminiscences, mostly on Ellie's part. But I have to admit…I've come up with a few memories of my own, too. There's so much *mustiness*, actual as well as emotional. So many things should have been thrown out years ago. Little personal things that make you feel you're trespassing when you deal with them.''

Claire sighed. ''Sometimes I think the Parmeters suffered from some kind of weird family phobia about not throwing anything away. Old letters and old postcards. Eyeglasses and broken watches, old prescriptions, you

name it.'' She laughed briefly and added, ''Even old un-
derwear and a set of gloriously yellow false teeth. Echoes
of the past Ellie and I could really do without. It gets depressing.''

''I can imagine,'' King said slowly. ''It's no good,
constantly dealing with cobwebs.''

''That's an excellent way of putting it.''

He glanced at her suspiciously, wondering if she was
being facetious. But Claire was watching him levelly, her
lovely face serious.

''The past,'' King said, staring down at his hands,
folded in his lap, ''should stay buried. There's no point
in opening closed coffins.''

Why, in God's name, had he blurted that out?

Claire hesitated, studying his face. Then she said,
''That's true, but only to a point.''

King knew she was hedging, but before he could
fathom why, she went on, speaking more rapidly than
usual, her nervousness apparent.

''The problem is that Thomas is insisting he's entitled
to half the contents of the house,'' she said. ''Whether or
not that comes to pass, it makes sense to find out what we
have and then to get some idea of the value.''

King nodded solemnly. ''I agree.''

''It's just that each drawer we open, each article we
find reminds Ellie of some little anecdote, some personal habit, that's all,'' Claire continued. ''As I've already said, King—''

''Yes?''

The way she spoke his name impelled him to meet her
eyes. She looked like a frightened child about to be
caught in some mischievous act.

He frowned. ''What is it?'' he asked, the question
sounding more abrupt than he'd intended.

Claire swallowed and it was plain that what she was about to say wasn't coming easily. She confirmed this when she stammered over the first words, and even when her voice had steadied, her tone still sounded strained.

"In general, King, I agree with you about not opening up the past. But . . . there is an exception."

Hearing this, King stiffened and sounded as strained as Claire as he asked, "Is there?"

"Yes," Claire said, and he could see her determination to go through with this, no matter how difficult it might be. "We need to open up *our* past, King," she told him steadily.

The silence that fell between them exploded with intensity. Then, gritting his teeth, King murmured darkly, "I don't think so, Claire."

Staring at his hands again, he said slowly, "It's too late. There would be no point in rehashing things. All of that was over such a long time ago. It no longer matters that you must have thought I wronged you, or you wouldn't have run off as you did. It doesn't matter that I couldn't deal with what I considered your desertion. The point is, I learned to deal with it and went on from there. You learned to cope with your own trauma and managed to make your own life. A very good one, I'd say, judging from the evidence."

King's smile was gentle. "When I look at you now, I see another person, Claire. Not the girl I once knew, but an entirely different person. Occasionally she reminds me of that girl, but this new person is still a stranger to me. You must feel the same way in regard to me. You *do* feel the same way, don't you?"

King saw Claire's lower lip tremble and knew she was fighting back tears. He hoped to God she'd succeed be-

cause the last thing he wanted now was the additional
burden of Claire's tears.

She said, her voice faint, "I don't really know how I
feel, King. I'd buried the past a long time ago, too. As
you say, I went on with my life and, yes...I've had a good
life. I truly believed I'd...forgotten. But coming back to
Lakeport has resurrected everything."

"That's natural, don't you think?" he queried gently.

"Yes, of course it's natural. But knowing that doesn't
make it any easier. For the first time, I've had serious
doubts about that day, about what I did..."

King shrugged slightly. "We all tend to feel plagued by
our own recriminations," he said. "It's easy to start self-
propelled guilt trips. But, in my experience, recriminations and guilt trips inevitably are exercises in futility. So
there's no point in either of us worrying about the past
now, Claire."

She stared at him, her face shades paler, her eyes
enormous. "Is it really too late?" she asked. "Are you
really so sure it wouldn't be better for both of us if...if
we talked it all out? Is that what you really believe?"

"Yes," King said. "Yes, to all three questions."

He willed himself to be firm because the fact was he did
believe what he was saying. His healing process had taken
a long time. He'd nearly wrecked his life because of this
woman who was looking at him now with eloquent gray
eyes that could wrench anyone's heart. But his wounds
had healed and the last thing in the world he wanted was
to disturb the scars.

He'd succumbed to blind anger when he had looked
down at her lying on the examining table in the emergency room. But that, he rationalized now, was because
he had been totally thrown off guard. He'd been stripped
to his raw emotions, seeing Claire so suddenly. Perhaps

if he had yielded to impulse and had gone back to her room that night he would have wrenched open that emotional coffin long nailed down. Perhaps he would have flung at her the question that constantly tormented him, night and day for many long months after her desertion.

*Why?*

The word tore at him now and he thrust it aside. There had been only one lapse, at the hospital. There would not be another. What he had told Claire was true: there was no point, at this late date, in either of them blaming the other or trying to absolve the other of guilt. They were two entirely different people now. They had moved on and fortunately, after a time at least, their moves had been in positive rather than negative directions.

Dr. King Faraday glanced at his watch. Thinking of the direction he had followed reminded him of his profession. "I should call the hospital," he said.

Almost nothing else he might have said could have induced such a feeling of hopelessness in Claire. At that moment, she could think of nothing but King. She was filled with him and with a paramount need to set things straight between them. But he didn't seem to care about that. At a time when she would have thought that he, too, was only concerned about righting past wrongs—no matter which of them had been responsible for those wrongs—he had remembered, above everything else, his dedication to medicine.

Claire felt emotionally defeated. Pride, if nothing else, made her seek a way out. She found a small escape route in asking, "Weren't you about to go for a swim?"

He grinned, and the vestige of boyishness in his grin made her heart ache. "The water's going to be cold," he confessed. "And after that good lunch you gave me, and the nap, I'm feeling awfully comfortable."

Comfortable? How could he possibly say he felt *comfortable* under these circumstances? Again, King's word choice instilled helplessness in Claire. She told herself ruefully that he could not possibly have demonstrated any better what he'd just said. King had most definitely moved on.

The ache deepened. But as bruised as she was feeling, Claire managed another small verbal escape, saying, "I thought this was your day off."

He looked surprised. "It is."

"You still need to call the hospital?"

"There are a couple of patients I want to check on."

"Don't you ever get away from it, King? From your work, that is?"

He considered this only briefly then said, "No, I don't suppose I do. Seldom, anyway."

"That's very dedicated of you," she said, and recognized how close to sarcastic she must have sounded.

"People shouldn't go into medicine unless they're dedicated," King responded calmly.

She didn't try to answer him. Instead, she reached for the beer and said, "It's still cool. If you're not going for a swim, would you like another?"

"If you'll join me," King agreed. "But I'll really have to get going after that."

Was he offering to stay with her only out of politeness? The thought stung, but Claire still handed him a bottle of beer then took one herself.

King appeared so relaxed as he sipped the beer that Claire envied him. She was so nervous it was all she could do to tilt the bottle to her lips without spilling the contents. Then she set it down carefully at her side and tried to find something to say. King might consider this a companionable silence; she didn't.

At length, she asked, "Do you find it very different, practicing in Lakeport?"

"Than being in a city?" he asked. "Yes, it's very different." She waited without commenting and after a moment he continued. "I went to med school in Rochester, I guess you know that," he stated.

Claire shook her head. "No, I didn't know."

"Well, I finished at the state university and went on to Old Rochester, as it's called," he went on. "I did my year of internship in Albany and my four years of surgical residency right in Manhattan, so I got a real taste of big-city medicine."

King in Manhattan? The shock was instantaneous, but if it registered in Claire's expression, King didn't let on.

He said, rather blithely, "I thought about staying in New York, for all the obvious reasons, but there was the offer of a staff position in Albany and I took it."

*All* the obvious reasons?

"Of course, Albany's nothing like New York City, though the atmosphere is definitely urban. So you might say I never experienced the personal quality of small-town medicine—as a doctor myself, that is—until I came back to Lakeport."

"Do you like it here, King?"

He reflected on this then said, "To my own surprise, I do. In one sense, I faced many more surgical challenges in New York and Albany than I do now. But the difference here is that when something comes along, *I* have to deal with it. There aren't very many colleagues I can turn to simply because we have such a small staff. And to call in a consultant from Albany or Montreal…well, there's never enough time, not if we're facing an emergency surgical situation.

"Aside from that," King added slowly, "the close-ness of small-town medicine does have its own unique rewards. And unique drawbacks, of course. It's hard sometimes, even for a doctor, to deal with patients objectively when they're also old friends or acquaintances. But on the other side of the coin, there's a very special personal reward..."

King broke off with a wry smile. "I'm rambling on," he said. "You shouldn't have asked me about medicine. It tends to become my favorite subject."

Claire could see that. Sensing the strength of King's quiet determination, a new feeling stirred within her. Something called admiration. She'd never viewed King in quite this light before.

He said, "We seem to do a lot of talking about me and very little about you. What *about* you, Claire? I understand from Ellie that you've become quite an art expert."

Claire shook her head. "Knowledgeable, yes," she amended, "but I still don't consider myself a real expert, not like Philip was..." She hadn't intended mentioning Philip in her conversation with King. She bit back the rest of her sentence.

But King said easily, "Tell me about your husband, Claire. Had you known him long before you were married?"

*Yes, we are on a new level,* Claire thought, hearing this. He was asking this question just as he might have asked a stranger at a cocktail party.

She said carefully, "Philip was my art instructor in college. He encouraged my interest in art and also my... small talent." She paused then went on, this easier than she had expected, "He was a widower, sixteen years older than me, with no children. I think, in the beginning, I was actually like a daughter to him. There was that kind of affection between us. . . .

"Anyway, Philip was a wealthy man in his own right, having inherited quite a bit of money from his family. Because he had independent resources, he'd always been able to travel as he wanted. He didn't need the teaching job, not for money. But he loved it, he loved discovering and encouraging new talent.

"He was a real friend," Claire said, "and I never expected our friendship to turn to love. Philip and I got married because of a mutual . . . need at that particular time. Later, I did love him, very deeply. He was a wonderful husband, a wonderful person."

Funny, Claire thought, how she felt she should say amen after that. As if she was ridding herself of some burden she'd not been aware of. At the least, she was enshrining Philip in a niche that was very much a part of her past now. Not unlike that long-ago day when she'd fled Lakeport.

She continued, glad to get on less emotional ground, "Philip always dreamed of owning an art gallery and, a couple of years after we were married he was encouraged by a man named Brent Underwood, someone he'd known for a long time, a real expert in the field. I was as enthusiastic as Philip, because during those two years we had done a lot of traveling." Claire smiled. "I became almost as familiar with the paintings in the Louvre and the Prado and the National Gallery in London as I was with the art that hung in our home. So, from day one, I worked very closely with Philip. I was his partner legally, too. And Brent . . . well, Brent was and is invaluable. He still works with me. In fact, I could not possibly be here now, except that he's holding the fort in New

York and is keeping a watchful eye on our other gallery in Florida.''

"You still travel much?'' King asked.

"A fair bit, by most people's standards,'' Claire answered modestly. "I was in Hong Kong in March, and I would have gone to Paris a few weeks ago had it not been for coming here. That's to say, I knew Ellie was going to need me and there were a few matters in New York that I had to take care of myself before I felt free to leave. Brent went to Paris instead, and actually I'm extremely lucky that he did. He stumbled on something I might never have had the fortune to discover.''

"An art find?'' King queried.

"Very definitely, an art find.'' Claire nodded, her smile radiant. "Brent learned that two relatively unknown Monets were being offered for sale. They've been in the hands of private collectors for years, and people don't generally brag about owning art that valuable. But Brent was given the opportunity to examine the paintings and told me there's no doubt they are genuine.''

Claire's eyes sparkled. "I spoke with him on the phone the other day and he's worked out virtually all the details toward our acquiring the paintings. Really, King, I don't know when I've been so thrilled about anything. They are winter scenes—Monet loved to paint snowy or rainy pictures. I think they must have been done close to the time he painted *Snow at Argenteuile*, around 1874. He'd rented a house in Argenteuil then and did many winter scenes in that vicinity during 1874 and 1875. Painters were inclined to paint their snow scenes either near their own homes or close to where friends lived, so they'd have the chance to dash inside occasionally and warm their frozen fingers and feet.''

Claire's laugh was wry, as King's had been earlier. "Now who's rambling on?"

"On the contrary," he told her. "What you've been saying is very interesting."

"Well," she said, feeling slightly self-conscious about her enthusiasm over the incipient purchase, "I happen to be very fond of the French Impressionists, and Monet is my favorite."

"Mine, too," King said, surprising her. "I saw *Snow at Argenteuil* at the Museum of Fine Arts in Boston. It was there when I did a three-month rotation at Mass General."

"It still is," Claire said.

"There was another painting quite like it. What you'd call a companion piece, I think."

Claire nodded. "*Boulevard St. Denis, Argenteuil, In Winter*," she said. "He painted it the year after he did *Snow*."

"I couldn't make up my mind which one I liked best," King admitted. "When I had time off, rare as that was, I used to wander around Boston, taking advantage of the culture it offers. The Museum of Fine Arts was my favorite discovery. It was nothing less than a transfusion, getting away from the hospital atmosphere and becoming steeped in such beauty."

He looked directly at Claire and added, "I should think it would be very difficult to have the Monets in your gallery and not want one for yourself."

Again he was surprising her. No one could be expected to appreciate how strongly she felt about those paintings, including King Faraday.

"It could be an impossible temptation," she admitted. "I've already told Brent I might have to have one for my very own. It would make a major dent in my personal finances, but I'd give up a lot, I really would. Can you imagine, owning a Monet?''

''What about you Claire?'' King asked now. ''Do you still do any painting yourself?''

''No,'' Claire answered. ''I haven't painted for years, which is no great loss as far as the art world is concerned.''

King didn't answer that. He was finishing his beer and Claire knew that in another moment they'd be parting. Still, she remembered how he had encouraged her in her artwork once. She'd shown him everything she did, from a sketch of Aunt Delia's roses to a watercolor of Lake Champlain. She had even painted on this very beach, setting up her easel and trying to capture the vista of the distant Green Mountains while King had explored for the Indian arrowheads that people still found in the area. But that, Claire reminded herself sadly, had been in another life.

## CHAPTER ELEVEN

AFTER HER BEACH ENCOUNTER with King, Claire stayed close to the old Parmeter mansion. She plunged into helping Ellie inventory the contents of the house, which proved to be a totally absorbing task.

Claire tried not to let the job get to her as it had prior to that afternoon with King. She attempted to inject some humor into the situation, and occasionally succeeded. Further, she persuaded Ellie to start throwing things out, like a drawerful of half-burned candles that certainly would never be used again.

"These," she proclaimed, holding up one of the candle stubs, "are of no earthly use to anyone."

They had done one of the bedrooms that morning, a second-floor room that had been used primarily as, to quote Aunt Delia, a spare room. It hadn't been occupied by a member of the Parmeter family, so the furnishings were sparse. But there was a nice Limoges china dresser set, a Hitchcock chair that appeared authentic rather than reproduction, and several other potential valuables, which they duly logged.

After lunch, she and Ellie again turned their attention to the dining room, this time attacking the Sheraton sideboard. It was there that Claire found the candles, but as she began tossing them into the green trash bag she'd brought from the kitchen, Ellie demurred.

"I don't know," Ellie said doubtfully.

"Don't know what?" Claire queried.

"We could melt those down and do something with them," Ellie said. "You can pour the wax into an empty oatmeal carton then peel away the cardboard and get a nice fat candle."

"Fine," Claire said nodding. "I'll put them all in a grocery bag and you can take them up to your room until you're ready to do that."

"You know very well there isn't an inch of space left in my room for anything," Ellie retorted. Then she broke out laughing. "You're right," she admitted. "I've become as much of a pack rat as the rest of the family. For heaven's sake, toss those candles out."

Claire grinned. "Here they go," she announced gaily, and made a big production of discarding one candle stub after the next.

That small incident changed the pace of their endeavors, and Ellie started throwing out worthless items on her own. After three productive hours, she paused, wiped her hands on her apron and stated, to Claire's surprise, "I could do with a drink."

She laughed at Claire's expression and added, "There's plenty of that rum left that Bill brought over, and some tonic. So how about it? It's hot this afternoon..." And it was, compared to what the weather had been since Claire's arrival.

"I think summer's finally here," Ellie called from the kitchen, getting out two tall glasses and ice cubes. "If it keeps up like this, it'll be swimming weather."

Claire started. Tomorrow was Wednesday, a fact she'd been increasingly conscious of as this day passed. She didn't know if King always took Wednesdays off, and had a hard time remembering what day she'd been taken to the emergency room. Crazy, that whole episode was so fuzzy. Still, she was pretty certain his day off then hadn't been a Wednesday, meaning it fluctuated. But even so...

As she and Ellie toasted each other with their drinks, a corner of Claire's mind embarked on a lecture. She must not make another excursion out to Baskin's Beach in the hope of encountering King. Once had been enough.

Last Wednesday, when she'd returned to the house, she'd found Ellie entertaining two women who had been their classmates at Lakeport High. Now both were married, with children. They'd become typical small-town housewives, Claire thought without censure, nor did she resent their frank curiosity about her.

She put herself out to be pleasant, for her own sake as well as Ellie's, realizing acutely that she had left quite an impression locally when she'd run away on her wedding day. Funny, until recently that was one facet of the whole thing she'd never dwelled on.

Also, it was a relief to have someone else in the house. For reasons Claire didn't try to define, she hadn't told Ellie about her meeting with King out at Baskin's Beach. As it happened, she was reprieved. Ellie had invited Bill Edgerly over for supper and he arrived not long after their old friends left. Once again, they got into a discussion about Thomas Haskell and Lottie's will. And once again the subject began to wear thin with Claire.

Now, remembering last Wednesday, Claire knew she couldn't hope for history to repeat itself. If she drove out to Baskin's Beach again, she'd have to think of something to tell Ellie when she returned to the house. And it made little sense to tell her anything other than the truth, if only because she hated lying.

*But I'm* not *going to Baskin's Beach,* she reminded herself.

"There are hot dogs and beans in the fridge, Claire. I thought we might just have that for supper. It only takes a minute to fix. Would that be all right?"

"Fine," Claire said, "unless I could persuade you to go out."

"Actually, that would be nice," Ellie said, to Claire's surprise. "Just as long as it's no place fancy. I don't feel much like dressing up."

Claire agreed, and they settled on a popular steak house on the highway west of town. The restaurant offered good food and a pleasant atmosphere, but was certainly not dressy.

The dining room was crowded. Claire and Ellie, standing in line, were deliberating about whether or not to wait for a table or try someplace else when a familiar figure loomed up in front of them.

"I've been trying to get your attention," Chris Talmadge complained, "but evidently my magnetic eyes aren't working tonight." Before either woman could reply, he continued, "We've got a table in the corner. How about joining us?" Chris was smiling at Claire, even though he was ostensibly addressing both women.

It was Ellie who answered. "That would be fine, wouldn't it, Claire?" Then she added quickly, "If you're sure it's all right, Chris."

"It would be a pleasure," Chris assured her smoothly. He placed one hand on Ellie's elbow and his other on Claire's as he spoke, then steered them toward the far side of the spacious dining area.

Claire, preoccupied with navigating around the tables under Chris's guidance, had no clue as to whom she would encounter at the end of her small journey. And before she knew what had happened, she found herself face-to-face with the tall blond man who had stood politely and was waiting for them.

For a moment of sheer panic, Claire felt like an adolescent, trapped in an especially awkward situation. She felt like turning on her heels and fleeing. She, sophisticated, worldly Claire Bailey.

Confronting King unexpectedly had the effect of not only leaving her tongue-tied, but also at odds with the movements of her body. When King held out the chair beside him she sat down as if she were a wooden puppet being manipulated by wires.

Chris was holding a chair for Ellie and, as she seated herself her eyes apprehensively swerved from King to Claire and back to King again. As if to reassure her, King smiled. But the smile didn't reach his intensely blue eyes.

Claire had the sudden, dreadful feeling that King probably thought she and Chris had *arranged* this meeting, just as she so obviously arranged the rendezvous at Baskin's Beach. She sat numbly, unable to speak.

Chris said easily, "This is really great. King and I were about to order some wine. We were saying we're both in a steak mood, so we thought we'd go for a carafe of burgundy. How does that strike you?"

"Fine," Ellie said promptly.

"Claire?" Chris queried.

"Burgundy would be fine, Chris," she whispered, her voice lost.

Why was she so damned *nervous*? Claire asked herself, knowing she was on the verge of starting to toy with the cutlery, tap her foot and wriggle in her chair. Any second now, she would unconsciously yield to this tremendously edgy feeling possessing her and reveal her inner turmoil.

Claire glanced at King while he was studying the menu. She concentrated on his hands, fascinated by their grace as they turned the long ivory pages. Comments about surgeon's hands were legendary, but King did have beautiful hands. Strong, not too wide across the palm, with long, slender fingers. Supple, capable hands.

Claire swallowed as the blood began pumping through her veins with an unexpected force. She felt the warmth of excitement racing through her body, felt herself responding feverishly to the sight of King's hands and the incredibly provocative imagery they evoked.

She wanted to feel his touch with an urgency she wouldn't have believed possible. She wanted King to caress her with those beautiful hands, wanted his fingers dancing over every inch of her, wanted him to make love to her. Not the King of her dreams. Not the golden hero of her past. Not the fiery idol whose feet had turned to clay. She wanted this man at her side, this man whose wonderfully sensitive face and mobile mouth were expressions of life, of vitality. This man who was attracting her more than anyone ever had before, though she scarcely knew him. And Claire could not have been more convinced that this King Faraday was a stranger.

Her thoughts were so treacherous, so unexpected, that very suddenly Claire felt giddy. She reached for the glass of ice water in front of her, then gulped it. Certainly, she must look as flushed as she felt, which meant her face would be beet red.

Ellie and Chris were talking and under cover of their conversation King murmured in her ear, "Is there something wrong, Claire?"

Her eyelashes fluttered as she became a butterfly caught in a net of her own making. She said hastily, "No. Why?"

"Wondered, that's all," King said easily. "You look awfully pale."

So much for feeling as if she'd started having menopausal hot flashes years ahead of time! Claire thought. She wanted to laugh aloud because it seemed, these days, she was wrong about everything. But not relishing the idea of fibbing—since an honest explanation for such an outburst would be out of the question—she choked laughter back. Instead, a sound closer to a cough emerged from her lips.

King leaned closer. "Hey," he prodded gently, "are you sure you're okay?"

"Yes," she managed to say, feeling herself bathed by his gaze, awash in his deep blue eyes. Even then, she was yielding. She was letting King's magic flood her, she was drowning in this wonderful weakness.

He said, his voice low, obviously not wanting Chris and Ellie to overhear, "Look, I told Chris I wasn't sure you'd want to join us, but he insisted on asking. Anyway, it did seem pointless, you and Ellie standing in line. From the looks of things, you'd have had a long wait. But I'm sorry—"

"No, King," Claire said quickly. "No, no," she repeated, keeping her voice low. "It's not that at all. I just thought . . ."

"Yes?"

"I thought you might think Chris and I had drummed this up together."

He frowned and looked honestly bewildered. "Why would I think anything like that?"

Honesty has a way of perpetuating itself sometimes, and Claire admitted, "Well, I went out to Baskin's Beach hoping I'd find you there."

"Yes," King said. "Yes, I know that."

His frankness shook her, and she was further taken aback when he added, "But I know why you did that, Claire. I think we worked our way through that. Tonight, on the other hand, was plainly coincidence. Chris has been in New York on business and—"

Chris caught his name and looked up. "What was that about Chris?" he asked.

"I was telling Claire you've just gotten back from a business trip to New York. And for once I managed to get away from the hospital at a decent hour, and I'm not on call tonight. So that's how we're here."

"It's a small celebration, actually," Chris said. "I landed an important contract while I was in New York. We've been doing well, but with this contract Champlain Plastics is going to have its banner year thus far. That called for a steak at the least. Don't you agree?"

"A steak, caviar, champagne, the works," Claire said with a nod. "That's wonderful, Chris."

"Chris has worked for it," King said. "He didn't get too much cooperation from the town fathers when he wanted to start a plastics factory within the town limits. They pressed him as far to the edge as possible, geographically and every other way. Now they're eating their words. They can see the positive impact that successful, well-managed businesses can have on Lakeport. Particularly when the buildings are aesthetically attractive, as well, as Chris's are." King paused. "Excuse me, Ellie," he said. "I realize you may not agree with me."

Ellie was sipping her burgundy and enjoying herself. She asked innocently, "Why ever not?"

King laughed. "Ellie, can you imagine what your grandfather would have said to the idea of having a plastics factory in town?"

"Claire's grandfather, too," she reminded him.

King's glance swerved to Claire. "So he was," he said, and added slowly, "I forgot that you're as much a Parmeter as Ellie is, Claire."

"Not really," Ellie said unexpectedly. "I mean, Claire's father left, and so did Claire. It was the rest of the Parmeters who stuck around and became old fuddy-duddies!"

"Now, Ellie," King said, lacing the smile he bestowed upon her with a full measure of charm, "no one could ever accuse you of being a fuddy-duddy."

Watching him, Claire was pleased to have this brief glimpse of a different side of King. He was showing the capacity to tease, to banter, and that was something she'd wondered about. For the most part, the exposure she'd had thus far to the new King Faraday had shown her a very serious person. It was good to know King also had a lighter side.

She could see Ellie visibly respond to his charm, and smiled. What woman wouldn't respond to King?

Lightheartedly, King led the conversation into more general areas, and the next hour passed very pleasantly. Then, when they had finished their steaks, King insisted on ordering champagne to celebrate Chris's latest success.

Once the champagne had been poured, King proposed an appropriate toast and they all clicked their glasses and drank. Then he added, "And we should also drink a toast to Claire's recent victory."

Chris looked surprised, hearing this, but Ellie's face was a study in stone. "What victory?" she demanded bluntly.

"The acquisition of two long-hidden Monets," King announced.

"What?"

"Please," Claire said quickly, stepping in before anyone else could speak. "I haven't acquired them yet, King. Bailey Galleries hasn't acquired them, that is."

"But you're virtually certain you will, aren't you?" King persisted.

"Well, yes," Claire hedged.

"Well, then... May a Monet soon hang in Claire's living room," King toasted.

There was nothing to do but follow along with him and sip champagne, though Claire knew that later, when she was alone with Ellie, she would have some explaining to do. And she was right.

As they ascended the stairs to their respective bedrooms that night, Ellie asked suspiciously, "How is it that King knows so much about your business?"

Claire sighed softly. She really didn't want to get into this, and also wished she wasn't always so conscious of Ellie's vulnerability. There were times when a person should be able to turn off someone's queries without hurting their feelings.

"King knows very little about my business, Ellie. The subject of the paintings came up casually. It seems we both share a fondness for Monet's work."

"I didn't know you and King had been seeing each other," Ellie said.

There was a sulkiness to Ellie's tone. Claire knew her cousin was already brooding, fancying she was being left out of something. Years ago, Ellie had behaved exactly this way time and time again. Ellie, inevitably, would be awake when she'd get home from a date with King—usually having sneaked in the back way because she was late, according to her grandfather's curfew. Ellie had always wanted to hear about where they'd gone and what they'd done.

*Because she was in love with King herself.*

The conclusion came unbidden, lodged so firmly in Claire's mind that she paused, looking up at Ellie, who had already reached the second-floor landing and was flicking the switch for the upstairs hall light.

Claire had toyed with the idea that King might be the mystery man who had impelled Ellie to break off her relationship with Bill Edgerly. She'd given thought to this notion and dismissed it more than once. Now it seemed so obvious she wondered how she ever could have had doubts. Even more, she wondered how Ellie felt about King now.

Was it possible that Ellie was still in love with King Faraday?

*No.* Claire nearly spoke the negative aloud. No, it wasn't possible. Because...love couldn't live without nourishment. Love had to be nourished or it slipped into the recesses of memory. That was where past love, lost love, belonged.

That was what King had really been saying the other day at Baskin's Beach, Claire realized now. People couldn't carry torches for years and years because torches burn out, the flames die. No flame could last forever without occasionally being relit. And once a fire had turned to embers, had dissolved into charred ashes, it could never glow again.

Ellie turned, peering down the stairs. "Aren't you coming up?" she asked.

"Yes," Claire told her then climbed the rest of the way.

Ellie was standing in her bedroom doorway. The room behind her was in darkness and the hall light was dim. She made a shadowy figure and Claire couldn't see her features as she said, "I know it's none of my business if you've been seeing King, Claire."

Ellie was speaking like a child who has just learned a bitter lesson, and Claire felt a mixture of sympathy and irritation toward her. She said patiently, "I haven't been seeing King, Ellie. I drove out to Baskin's Beach the other day and King happened to come by later. We…talked for a while. That's when the subject of the paintings came up."

Ellie, still standing in the shadows, said, "King's never had eyes for anyone but you. Not since the first day he saw you, I'd wager. It's still that way. I was watching him with you in the restaurant tonight."

"Don't be ridiculous!" Claire said sharply, suddenly not caring whether or not she hurt Ellie's feelings. "King was being polite tonight. Nothing more."

"That's not the way I saw it," Ellie said stubbornly. "From the looks of it, Chris Talmadge feels something for you, too. They're good friends, Claire. You shouldn't play one against the other."

Claire's eyes narrowed and she couldn't hold back the words that followed. "Maybe you *should* mind your own business!" she hissed.

She heard Ellie's gasp and was sure the tears would come next, moist crystal beads trickling her cousin's plump cheeks. For once, she didn't give a damn. Never before had she recognized one advantage Ellie had: perhaps involuntarily, perhaps subconsciously, Ellie, for years, had been making people feel sorry for her. Of her own doing, she'd been the drudge in the Parmeter household, but hers had been a drudgery that ensured a star in her crown. She'd been the daughter-niece who'd stayed home to take care of the old folks. Another star. A couple of stars. Maybe even a whole halo. But this was a kind of martyrdom that had always offered Ellie a lot of protection. She'd never had to make major decisions on her own, never had to go out in the world and assert herself. In so many ways, she'd never fully grown up.

Claire's simmering anger dissipated and she managed to say gently, "I'm sorry, Ellie. I didn't mean that. I guess I'm tired, I think we're both tired. It really hasn't been much fun, going over the things in this house. It's been a bad trip for both of us. No one should ever have to wade through the personal stuff we've been wading through. People should get their acts in order at some point. I know it's taught me a lesson. I'm never going to subject anyone else to doing what we've been doing...."

Claire was walking along the hall as she said this and was almost abreast of Ellie's door. She was startled when Ellie said nastily, "You always did hate them, didn't you?"

Puzzled, she asked, "Hate who?"

"Grandfather and Aunt Delia and Aunt Lottie and my father," Ellie retorted. "They took you in when you didn't have a place to put your head, but you never appreciated that, did you? You always thought you were too good for Lakeport, too good for any of us."

"Ellie—"

"Don't 'Ellie' me! I lived here with you, remember? If you don't remember, I do. I remember exactly the way it was, every minute. And you did the dirtiest thing anyone could ever possibly have done when you ran out on King." Ellie was working herself up, and Claire was close enough to hear her chest heaving. "You didn't deserve King," Ellie accused, her words laced with venom. "You never deserved King. You still don't. But you'd only have to crook your finger—"

"That's enough!" Claire commanded. She faced her cousin, feeling as if she'd turned to ice. She said, her voice level, controlled, "You're wrong about everything, Ellie. I loved my family. And yes, your family was my family. Even Grandfather. I loved him. I used to wonder what I could possibly do to make him feel differently about me. To make him forgive me for being my father's child. But I could never reach him all the way.

"With Aunt Delia and Aunt Lottie and Uncle Ralph, it was different. They knew I loved them. I showed my love to them in many ways, and they responded to me. Where were you, that you were too blind to see that? And as for King, as for my leaving King, that really *is* none of your business, Ellie. If you loved him yourself, if he didn't return your love, that's none of *my* business, either... except when you start making accusations that aren't true."

Claire drew a long breath. "I left that day for reasons I'm never going to tell you," she stated firmly. "That's my secret, and it's going to remain my secret. The only person in the world who has the right to know why I left here is King—and he doesn't want to know. Believe that or not as you wish, but it's true. And as for my playing King and Chris against each other, that isn't my style. I'm not that devious, Ellie! I admire Dr. King Faraday tremendously. And I like Chris Talmadge very much. I would like to consider both of those men my friends, trite as that may sound to you. But as soon as you and Thomas Haskell can come to an agreement I'll be leaving here. And I won't be coming back again. That you can count on. So you see, there's no need for you to worry about Chris Talmadge or King Faraday."

As she brushed past Ellie, she felt her reach out. And drawing away from her cousin's outstretched fingers, she saw Ellie flinch in shock.

"Claire!" Ellie implored. "Please! I'm sorry, I'm so sorry."

There were tears flowing down Ellie's cheeks as she stood, shaking. Claire's cheeks were wet, too, but this time she didn't hold back. Her voice choked, she tried to say, "I'm sorry, too."

She held out her arms and Ellie rushed into them. Then Claire clutched her close and the two women rocked together, sobbing.

For more than a minute they held each other, as only two people who'd shared so much emotional trauma can do. Then Claire pushed back tenderly and said softly, "Let's go downstairs and make some cocoa."

Sitting at the kitchen table together, their eyes puffy, their faces tear-stained, Claire and Ellie talked as they'd never talked before—about the family, about the turns their two lives had taken. They talked on into the first hours of a new day, covering everything there was to cover between them. Except King Faraday and the reason that, fourteen years ago, Claire had left him on their wedding day.

## CHAPTER TWELVE

THE NEXT AFTERNOON Claire and Ellie were working in the front parlor, an especially memory-filled room because in older days it had doubled as a teaching studio for Aunt Delia.

The time passed slowly and the hours were difficult for Claire. She wished she could banish the constraint between Ellie and herself, but didn't know how. Unfortunately, one thing was certain. Last night's exchange of confidences had not effected the kind of catharsis she had hoped for.

Claire had awakened this morning glad that she and Ellie had finally opened up, even though it had been painful for both of them. She felt their letting it all out had cleared air that badly needed clearing. But when she went downstairs, she found Ellie subdued and withdrawn.

Later, as they worked together, Ellie was abstracted, speaking only in monosyllables, mainly to answer questions Claire asked. Dark circles ringed Ellie's eyes and she seemed edgy. Claire pondered whether or not she should say anything about this and decided to keep quiet. Better to let Ellie work out whatever was bothering her by herself.

Despite Ellie's attitude, Claire felt she'd had a burden lifted that had been weighing her down subconsciously for a long time. She'd finally gotten a great deal out of her system. She had vented feelings about her grandfather, her aunts and her uncle. Feelings that until last night had been suppressed for as long as she could remember. She had even let slip her suspicion it was King with whom Ellie had been in love in high school. Ellie hadn't confirmed this, but she hadn't denied it, either.

It was too bad Ellie evidently didn't feel the same way about last night, Claire thought now, as she listed a Chinese porcelain vase and an oil painting that looked like an original of the Hudson River School.

Dusting off a venerable mantel clock ornamented by a reverse painting, she said, "We need to get a more comprehensive antique guide than the one you have, Ellie. You're right, we should have an idea about the value of some of these pieces before we call an appraiser. Both this clock and that painting look very valuable. Especially the painting."

Before Ellie could answer, the doorbell pealed.

Ellie asked distractedly, "Now who could that be?" She peered out the front-parlor window. "It's a black sports car," she reported. "I can't think of anyone who owns a black sports car," she added flatly, turning her attention back to her notes.

Neither could Claire. During the two encounters with King Faraday when she might have noticed the kind of car he drove, she hadn't had the opportunity. At the garden center, she'd left first. At Baskin's Beach, he'd left first.

So, as she opened the front door, she was completely unprepared to find King standing on the threshold. Seeing him immediately had the same sensual effect on her that it had in the restaurant last night. She stared at him numbly, realized she was staring at him and managed a smile.

"Hi," King said easily, returning the smile.

He was wearing faded jeans and a pale-yellow T-shirt, and he looked as if he'd spent some time outdoors. There was more color in his face, more sparkle in his eyes. In fact, he looked wonderful. Handsome, energetic and confident. A thought crossed Claire's mind. Certainly King hadn't spent these past fourteen years carrying a burnt-out torch for her.

"Hi," she said, wondering if she'd camouflaged her surprise. "Won't you come in?"

"Thanks," he said. "I hope I'm not interrupting anything."

"You're offering Ellie and me a reprieve," Claire told him, leading him into the front parlor. "We've been inventorying most of the day and I, for one, am beginning to feel bogged down."

As she spoke, Claire was noting Ellie's flustered reaction to this unexpected visit by King. Ellie unconsciously smoothed the front of her apron with both palms, then touched her hands to her hair. She had pinned it up in a bun and wisps were darting out everywhere. Helplessly, she lowered her hands and said, in a curiously toneless voice, "Hello, King."

King was looking around the room. His eyes fell on the grand piano that dominated one corner. "Do I ever remember that!" he exclaimed. "I took lessons on it when I was about nine years old."

Diverted, Ellie pondered this then admitted, "I'd forgotten you'd ever taken lessons."

"I was a most reluctant pupil," King confessed. "I had your Aunt Delia as my teacher for about six months. We were getting nowhere fast, because I'd do anything rather than practice. So she had a conference with my dad and they switched me over to your father. I took violin from him for about four months, but even my dad couldn't stand the screeching when I tried fingering the scales. I never got much beyond those damned scales!'' King grinned. ''So much for my musical talent.''

Claire was picturing King, at age nine, trudging into this room and taking his place at the keyboard under Aunt Delia's watchful yet indulgent eye. She'd sat there herself on many occasions, and always felt she'd let Aunt Delia down because she'd been such a poor student, too. Like King, she'd do anything rather than practice, even though she loved music. Probably this had been a small act of rebellion aimed at her grandfather, she analyzed now. Unfortunately, it had been hard on Delia, too.

*Another potential guilt trip,* Claire warned herself, turning her attention back to King.

He was asking, ''Are you two listing absolutely everything in this house?''

''Everything that might have value,'' Claire answered. ''We're also throwing out a lot of junk and filling up cartons with old clothes to give to the Salvation Army. In short, we're trying to get down to the nitty-gritty.''

''But there's so much gritty,'' Ellie complained, sounding more relaxed.

King laughed. ''Maybe you should turn this place into an antique shop,'' he suggested.

''I was thinking that also,'' Claire agreed. ''Matter of fact, I was just telling Ellie we should get a few trade guides and look up some current prices before we call in an appraiser.''

''You really plan to sell things off?'' King queried.

''That's up to Ellie,'' Claire said quickly. ''Everything belongs to her. I'm just here to help out.''

"These things are just as much yours as mine, Claire, and you know it!" Ellie protested. "The problem's with Thomas Haskell," she told King, "but you've probably heard about that."

"Yes, I've heard," King admitted. "It's too bad he's making such a stink."

"It'll get straightened out," Ellie said. "Bill Edgerly's our lawyer. He'll work things out for us."

"Once it *is* straightened out, what will you do?" King asked. "Have an auction?"

"I guess it depends," Ellie said. "We haven't gotten that far, though I suppose it's something we should talk over. I know I'm too sentimental about family things. Claire keeps telling me that, and she's right. We certainly should whittle things down, to say the least. Maybe an auction would be the best solution. We could deal with everything all at once. But . . . I don't know," Ellie concluded unhappily.

"I didn't mean to stir anything up," King said. "I had an idea, that's all."

"You haven't stirred anything up," Claire told him quickly. "Bill's having a conference with Thomas Haskell's attorney any minute now, so maybe we'll know something definite by the end of the day. Hopefully, we can settle things without going to court, though Thomas has been anything but cooperative so far. Unfortunately, there is more than a chance he'll be legally entitled to whatever share would have been Lottie's. So to me it makes sense to convert everything Ellie doesn't really want for herself to cash."

"In that case," King said, "may I make an early bid?"

"A bid about what?" Ellie asked curiously.

"A while back," King said, "I started picking up old pewter pieces." He added modestly, "It just happened.

I was driving around the country one day and came across a barn sale, and this old coffeepot attracted my eye. I bought it on the spur of the moment, and that's when the bug bit me. I wouldn't say I'm a true collector, but I've sort of gotten into old pewter and flow blue china and a couple of other things along the same line. So if you're going to offer anything like that for sale, I'd appreciate having first refusal.''

"As far as I'm concerned," Ellie said, to Claire's surprise, "you can take all the pewter and flow blue—and anything else you want—with you right now, King."

He grinned. "That would be nice, but I don't think it would be the wise thing yet, Ellie. Since there's the possibility of a court hassle with your uncle, you'd probably better keep your possessions intact for the time being."

"I suppose so," she said. "But you definitely have first refusal. Is that okay with you, Claire?"

Claire was about to say, yet again, that she wanted no voice in the matter, but bit back the words. She didn't want Ellie to become insistent so she merely nodded.

"Look around, King," Ellie invited. "We could tag the things that interest you and see no one else gets them."

Ellie was untying her apron as she spoke. Folding it over the back of a chair, she added, "Look, would you two excuse me? I have a splitting headache. I'm going to take a couple of aspirin and lie down for a while."

"You should have told me," Claire protested.

"It wasn't that bad, Claire."

"Do you have headaches very often, Ellie?" King asked.

She managed a weak smile. "Actually, I seldom have a headache," she said. "I'm kind of tired, that's all."

"Would you like me to bring you up some tea?" Claire asked.

"No. Nothing, thanks. I'll be fine. But there's still some rum and tonic. You might offer King a drink."

Ellie left with this. Claire, staring after her, couldn't decide whether she was being hospitable by suggesting that King be given a drink or whether she was trying to patch up things past patching.

At her elbow King said, "I'm afraid I stopped by at the wrong time. Look, I'll run along. I can check out the pewter some other time."

"No!" Claire said quickly, turning to face him. "What I mean is, there's no reason for you not to look at the pewter now. And a rum and tonic would taste good, don't you think? To tell you the truth, I wouldn't mind one myself."

King smiled. "I'd hate to force you to drink alone," he teased. Then more soberly, he said, "You look pretty done in yourself, Claire. Is there something wrong?"

"Not wrong, exactly," she hedged. How could she possibly tell King about the episode between Ellie and herself last night? King, of all people?

She said, abruptly, "There's some pewter and some of the blue china you like in the china cabinet. Why don't you look it over while I make our drinks?"

"Why don't I make our drinks while you take a few minutes off and sit down?" King returned.

Claire nodded and led the way to the kitchen. She got out two glasses, put the rum and a bottle of tonic on the counter and let King do the rest. There was an unreality to sitting at the kitchen table watching him mix drinks for them. An unreality to his being here at all.

Two weeks ago she wouldn't have believed it possible that she and King Faraday would ever again be sharing the same space. She still couldn't fathom this completely. It was as if the past had collided head-on with the present, and Claire still wasn't prepared for the situation unfolding in front of her. Yet she admitted to herself, *I've never in my life been more glad to see anyone.*

King made a hefty drink, Claire discovered, flinching when she tasted it. She looked at him quizzically and he laughed.

"Prescription," he said. "Medicinal therapy."

"I'll just bet," she scoffed.

He pulled out a chair, turned it around and straddled it. Facing her, he said, "Frankly, you look as if you could use a drink. I'd say the same about Ellie, except that with a headache she's probably better off settling for exactly what she's doing." He took a sip of his rum and tonic, then continued, "I can see what you meant the other day when you told me the house was getting to you.

"This place," he said, looking around, "really is permeated with Parmeters, isn't it? If I believed in ghosts, I'd say this house must be full of them. I imagine you'll be glad to get away again. This must be a tremendous contrast to your life in New York."

It was, of course. Yet . . . it wasn't a question of getting away again. Suddenly Claire knew that. Rather, it was a question of coming to terms with the past and the present so she could live fully *now*, without shadows, without cobwebs. It was so easy to get enmeshed in cobwebs and regress. . . .

"What about your life in New York, Claire?" King asked. "Do you live in an apartment?"

"A condo," she said, "on Central Park West. It's in an old apartment house that Philip's parents owned before him. It's quite spacious for an apartment. Big rooms, high ceilings and windows in the living room and master bedroom that look out over the park.''

"Sounds like a great place to entertain," King remarked perceptively.

"Most of my entertaining combines business with pleasure," Claire confessed. "Cocktails or small supper parties for people involved in some way with the art world. Collectors, artists, other dealers and publicity people. We have to pay a fair share of attention to the media. There are so many galleries in New York. Excellent galleries. Competition, always. So we try to consistently put our best foot forward."

"And I'm sure you succeed," King told her.

"I try," she murmured, not knowing quite how to answer. It was true she usually succeeded at what she did with Bailey Galleries, including her entertaining, but it was equally true that success carried with it a price tag. Sometimes Claire yearned to escape from the formality that went along with so much of her life. Sometimes she wanted to kick up her heels, to express herself, to be young again....

It was so long since she'd been young. She had sacrificed certain aspects of her youth when, at twenty, she had married a man so much older than herself. It had been impossible for Philip to act her contemporary. So in many ways, she'd become his.

A crazy memory surfaced, and Claire asked King wistfully, "Do you remember the day we climbed Pocomoonshine?"

King's head jolted backward. Briefly, just briefly, his blue eyes glazed. Then they cleared and he smiled. "I remember it very well," he said pleasantly. "It proved, conclusively, that you were not cut out to be a mountain climber." He paused then continued before Claire had a chance to comment, "You haven't become a mountain climber, have you?"

"No. I'm as much of a dolt about heights as I ever was."

"What do you do for exercise, then? Ever take up skiing?"

"Skiing usually requires going up on mountains," she reminded him. "Actually, walking is my thing. New York is really a great place for walking, if you avoid certain areas during rush hour. And I swim. I belong to a health club and try to swim there three afternoons a week."

"Do you dance very often?"

It was an odd question, and Claire looked at King curiously. "No," she said. "Matter of fact, the first time I'd danced in quite a while was when I went out to dinner with Chris last week."

"How about going out to dinner with me this week?" King suggested.

Claire's eyes widened. She couldn't believe he was actually asking her for a date. King Faraday, asking her for a date!

She said feebly, "I'd like that." God knows, this was the truth. She couldn't imagine anything she might like more than going out to dinner with King. Just being with King. Just...

"How about Saturday?" King asked. "I'm reasonably certain I can get away on Saturday."

"Saturday would be fine."

"Great. Now, if you don't mind, I'd like to take a look at the pewter before I go."

Claire nodded and, in a daze, led the way into the dining room. Opening the china cabinet, she tried to keep her fingers steady as she brought down a selection of pewter and flow blue china, placing each piece on the dining-room table so that King could look them over.

Very quickly, he became deeply absorbed. Claire was surprised at his interest in these old things, lovely as they were. She was seeing yet another side of King Faraday, a side she'd never imagined.

A strand of thick blond hair fell across his forehead as he bent to examine a large pewter pitcher. He turned the pitcher upside down, studying the maker's mark on the bottom, while Claire fought the urge to reach over and smooth the truant hair into place.

A dangerously sensual feeling for this man suffused her. In fact, Claire told herself, it might be best to simply admit how sexually exciting King was and let it go at that. But she felt something else, too, something deeper. Something that frightened her.

Was she falling in love with Dr. King Faraday? The question couldn't be avoided, not by anyone as intrinsically honest with herself as Claire. Immediately, she told herself she couldn't afford to fall in love with him . . . for so many reasons. She told herself it would be far safer to yield to her physical yearnings than to let this deeper current flow uncontrolled.

She winced, watching King . . . and wanting King.

He looked up at that exact moment and met her eyes, and Claire would have sworn that his eyes darkened, becoming a shade of blue like Lake Champlain in August, in places where the water was very deep.

He sounded casual, though, as he said, "This is an excellent piece, Claire. A classic example of early American pewter, made by Daniel Curtiss, Albany, 1822. See?" he said, pointing to the information printed on the bottom of the pitcher. "I'd very much like to acquire this, if Ellie wants to let it go."

Claire, needing to occupy herself with anything impersonal, fighting to get her emotions back into a safer, saner focus, searched for and found a notepad and pencil. "I'll mark that down."

He'd turned his attention to a flow blue china platter. "There's something about the color of these pieces, the way the blue sort of melts, that appeals to me very much," he confessed.

"Somewhere," Claire said, memory nudging, "I think there's a whole dinner service of flow blue. Quite a number of pieces, anyway. I remember Aunt Delia packing them away after she won a set of brand-new china at a church bazaar. She was so proud of the new stuff. Funny, isn't it? How often we don't appreciate the things we have right before us, things like antiques."

Claire hadn't intended to turn philosophical and quickly added, "I'd bet the majority of the blue pieces were never taken out of the cartons again. She kept a few platters out, but the rest—"

"Where do you suppose the cartons are?" King asked.

"I don't know. It's just dawned on me that Ellie and I have the attic and the cellar to go through, too," Claire said. "I don't think Ellie's even thought about *that*."

"Now you really look as if you could use a breath of fresh air," King joked. "I'd suggest we make our dinner date tonight, except there's something I have to do after I leave here."

Claire stared at him helplessly. "It's overwhelming," she admitted. "Do you suppose everyone's old family home is like this?"

"I'd say yes, when you're talking about people who have family homes like this one," King told her.

He glanced at his watch as he spoke. He'd promised to visit Mary Clayton this afternoon, and knew he should be getting along. Mary, a woman in her sixties, had been his high-school English teacher. This past spring he'd referred her to Albany for coronary bypass surgery, feeling that the hospital there was better equipped to handle a case like hers. Mary had done well and had come home the past weekend. She phoned King and he'd promised to stop by on his next day off.

It occurred to him now that Mary had also been Claire's high-school English teacher. Ellie's, too, for that matter. He was tempted to ask Claire to come along, knowing this would give her a chance to get out of the house for a while. Then they could go to dinner from Mary's house....

King corrected himself. They couldn't go to dinner from Mary's house. He remembered that he and his father were invited to dine tonight at James Faraday's home. Uncle Jim and Aunt Alice. Good people. Still, King couldn't convince himself that he really wanted to spend the upcoming evening with them.

Claire interrupted his thoughts, saying, "King, if you're in a hurry, I don't want to hold you up. You can look at these things another time."

King realized he'd been staring at his wristwatch. He said quickly, "You're not holding me up, though I do have to get going. Tell Ellie I'd like to buy all the flow blue china, would you?"

"The cartons, too, assuming we find them, or just these pieces?" Claire asked.

"The cartons, these pieces, everything."

Claire wondered what King planned to do with all the antiques he was amassing. Set up his own home at some point? She couldn't quite imagine that, since his prime reason for returning to Lakeport had been to be with his father.

She remembered dining in the Faraday house, years ago. It was Victorian in style and quite formal, the furnishings echoing the Victorian way of life. It wasn't a family homestead, like the Parmeter mansion. If her recollections were correct, George Faraday bought the house when King was a child, just after his wife left him. King had said something once about his father not even liking to drive near the street where they'd lived before. It evoked too many painful memories.

The Faraday house, Claire remembered, hadn't been crammed with belongings like the Parmeter mansion. Nor had it been underfurnished. There had been an adequate supply of china, silver and all the rest. Dinner had been served in a gloomy, dimly lit dining room, the serving done by the Faradays' housekeeper, a sallow-faced woman who looked as if she never smiled.

King was replacing the pieces in the cabinet, and Claire said hastily, "That's all right, King. I can do that later."

He nodded. "Okay. Tag the pewter pitcher for me, too, will you, please?"

Claire followed him around to the front door. He asked, "Shall I pick you up at, say six-thirty on Saturday? I should be able to break away from the hospital by then."

"Six-thirty," Claire repeated, suddenly feeling awkward again. She watched him take the front steps two at a time...and remembered how the King she'd known long ago had always taken those steps two at a time.

*The King she'd known.* She was making a sharper and sharper distinction between the King she'd known and the man who just left.

Saturday night should be an experience, a fascinating experience, Claire told herself, as she walked back to the dining room and began returning the pewter and china to the cabinet. Until then, each hour would pass like molasses in winter, Claire feared, groaning at this frustrating thought.

When Saturday came, though, King didn't take her to dinner at all. It was nearly six when he telephoned to say, "Claire, I'm terribly sorry. I'm going to be held up in the OR until at least midnight. A complicated case. Look, I'll call you tomorrow and maybe we can have brunch."

He said again, "I'm terribly sorry," and Claire nodded, as if he could see her through the phone receiver.

"That's all right," she assured him. But as she hung up she knew it wasn't all right. That King had to break their dinner date she could accept. She had a good idea of the demands his profession made on his spare time, and was sympathetic. What bothered her was the tone of his voice. There'd been no real regret as he'd told her he was sorry. She'd sensed his mind was not with her at all, only on the patient in need, waiting his skill.

King was a doctor, foremost and always. A surgeon dedicated to medicine, a man thoroughly in love with his work. Claire told herself firmly that it would behoove any woman on the verge of loving him to remember that and never forget it.

# CHAPTER THIRTEEN

BRENT UNDERWOOD CALLED CLAIRE first thing Monday morning.

She and Ellie were having breakfast when the phone rang. Claire was nearer and took the receiver, aware that Ellie was going to listen intently to every word she said. She saw the look of apprehension on Ellie's face as soon as it was clear the call was from New York.

When the whole unhappy mess with Thomas Haskell was finished, it was going to be very, very difficult to leave Ellie. Claire, this past weekend, had been increasingly convinced her cousin was becoming overly dependent upon her. Once she'd rallied from their emotionally charged confrontation, Ellie had become almost too docile, too willing to go along with anything Claire suggested.

Wishing something would happen to make Ellie leave the kitchen, Claire said, "Yes?" into the receiver and was greeted by Brent's familiar voice.

"What are you doing up at this hour?" she asked, surprised. Brent was not an early riser. Nor was it ever easy to get him to leave the gallery once he'd arrived. He liked to linger late, insisting that some of his most productive work was achieved after everyone else had gone home.

"Claire, I don't like to add to your problems, but we need you here in New York," Brent said. "Briefly, just a fleeting visit. The Monets are ours, but I need your signature on the purchase agreement. I could bring the paperwork up to you—''

"No," Claire cut in hastily.

She heard the amusement in Brent's voice as he asked, "Need to get away, sweetheart? Back to the bright lights? Thank God! I was afraid you might go rustic on me and try to escape this net altogether."

"Not a chance," Claire told him. In truth, her allegiance to Bailey Galleries was far too great to permit her to seek an escape route. Not that she wanted one. And what Brent said was true. She did need to get away from Lakeport and the Parmeter house. She needed to get away from King, for that matter. Over the weekend, she had given herself some stern lectures. There was absolutely no point in cultivating even a casual relationship with someone whom she found as attractive as King when the only possible path offered was a dead end.

She said, "I can fly down this afternoon, Brent. It would be the quickest way. I change planes at Albany—''

"Get back to me with your arrival time and I'll meet you at the airport," Brent returned immediately.

"Nonsense. No need to drag you out to Long Island," Claire teased, knowing that anything beyond the confines of Manhattan was outside Brent's realm. "I'll take a taxi directly to the gallery. When I get the flight information, I'll call you back and tell you approximately when to expect me."

"Don't bother, as long as I know you're coming," Brent said. "I can't find enough words to tell you how fantastic it will be to see you," he added. "How long have you been gone? Three weeks? Something like that? My God, it seems like a century."

Claire was inclined to agree as she said goodbye and hung up. This space of time spent in Lakeport was immeasurable. It stood by itself, apart from the rest of her life.

She turned and faced Ellie and was struck by the quiet despair etched on her cousin's face.

Ellie said, "You're going back."

"Only to attend to some necessary business," Claire assured her. "Ellie, don't look like that! I'll be in Lakeport again before you know I'm gone."

"I doubt that," Ellie said dryly. "Oh, Claire, I don't mean to be such a…frump! You must get disgusted with me. I wouldn't blame you if you didn't come back at all."

If this was a cry for help, Claire was going to answer it in her own way, she decided. She said firmly, "I don't consider you a frump, Ellie. But I wish you'd straighten up. I'm coming back, I promise you. But I can't stay forever. Fortunately, we're into a slow season at both of the galleries, but in a few more weeks we'll be getting ready for the fall shows and exhibitions. I really can't miss any, so by then I'd like to see you standing on your own feet. It's high time you became your own person, cousin."

Ellie was looking at her as if she'd been slapped in the face, and briefly Claire felt ashamed. Still, these things had to be said, just as she'd had to say what she'd said the other night.

Claire tried to choose the right words, wanting to make each one count. "You're such a terrific person, Ellie, but you're so damned unfair to yourself. I don't care whether or not you ever lose a pound, personally. You're dear to me now, and you'd be just as dear to me if you were as skinny as a rail. But it might do your health some good if you pared down a little. Meantime, you could spruce up your appearance in all sorts of ways. Try using a cover-up rinse on your hair, for example. It would be one thing if your hair was a lovely silver gray, but it's a mixture, and apt to stay that way for years. I can't recall any other Parmeters going gray when they were as young as you are.''

"Young?" Ellie laughed, a strained little laugh. "Have I ever been young, Claire?"

"If you haven't, it's your own fault. At least…it's your fault now, and that's another thing. You've got to put the past behind you, Ellie, and start living for today. You can't keep harking back to a time long gone, to people long gone, no matter how much you loved them. You owe something to *you*, damn it! Now, I'd like to drop off my rental car on the way to the airport. If you'll follow me, we can stop at the mall before it's time for me to catch my plane. I want you to buy yourself a couple of colorful items that will play up those gorgeous eyes of yours, and your lovely coloring. I want to hear you make an appointment at a beauty shop. When I come back, I want to see you with hair that doesn't show a touch of gray, a new hairstyle and something pretty on your back. Okay?''

"Okay," Ellie said shakily. Remarkably, she was actually smiling.

Claire followed through with what had sounded like more of a threat than a promise. They stopped at the Champlain Mall en route to the airport and bought Ellie a loose-fitting blouse in a shade of deep tangerine that did wonderful things for her coloring. Their second choice was a lacy cotton top in a vivid shade of pink. And Claire insisted that Ellie indulge in some tapered white slacks to go with her two other purchases.

Claire had a layover in Albany, so it was early evening when she arrived in New York. She'd brought no luggage with her, as she had changes of clothing for every season back in her apartment. She'd simply tossed a few essentials into a tote bag, and when she got to the airport terminal she was especially glad she'd traveled light, as it meant being able to go directly out to curbside where she was lucky enough to quickly snatch a cab for the trip into Manhattan.

Sunlight still splashed the city streets, though the giant golden orb was descending into the west, where it would sink into oblivion back of the Palisades on the New Jersey side of the Hudson.

The cab made its way along Fifty-seventh Street, one of Claire's favorite midtown streets, then crossed Park Avenue, another of her favorites with its grassy center strip running all the way to the tall building that housed Grand Central Station. They pulled up in front of the gallery, where a bright-blue canopy stretched out from the front entrance, spanning the sidewalk. Claire paid the cab driver and tried to decide whether or not this was a homecoming.

Lakeport was already part of another world. And the disparity between that world and this world intensified for Claire as she was greeted by her sales staff. She knew their pleasure at seeing her wasn't something assumed because she was their boss. She liked the people who worked for her, and they liked her.

She took the small private elevator up to her suite of offices and saw that the lights were still on. But when she glanced inside the first room she found it empty, and her secretary wasn't at her desk. Brent, bless him, had undoubtedly sent the office people home.

Brent was in his spacious corner office, and he rose from behind his desk to greet her, both hands outstretched. His eyes sparkled with genuine enthusiasm as he kissed her cheek. Then he stood back and surveyed her critically.

"I expected to find you rosy cheeked and pounds fatter after breathing all that clean air and eating all that country cooking," he said, frowning. "And, more important, well rested. Not true, I see. Have you had *any* sleep since you've left here, Claire?"

"Most of the time, I've felt like quoting Hamlet," Claire admitted. " 'To sleep, perchance to dream . . . aye, there's the rub!' You might say my days and nights have been filled with dream sequences, Brent."

"Nightmare sequences, I'd say," Brent told her. "Has it been that bad?"

"In many ways, yes. Emotionally traumatic, at the least. Constant excursions into the past."

Brent went to a wall cabinet that concealed a small refrigerator and procured a bottle of champagne and two stemmed glasses, chilled.

"Having you back calls for a celebration," he announced, extracting the cork from the bottle with only the slightest of pops. "Anyway, you look as if you could use a touch of bubbly."

Claire smiled wanly. "Not too much has been bubbly since I left here," she admitted.

Brent handed her a glass of liquid gold, filled with escaping bubbles. They clicked a silent toast, then he resumed his place at his desk while she took a chair across from him. Over the rim of his glass, he said quietly, "You've seen him again, haven't you? Since that day when you collided with him in the hospital emergency room?"

Claire knew she shouldn't be surprised at Brent's perceptiveness, yet he always surprised her in this respect. He was the most intuitive man she had ever known, and extremely compassionate. His was much too good a shoulder to cry on, something she'd already done too often.

Nevertheless, it was impossible to dissemble with him, so she nodded. "Yes."

"And?" Brent asked softly.

"Well, as I think I already told you, King went on to become a doctor," Claire said slowly, studying the bubbles in her glass. "He's a successful surgeon now. He was practicing in Albany, but a couple of years ago he returned to Lakeport because his father needed him. The elder Doctor Faraday had a stroke. King lives with him, in fact, and he's on the staff of Lakeport General Hospital. Dedicated to his profession...."

Brent's tone was lower still. "You're telling me that he's changed dramatically. That is what you're saying, isn't it, Claire?"

"Yes, I guess that's what I'm saying," Claire agreed. "Yes, King certainly has changed dramatically, as you put it."

"How would you feel about him if you met him for the first time?" Brent asked bluntly.

The question startled her. She looked up, meeting Brent's pale-blue eyes, and found in them—as she always did—only empathy, understanding and the desire to help her in any way he could.

Brent leaned back in his chair, champagne glass in hand. As usual, he was so perfectly groomed he could have gone before the camera immediately to pose for a successful fashion ad. He had the silvery gray hair she'd been thinking of when she'd spoken to Ellie about hair color. And his pale-gray suit complemented him perfectly. He was tall, slender and fine featured, and possessed a certain elegance. A casual elegance, paradoxical though that might seem.

She said, being honest with him because there was no other way to be, "If I were to meet King today, I would find him overwhelmingly attractive. I used to think he was the handsomest man in the world. But he's even better looking now, though in a different way."

"He's grown up, perhaps?" Brent suggested.

"Oh, yes—" Claire nodded "—he's grown up. The first thing that struck me was how all his boyishness had disappeared. He's mature, maybe a shade too mature for a person his age since he's still only in his mid-thirties. But maturity becomes him. You sense his competence, his capabilities. There's still that gentleness I remember so well, but there's a firmness, too. There's nothing soft about Dr. King Faraday."

Claire paused to sip her champagne, then continued more slowly. "He still mountain climbs and skis and Windsurfs, among other things. From what I hear, he isn't much for the social life, though he's not a hermit, either. Matter of fact, he asked me out to dinner just Saturday night."

"Did you go?"

"No." Claire shook her head, thinking about last Saturday night, wishing they had gone out. "A surgical emergency came up," she said, "and he had to cancel. He was going to call me yesterday—he'd mentioned that perhaps we could have brunch together—but his secretary called me up instead and told me he was so involved with the patient he'd operated on the night before he couldn't get away."

"So," Brent obversed, "he's interested in you."

"I'd like to think so," Claire mused. "My intuition tells me that. Though he's very self-contained and not at all easy to read, I suspect that King is as...well, as aware of me as I am of him. But only on one level."

"What's that supposed to mean?"

Brent reached for the champagne bottle as he posed the question and, leaning across his desk, refilled Claire's glass, then his own.

"King behaves as if we just met," Claire said. "I have this funny feeling he'd like to have an affair with me. But it would clearly be just a summer romance. What I'm saying...well, it's obvious that King doesn't want me or any other woman in his life on a permanent basis."

"Does that mean you have some tantalizing little wishes about becoming a permanent part of King's life, but you're trying to hold back because you fear he'll frustrate them?" Brent challenged.

Claire laughed. "You do have a way of putting things," she said.

"Yes, and if I were anyone but myself you'd tell me to mind my own damned business," Brent told her. "But you know and I know that I care deeply for you, Claire, dear. I cared for Philip, I care for you. I suppose I tend to feel he entrusted you to me."

"You make me sound like a dreadful burden," Claire protested.

"A beautiful burden," Brent corrected. "Actually, not a burden at all—burden's a terrible word. Looking after you, thinking about you, concerning myself with your welfare, is a privilege, and I love it."

Brent raised his glass, then added, "I take it you saw King now and again before he stood you up Saturday night."

"A couple of accidental encounters, and at least one deliberate, by each of us," Claire said.

"Have you explored the past with him? Have you ever found out whether he stands guilty as charged? When you talked to me, I had the impression that although initially you were sure of your ground, time may have changed your mind. There seems to be room for doubt, anyway. But I'm not sure you've ever fully admitted that, even to yourself."

"I hadn't," Claire conceded. "But I have now. And yes, I tried talking to King about the past, but he's shut the door. I believe he called it closing the lid on a coffin. And he doesn't want that coffin reopened."

"And you agreed?"

"I didn't have much choice, Brent," Claire confessed. "I could feel myself up against a stone wall. In a way, I guess he convinced me that there'd be no point in either of us rehashing everything. King infers we're two entirely different people than we were fourteen years ago. So most of the time, you see, it really has been like meeting him for the first time."

"Ah, but it can't be," Brent interposed. "That's to say, I believe it's impossible for either of you to be happy with this present-day mutual attraction you're speaking of until you've settled the past. We're not speaking of small misunderstandings here. Your misunderstanding was the stuff revolutions are made of, Claire, and had almost as great an effect. It changed the courses of both your lives. So you're two new people now. You are also the two people you were then. Leopards age, but they never lose their spots."

With that, Brent set down his empty champagne glass. "I'll say only one thing more," he told Claire. "I think it would be easy for you to fall in love with this new man.

He'd be a new love...yet at the same time he'd be an old
love, if you follow me. Be cautious, that's all. I'm terribly afraid you're apt to get hurt again. And wounds of
the heart are even more painful when the heart has matured."

Brent edged his chair closer to the desk and reached for
a folder. And Claire, still mulling over what he'd said,
knew that the subject of King was terminated for the time
being. Brent was one to make his point then let it go.

"Now," he said, "to the lovely matter of the Monets.
They are arriving from France day after tomorrow, darling. Their previous owner is escorting them personally.
He's a charming Frenchman, complete with title, and he
yearns to meet you. I think it's advisable, under the circumstances. Frankly, I doubt the Monets are the only
treasures in his château, and if we handle this adroitly we
may have the chance for future acquisitions that would
make our competition *green*."

"Well if that's the case, let's go for it!" Claire said
enthusiastically.

Brent smiled. "Good," he said, "because I've taken
the liberty of inviting him to an intimate little supper at
your place on Thursday. We can give him time Wednesday to recover from jet lag. Then we can finalize business details here on Thursday in the daytime and
entertain him that evening. I've asked a few very choice
clients to be present—"

"Brent," Claire interrupted, horrified. "How could
you? The apartment's going to be dusty, to say the least.
This will mean thinking up a special menu and..."

Brent waved a deprecating hand. "All taken care of,
my dear," he assured her. "I've arranged for a caterer,
we've selected the menu, the apartment was thoroughly
cleaned today and will be gone over again on Thursday

while we're occupied here. You have only to appear Thursday evening and be your usual charming self.''

Claire sank back, not entirely mollified, but there was really nothing she could say. Brent was right. Regardless of the prospect for future art acquisitions, the gracious thing would be to entertain this gentleman from France. And her apartment was the perfect setting for the intimate kind of supper Brent was suggesting.

What troubled Claire most, though, was that she'd had no intention of staying in New York so long. She'd thought that she could get back to Lakeport by Wednesday morning at the latest. Now it would be Friday at the earliest.

Still, there was nothing labeling her return to Lakeport an urgent priority, she reminded herself. At last report, Bill Edgerly and Maury Fletcher were still conferring about the alleged second will. Bill had examined the document and reported to Ellie only that there were some things he wasn't satisfied with. He'd added that he was planning to meet with Fletcher at least one more time. After that, he advised them to get together with Thomas Haskell again. Provided Thomas had recovered from his pique, and was ready to discuss things on a more rational level.

So there was really no need to return to Lakeport until next week. No need . . . yet Claire found herself *wanting* to go back. Wanting to so much, in fact, that it frightened her.

King was the real reason for going back to Lakeport, she admitted. Her King, with whom she was not yet finished. Ellie, at this stage, might actually do better without her than with her. Maybe if Ellie had to face things on her own, she'd stand on her two feet the way Claire hoped.

Claire turned her attention to Brent and to discussing the Monets. He already knew how delighted she was with the purchase, but she told him again. Then they briefly went over the other gallery business Brent felt was worth her consideration. After that, he insisted they stop at a Japanese restaurant he had just discovered for "something light." Later, he accompanied her home.

The apartment, as she'd known it would be, was spotless. The rooms were filled with fresh flowers in lovely arrangements. Brent fussed over Claire, shared a nightcap, and she was sure that with a little encouragement he would have tucked her into bed, only to kiss her on the forehead and then leave her with her dreams.

But Brent finally did take his leave and Claire finally fell asleep, though she'd felt certain she was going to stay awake all night thinking of King. At some point, she had a dream about him. A vivid dream. She awoke to find moonlight streaming through her windows and her palms damp, not from the almost-July heat in the city—the apartment was air-conditioned—but from the grip of her own emotions. Her cheeks were wet, too, and she wondered what she'd dreamed about King that made her cry in her sleep.

EDOUARD DE CASSET, who was a marquis—or would have been, had royalty still been in order in France—arrived on schedule. The Monets were displayed on Thursday afternoon in a very private showing at the gallery. The winter scene was much like *Snow at Argenteuil*. Looking at it, Claire thought of King, as an intern in Boston, making a lonely pilgrimage to the Museum of Fine Arts on a Sunday afternoon and responding to Monet's work the same way she did.

The dinner Thursday night was an unqualified success. Friday morning, the florist delivered a massive bouquet of flowers from Monsieur de Casset, and a note even more flowery—and more suggestive—than Claire would ever have expected. She'd obviously made an impression on the Frenchman. He hoped, he said, she would be in Paris before long, so he could show her the private art collection in his château.

Claire recognized this as the real opportunity it was, professionally. She was also fully aware of the strings that might be attached to such an offer. She decided that if there were any business trips to France in the foreseeable future, she would ask Brent to go. The Frenchman was charming, but Claire wasn't about to set herself up for the kind of involvement she was sure he contemplated.

Friday became an impossible day. Brent seemed determined to keep Claire in New York through the weekend. She sensed he really considered it a mistake to return to Lakeport, though he admitted Ellie probably still needed her. He didn't come right out and say so, but Claire was sure he was acting this way and presenting her with business details he could have handled himself because he was against her becoming involved with King.

She couldn't blame him. She was against becoming involved with King herself. She was more afraid than Brent that any new relationship with King Faraday could only lead to further heartbreak for her. King was his own man, he'd made his own life. She had her own life, her work, just as he had his work. She could see no logical way they could compromise their time to permit any real relationship, even if they actually could start over, negating the past.

In her heart, Claire knew that no matter what King said, no matter what she might say, the past couldn't really be forgotten. King might become her new love, but Brent was right. He would always be her old love.

An old love, a new love. Claire doubted she could handle both, when the package was the same devastating man.

## CHAPTER FOURTEEN

CLAIRE WASN'T ABLE to get back to Lakeport until the third of July. Air travel was heavy due to the impending holiday. Then her flight out of Albany was delayed, so by the time she reached Lakeport's Champlain Airport she was tired and out of sorts.

The afternoon was blazing hot. Claire, descending the airplane steps, felt the heat rising in waves from the concrete apron, and this did nothing to improve her mood. She wasn't looking forward to being in the Parmeter mansion again. She didn't want to deal with Thomas Haskell, Lottie's will or the endless possessions she was beginning to wish she'd never seen. New York had given her a new perspective. She could do without family heirlooms. Most material possessions—except, perhaps, a Monet, she admitted with a wry inner smile—were not worth fighting over.

Claire scanned the small cluster of people waiting at the outside gate, searching for her cousin's familiar face. Instead, another familiar face loomed within her field of vision.

King Faraday was standing behind the chain-link fence.

Claire did not immediately conclude that King was there to meet her. The plane had been filled to capacity, so she assumed he was meeting someone else. Only when he came forward and said, "Hi," then reached for the tote bag she was carrying, did she realize he'd been waiting for her.

"Where's Ellie?" she asked, flustered.

"She's tied up in a meeting with the vestrymen at the Episcopal Church," King said. "They're contemplating the purchase of a new organ and they wanted her input." He added, "I happened to call the house this morning to see if you were back, and Ellie told me she was in a bind because she was supposed to come out here to get you, but wasn't sure her meeting would be over by the time your plane arrived. So I volunteered."

"That was very nice of you," Claire managed to say.

"My pleasure," King said, smiling quizzically. "Shall we get your luggage, then move on to better things?"

Claire couldn't imagine what he meant by better things but said only, "I don't have any luggage."

He glanced at the tote bag. "That's it? You do travel light!"

"I've learned the hard way," she admitted. "Anyway, I didn't need to take much. I have plenty of clothes at my apartment."

King was leading her around the small terminal building, and said, "My car's right over there. Whew, it really is hot, isn't it? Was it this hot in New York?"

"To tell you the truth, I didn't really notice," Claire told him. "I spent most of my time in air conditioning, except for a few cab rides, and those were in the evening. This kind of heat's unusual for Lakeport, isn't it? I remember summers here being perfect, temperature-wise."

Talking about the weather was the safest track and, though Claire knew she was taking refuge in safety, she wondered if King was, too. She wondered if he was even remotely as *aware* of her as she was of him.

Again, his physical presence was overwhelming. Claire felt herself wanting to sway toward him, to touch her skin to his, to discover with her hands whether his well-developed arms, his muscles exposed by the short-sleeved shirt he was wearing, were as hard as they looked.

King, continuing with the weather, observed, "Well, we had a rather cool June, so now it looks as if we're in for a blazing July." As he spoke, he opened the passenger door of his low black sports car and waited for Claire to slide in.

As he concentrated on weaving through the tangle of cars in the parking lot, Claire stole a long look at him. There were beads of perspiration on his upper lip and his blond hair was damp at the edges. The blue cotton shirt he had on was almost exactly the color of his eyes, and he'd left the top three buttons undone, giving her a tantalizing glimpse of golden curls, a shade deeper than his hair, on his chest.

He was wearing faded jeans again, and the fabric hugged his thighs. He had powerful legs. Probably mountain climbing, skiing and Windsurfing were responsible for those well-developed muscles, she thought. Whatever their cause, the ultimate result was sexy. Very sexy.

Swinging onto the main road into town, King said, "I have an idea."

"Oh?" Claire's thoughts were so intensely centered upon one dimension of him that for a moment she wasn't sure just what he'd said.

"Why not stop at my house and I'll change into a bathing suit. Then we'll stop by your place and you can slip into your best bikini," King suggested. "Baskin's Beach beckons, don't you think? At the moment, I feel

like I could swim all the way to Vermont. It would probably take that long to cool off, in this heat.''

Claire nearly laughed. She needed to cool off for an
entirely different reason. And that reason was sitting
right next to her, dangerously close. Sobering, she said
thoughtfully, ''I shouldn't, really. Ellie will expect to find
me at the house when she gets back.''

''Maybe she'll be back by the time we get there ourselves,'' King said reasonably. ''If not, we can leave a
note. She can join us, if she wants.''

The thought of Lake Champlain's cool waters was
tempting, but the thought of spending time with King
tempted Claire even more. New York, despite the thrill of
acquiring the Monets, had not been very relaxing. It
wasn't the business she'd conducted during her stay that
had tensed her, it was Brent. His attitude about Lakeport and her returning here and his comments about King
were very disturbing, because she respected Brent's
opinion. In fact, she loved Brent like a favorite uncle. She
knew he'd been putting her interests first for years, and
that made his present negativity all the worse. She'd told
him insistently that she had no intentions of getting
deeply involved with King Faraday, and she was certain
that King didn't want to become deeply involved with
her.

At her side, King asked, ''Well, how about it? If we're
going to stop at my place I'll have to turn at the next
corner.''

Suddenly Claire's spirits lifted. She reflected on what
she'd just been thinking, and it was all to the good. If
King didn't want a deep involvement, neither did she. But
that was no reason they shouldn't enjoy each other's
company.

They *were* enjoying each other's company, and had been increasingly, each time they'd been together, Claire realized. And if, within that sphere of enjoyment, there came a sexual rapport, why should they not go with the dictates of their own psyches? she concluded, amused at her choice of words.

"The thought of a swim is irresistible," Claire told him. "Turn, King."

King handled the powerful sports car with a racer's skill, but it was not until they were mounting the front steps of the Faradays' gray Victorian house that Claire remembered this was George Faraday's house, not King's alone.

"Will your father be home?" she asked, pausing behind him.

He turned and looked down at her, frowning slightly. "Dad?" he said, seemingly puzzled. "Yes, I suppose so. Why?"

Claire hesitated, wondering how to phrase this. "I don't think he'd especially like seeing me here, King," she said finally.

King was already opening the front door and motioning her toward the shadowy interior of the front hall. "As far as I'm concerned, Claire, you're meeting Dad for the first time," he told her. "At least, that's the way it's going to be. All right?"

It was anything but all right, and Claire was actually trembling as she preceded King inside. She was remembering her earlier encounter with Dr. Faraday at the pharmacy. He'd been polite, true. But cool and distant also.

King said, "Come on out to the kitchen. There's some lemonade in the fridge. I'll pour you a glass, then I'll go change."

The kitchen was a big, square, high-ceilinged room, centered by a white wooden table with four matching chairs. The refrigerator, the stove and the sink were old-fashioned but spotlessly clean. George Faraday was standing at the counter, his cane propped by his side while he finished making himself a sandwich.

He turned when King greeted him and his eyes narrowed only slightly when he saw Claire. Then he said, "Well, hello, Claire." Again, his voice was cool but not unfriendly. Nor did he seem surprised to see her here.

Had King told his father he'd met her a few times, that they'd talked? Just what had King said? And how had Dr. Faraday reacted?

Questions tumbled, none to be answered. King was already getting a pitcher out of the refrigerator and filling glasses with the frosty lemonade. "Why don't you sit down and talk to Dad while I get ready?" he invited.

Claire felt herself begin to freeze despite the heat. She moved gingerly toward the white kitchen table and lowered herself carefully onto a chair, her back erect. She seldom felt so unsure of herself, and didn't know how to handle the feeling.

She watched Dr. Faraday place his sandwich and a glass of iced coffee on a small tray that he could carry with one hand. Then, using his other hand to support himself with his cane, he moved slowly across the room. Claire, not wanting him to see how closely she was observing his efforts, hastily sipped her lemonade. It was cold and tart and tantalizingly sweet.

"This *is* refreshing," she said awkwardly.

When he didn't answer, she couldn't help glancing up. His eyes, almost as blue as his son's, were fixed on her face. Then his mouth lifted in a slight smile.

He said gently, "I'm not going to bite you, Claire."

Totally confused, Claire set her glass down with a thud. "Dr. Faraday..." she began, stammering over his name.

"It was a shock, seeing you in the pharmacy that day," he admitted. "I knew you were back, but it was still a shock. I wished, later, that I'd stopped you so we could have talked for a few minutes. Meantime, King told me the two of you *have* spoken. I'm glad, Claire. It's time that past misunderstandings were cleared up and all the old ghosts laid to rest," Dr. Faraday continued. "I'm glad that's happened, Claire."

Claire stared at him, her confusion increasing. The past misunderstandings hadn't been cleared up.

*What had King told his father? More importantly, why had he lied?*

"Time marches on," Dr. Faraday said, gazing thoughtfully at his sandwich. "That's not a very original expression, I know, but it's one of the truest ever spoken. We can't stop time. We can't go back. What's done is done...."

He smiled, an appealing smile that reminded Claire of King. Watching him, she felt her heart being wrenched out of place by this formal older gentleman who might have been her father-in-law once.

Dr. Faraday said, "I'm saying this badly, Claire. What I want you to know is that I'm glad you came back. Glad for King. Glad for you." He raised his glass to her. "No more ghosts, eh?" he said.

She numbly watched as he drank his small toast, but couldn't respond. She couldn't possibly say, "No, no more ghosts." That would be such a patent lie.

King breezed into the kitchen wearing the same blue shirt over a pair of black swim trunks. His legs were slightly sunburned, the fine golden hair covering them somewhat bleached. He'd thrust his feet into leather sandals and draped a beach towel over one shoulder.

Downing the rest of his lemonade, he set the empty glass on the counter, then turned to take Claire's. "Hey!" he said, "You've hardly touched this."

"I feel a little bit queasy," she murmured. "Flying does that to me, sometimes. Plus the heat . . ."

She met Dr. Faraday's eyes and was certain he could see right through her. She wondered if he suspected why she'd been unable to respond to his toast and hoped she was wrong. Better that King's father thought the old ghosts had been laid to rest. Much better.

She managed a mumbled goodbye to Dr. Faraday as King steered her out of the kitchen. Then she settled down in the front seat of King's car, and it was true . . . she did feel a bit queasy.

King, watching her, asked, "Sure you're up for a swim?"

"Yes." She nodded. "I'll be fine in a minute."

But she wasn't fine. At the Parmeter house, where there was no sign of Ellie, she went upstairs and slipped into her swimsuit, choosing a green maillot rather than a bikini. She donned a short terry robe and took an over-size bath towel from the linen closet. The Parmeter ménage didn't boast any beach towels, she noticed. All the while, she felt shivery and unsure of herself. Maybe she *was* coming down with something.

Claire diagnosed her malady as she descended the stairs: Faraday-itis! Both King and his father were getting to her.

King was waiting in the front hall. "Better?" he asked.

"I think so," she fibbed.

"I left a note for Ellie on the kitchen table telling her where we'll be."

"Fine."

It was relatively cool in the old house, but the heat assaulted them again once they stepped outside. As they drove toward the lake, King complained, "That's one thing this car lacks—air conditioning."

"I wouldn't think you'd need air conditioning in a car in Lakeport," Claire commented.

"True."

King, she realized, was turning onto a secondary road. "Thought I'd drive you past Chris's plant," he explained, noting her curiosity. "He's done a great job, if you ask me."

Chris had indeed done a great job. The low buildings were cinder block, painted a creamy white. The design was primarily functional, but Chris had softened the rectangular contours by adding window blinds in a rich forest green and by planting flower beds everywhere, stocked with annuals. The resulting riot of color was eye boggling.

"Chris's got about fifty people working here," King informed her. "He hopes to expand next year and take on forty more." As they passed the last building, he added, "I'm glad to see him succeeding. He's gone through some bad times, so it's good to see something positive happening to him."

Claire wondered if King might mention the subject of Chris's unhappy marriage, but he didn't. Along their way, he pointed out a few other places that had been built since she'd lived in Lakeport, and then they were turning onto the dirt lane to Baskin's Beach.

Amazingly, the beach was deserted, even though tomorrow was the Fourth of July. They chose a spot close to the grassy area where Claire had taken her picnic that other afternoon. After spreading out their towels, Claire shrugged off her terry robe and tossed it over a nearby boulder. When she turned, King had divested himself of his shirt, and the sight of his broad chest gleaming in the sunlight stole her breath.

Long ago, she'd thought King must rival Adonis, the Greek youth of legend whose masculine beauty was considered supreme by no less than Aphrodite, the goddess of love. Now, Claire decided, this man before her surely surpassed Adonis. There was not an ounce of fat on his body. His muscles were taut and disciplined, like the man. And he was so totally disciplined. Only those eyes, blazing like blue fire as he looked at her, gave away any measure of passion.

He drew a deep breath, and Claire sensed he was not as calm as he was pretending. For an instant she felt deep relief. God knows he moved her, so it balanced the scales a little to have visible evidence that she was affecting him.

This moment of sensual tension was suspended between them like a high wire, stretched precariously thin, vibrating when touched by the wind of incipient passion. But King didn't prolong the moment.

"Last one in..." he challenged, as he had long ago. He'd never said what would happen to the last one in, but he'd never needed to. Claire was always last, and he'd catch her and dunk her thoroughly, then scoop her up in his arms and kiss her with the fervor and ecstasy of youth. All the while his hands would rove over her body—almost, but never quite, reaching that magical center from where explosions of all sorts could have been ignited...as Claire knew now. As she had suspected but not thoroughly known then.

She followed him, stepping across the patchy dark sand until she got to the water's edge. Then, more slowly, she picked her way over the round pebbles, muttering

"Ouch" as they bruised her tender feet. She voiced another exclamation as the water, feeling especially cold against the heat of the day, shocked her skin.

King was already standing in water up to his waist, watching her. A gentle breeze riffled his hair and he was laughing...and, in a moment so poignant it made her ache, time *did* move backward for Claire. They were young again, engaged, about to be married, so much in love.

She stumbled toward King, captured by her own illusion, waiting for him to splash her because that's what he'd always done.

But not this time. When Claire reached him, the water was up to her chest. And, as she swayed giddily, he reached out and pulled her against his body in a sudden, savage movement. Without further warning, his lips plundered hers in a jolting kiss designed to strip away the extraneous and get to the basics between them. It was the first step on this course King was charting, and Claire's mouth moved with his, twisting, opening, inviting him to explore.

They rocked together, their bodies cooled by the lake water yet completely on fire inside. After only a minute, King slipped the straps of Claire's bathing suit over her shoulders and then bent down, his face half in the water as he sought her breasts, discovered them and began feasting upon them wildly.

Though many long months had passed since a man last touched Claire, she knew she had never felt the instant fire scorching her now, burning hot red-orange and gold. This fiery tongue of passion, its licking flames matching the caresses of King's mouth, hypnotized Claire into wondrous submission. Then he drew away long enough to gulp some air and delved into the water once again, this time beginning with the hollow between her breasts, then moving lower and lower, tugging her bathing suit as he went, until with a last flick he pulled it off altogether. Emerging triumphantly, he held it out of the water and asked with a wicked grin, "And what shall I do with this?"

Claire, spinning out of control, couldn't possibly have formed a sensible answer. King's grin widened as he plunged both hands into the water, still holding her suit, and in another moment was holding his own suit next to hers. She watched him twist them together and start toward shore. His back was to her and she saw the tautness of his buttocks, the straightness of his back, his beautifully shaped head held high upon proud shoulders.

She watched him heave with all his force and glimpsed black and green banded together in the sunlight, then saw the suits land above the high-water mark.

King turned toward her, now submerged enough so that his most intimate flesh was hidden from Claire's view. But as he closed the gap between them, as he reached out and drew her into his arms, there was nothing left to her imagination. He was aroused, fully aroused in the most masculine of ways. He was at once hot and cold against her as he said, his blue eyes darker than the lake, "I want this. Do you?"

The words would have sounded too blunt, except for the tenderness of his tone. Except for his gentleness, except for an inner knowledge, on her part, that if she were to say no he would let her go, no matter how reluctantly.

Claire couldn't speak, so she nodded. And there, bathed by the lake's cool waters, King began making love to her. The small act of throwing their bathing suits onto the beach had been enough diversion for him to get a grip on himself. Now he was totally in control, just as she was totally out of control, wanting everything he could give. Wanting so badly to give similar passion to him.

She clung to him, gripping his shoulders as he sensuously read every inch of her body with his hands. Then, lingering skillfully, he moved to reread certain passages, spelling out new stories as he plunged her into a sea of emotions.

King led her through whirlpools, plunged her into rapids, until finally everything in Claire fused to an exploding climax, bottomless and unending. Then he left her alone, in quiet emotional waters, but soon began all over, bringing her all the way again, and still again. Only then did Claire see through glazed eyes that King was reaching the end of his astonishing control and, pressing her fingers into his shoulders, she opened herself to receive him.

He plunged into her, his thrusts deep and wonderfully searing. Claire, taking all of him, began moving with him in perfect rhythm, keeping pace, climbing this mountain she didn't fear, sharing the beautiful agony of striving for the ultimate until, beyond control, they exploded together as one.

In timeless harmony, they floated on their backs, hands clasped, staring at the white cloud puffs decorating the pure blue sky. Then, suffused with new life, they swam in deeper water well over their heads. Circling back to the shallows, they came together this time in water just ankle deep, lying on the damp sand just beyond the pebbles. Only then did they retrieve their bathing suits and wriggled into them. And Claire realized just how daring they had been.

''My God!'' she exclaimed, watching King give the final tug that put his trunks into position. ''Suppose someone had come down here when we were...out there." She pointed toward the water.

King laughed. "We took a chance, didn't we?" he asked.

"But suppose someone...suppose Ellie!" she insisted.

"Ellie...might have been a problem," King admitted. "Other than her, you could have kept your back turned to shore. I would have gone up and gotten your suit, and the people, whoever they were, would have been so embarrassed they would have fled the scene immediately."

Claire shook her head. "Do you always take chances, King?"

"I can't say I've ever been given this same opportunity."

"Maybe that's just as well! You'd be the talk of the town."

King's eyelids flickered. He said, momentarily distant, "I've been the talk of the town."

Quickly he added, "Sorry. That slipped out." He tossed Claire her towel then began drying his hair with his own. He said, "We should have brought along something to drink." And glancing at the sun, added, "I wonder what time it is. I'm on call tonight."

The sun was slipping behind the pines that separated the beach and the Baskins' farmland. Claire estimated it must be close to five, though she'd never given herself any points for accuracy when it came to guiding herself by the sun or the stars.

King said, "I guess we'd better get going."

Was it her imagination, Claire wondered, or did he sound more relieved than regretful?

She wrapped her towel around her hair, twisting it into a turban on top of her head, and they started up the path toward the spot where he'd parked his car. "You look like Cleopatra," he teased.

Claire didn't feel like Cleopatra in the least. She couldn't analyze how she felt. She'd experienced sex with King as she'd never experienced sex before. The problem was there had been more than just a physical union. There had been an added dimension in her response to him. Facing this fact, she made a grim self-confession.

She loved King. She truly loved him.

The wetness of her hair reminded Claire that she'd washed a youthful fiancé out of her life a long time ago. But it would be far more difficult to forget the man beside her who, at this moment, looked as if he couldn't wait to get back to his hospital.

## CHAPTER FIFTEEN

AT BREAKFAST, ELLIE SAID, "They're having a fireworks display from the state beach out on the point. Bill has a friend with a boat, and we thought we might anchor offshore to watch. That would be the best possible view."

Claire, finishing her coffee, took her cup and saucer to the sink and said, over her shoulder, "You go, by all means, Ellie."

"What do you mean? Bill asked both of us."

Claire turned and faced her cousin. The new Ellie was still a surprise to her. Ellie hadn't done anything radical to change her appearance. But she'd had her hair styled, the gray covered with a soft brown rinse, and she was using lipstick, in a pretty pink shade. These small transformations were a step in the right direction.

"I think there are times when Bill really would like to be alone with you, Ellie," Claire pointed out. "I'm almost always around. He must be tired of that."

Ellie laughed. "You just got back from New York, remember? Bill and I went out to dinner twice while you were gone, and to the drive-in last Saturday night, and—"

"You don't have to list every place you've been with Bill," Claire said. "I'm glad the two of you have been going out together. You . . . well, frankly you've seemed oblivious to the fact that Bill likes you."

"We're old friends," Ellie replied. "And, if the truth's to be known, Bill's still in love with his wife."

"In love with his wife?" Claire asked, surprised.

Ellie nodded sagely. "He carries her picture around with him. I saw it accidentally the other night when he opened his wallet at dinner. Anyway, he still wears his wedding ring. Haven't you noticed that?"

It was strange, but Claire hadn't. Admittedly, she hadn't concentrated fully on Bill Edgerly when he'd been around, though she liked him. "It's probably a reflex action."

"You don't wear a wedding ring, Claire."

Claire glanced at her ringless finger. "No, but I did for almost a year after Philip died. Then one day I decided it was time to take it off." With that, Claire turned back to the sink and began to rinse out her coffee cup.

There had been a man Claire thought she might become interested in. The first man after Philip's death. She had taken off her ring because somehow it seemed the right thing to do. Nothing had come of the relationship and it was she who had said goodbye in the end, opting for the cliché of offering her friendship instead of something more serious. She enjoyed pleasant, casual relationships, but hadn't wanted any commitments. Inevitably, whenever she felt lonely and gave thought to casting her lot with someone else, a cloud of caution appeared on her horizon. A cloud? A whole sky full of memories, she thought wryly.

Memories of King? Claire wondered if King had been the invisible barrier that stood between herself and giving herself fully to another man. And fully, in that sense, had little to do with sex.

Claire had been devoted to Philip. She loved him, in part because he'd taken her in when she needed emotional support so desperately. In return, she had given her love, given herself to Philip. But the giving had never been with Philip as it had been with King yesterday afternoon.

Claire shut her eyes tightly, hoping temporary blindness could blot out memory.

Behind her, Ellie said impatiently, "Honestly, Claire. I wish you'd come with us ... unless you're tied up with King. You're not, are you?"

Definitely, she was not tied up with King, Claire thought ruefully. King was on call again at the hospital. He had mentioned in passing that he hoped too many local kids hadn't made the short trek up to Canada and bought fireworks. If so, there might be some bad burn cases in the ER before the Fourth was over.

As they parted, she had wished him a quiet holiday. He had answered he'd be happy if it was so quiet he fell asleep.

Before she had a chance to think any further, Claire said, "If you're sure Bill won't mind, I'd love to go, Ellie."

Ellie beamed. "Maybe I should make some sandwiches. Bill said not to bring anything, but even so—"

"Let's go with what Bill said," Claire advised. "We can always pick up something along the way if we need to. That deli in the mall will probably be open, and they make excellent sandwiches."

She had a vision of King munching on one of the deli's sandwiches, and forced herself to block it out. She told herself she was damned if she was going to let thoughts of King Faraday ruin her holiday.

Bill's friend had a handsome cabin cruiser. He, Ellie and Claire boarded her at the town dock, pausing for a get-acquainted drink before casting off. Then they motored around the lake lazily, finally anchoring in the shadow of an offshore island. There were about a dozen people on board, and several went for a swim. Claire hadn't brought her swimsuit, nor had Ellie. In any event, she was perfectly content to stretch out on a comfortable deck chair and watch the others as she sipped a gin and tonic.

One man, who happened to have blond hair, dove into the water from the end of the deck. His hair glinted in the sun and, inevitably, Claire thought of King. Throughout the afternoon and into the evening, as they headed back toward Lakeport and dropped anchor off the point, Claire thought of King again and again. She remembered one special Fourth of July long ago, the cookout with their friends, the corn on the cob dripping with butter. She'd made a mess of eating the corn, and King had teased her and had kissed the butter off her lips. Then he'd said, judiciously, "I don't know whether you taste better plain or seasoned."

Now, as darkness fell, the fireworks streaked into an enormous sky where the crescent moon suspended low in the east seemed only a spectator. Claire watched the bursting rosettes in green and red and the silver stars tailing off like manmade comets and sighed her oohs and ahs with the rest. But all the while she wished King were near her, yearned to reach out and touch his hand, missed him until she physically hurt.

Ellie's stint at the hospital thrift shop was the next day, and she headed off with her standard apologies. Claire, as usual, said she'd be fine alone, and would get on with more of the inventory.

She dallied, writing a couple of letters that should have been written ages ago, then finally faced the Orchestra Room and started listing its contents. There were several excellent paintings in the room and, as she jotted down the artists and subjects, Claire resolved to get in touch with Brent. He could begin researching their ages and potential values using the gallery library.

She was studying a painting that depicted Lake Champlain with the Green Mountains in the distance when she heard the front door close. The piece was almost certainly the work of a local artist, but the signature in the corner meant nothing to her. And though the painting looked old, she couldn't be sure. Often, this illusion was fostered by the use of an antique gold frame. Definitely, this was something worth looking into.

She made this notation and turned, expecting that maybe Ellie had finished early at the thrift shop, as she sometimes did. There, in the doorway, stood Thomas Haskell.

He was the last person Claire expected to see, and she stared at him, baffled. He stared back boldly, then he laughed.

He looked bigger and more coarse than ever. His plaid shorts revealed meaty, hair-sprinkled legs, and a sweat-stained T-shirt covered his ample chest and belly. They were still in the throes of a heat wave, and Claire's uncle looked as if he were feeling its effects. Maybe in more ways than one, she thought suddenly. Thomas's flushed face and damp forehead could be attributed to something else, she knew. Perhaps he had been drinking, and the thought made her instantly tense. Thomas, she remembered uneasily, could be difficult enough to handle when he was sober.

"Well!" he said jovially. "I was hoping to find you girls home. Thought it was about time the three of us talked things over without those legal beagles getting in our way. Where's Ellie?" he asked, looking around.

Claire hesitated. A glance at the mantel clock told her it was only three, and usually Ellie wasn't home before five. She had no intention of telling Thomas Haskell this, though.

She hedged. "Ellie had to go out for a few minutes. She should be back soon."

"Good enough," Thomas answered. "To tell you the truth, you're the one I really want to talk to anyway." Again he looked around. "You wouldn't have a cold beer handy, would you?"

Claire was tempted to retort that to her knowledge beer had never been kept in the Orchestra Room, but there was no point in needlessly antagonizing him.

Also, Bill had bought beer for the outing last night, but had forgotten to take it out of his car, to his host's amusement. When he'd driven Claire and Ellie home, he'd suggested they stock their fridge "for future reference." In fact, he'd carried the beer in the house and put it in the fridge himself.

Claire said reluctantly, "There's beer in the refrigerator, Thomas."

Haskell nodded. "Lead the way."

Again, she was tempted to snap at him and retort that he knew the route to the Parmeter kitchen only too well. Instead, she walked ahead of him, nervous that he was following close behind. She imagined she could feel his warm breath on the nape of her neck and had the jittery feeling that if he came even an inch closer she'd scream. She wished she was a stronger believer in mental telepathy, so she could send a silent message to Ellie, urging her to come home now.

She took a beer from the fridge, opened it and handed it to Thomas. "There's a glass in the cupboard," she told him, knowing he knew very well where the glasses were kept.

"Don't need one," he said, already seating himself at the kitchen table, his legs spread wide. He took a swig of beer than wiped his mouth with the back of his hand. "Going to join me?" he asked.

"No," she said. Then, watching her step, added more pleasantly, "I had a glass of iced coffee just a little while ago."

"Hot as hell out," Thomas commented. "Got to drink fluids to keep your body up to par."

Temptation again. Claire wished she could come out and tell him that was something he didn't have to worry about.

He was watching her closely, too closely. He said impatiently, "Sit down, why don't you? There are a couple of things I want to say to you."

Claire sat down and tried not to fidget. She asked, "What is it you want to say, Thomas?"

"That there's no reason we can't come to a settlement, that's what!"

It occurred to Claire that this statement should make her feel relieved, but it didn't. She said cautiously, "Have you told Ellie that?"

Thomas snorted. "Hell, no!" he said bluntly. "That Edgerly fellow's got Ellie wrapped around his little finger. Any fool could see that. That's how lawyers make their money. There'll be a big cut for him if the three of us have to go to court."

"I don't think Bill wants to go to court any more than Ellie and I do," Claire said quickly. "He'll do what's best for Ellie's interests, that's all."

"What about your interests? You got as much right to all of this as Ellie has," Thomas said, waving a large hand around the room. "Hell, your father got shafted by old man Parmeter. Why should you give a damn about being so careful Ellie gets her share? As for me—"

"Yes?" Claire asked cautiously. "What about you, Thomas?"

"I took care of Lottie when she was out flat," Thomas said thickly, and Claire had no doubt now that he'd been drinking before he arrived. "She was out flat for a long time, mind you. Helpless as a baby. She couldn't eat by herself, couldn't go to the bathroom by herself. And did she have anyone else to help her? Let me ask you that. Did your precious cousin Ellie ever lift a finger to help Lottie?"

"Ellie couldn't," Claire protested. "Her own father was sick, and she was running this house as well as caring for him, plus keeping up with the orchestra."

"The orchestra!" Again, Thomas snorted. "I could say a few fine words to you about that orchestra, but I won't hurt your pretty ears. And about your precious grandfather, and your sainted Aunt Delia, and your Uncle Ralph who was nothing more than a goddamned parasite!"

Thomas's face was beet red. He pulled a soiled handkerchief out of his hip pocket and mopped his forehead. "Hotter than the hinges," he complained again. "Look, Claire, like I said before, you and I can settle this whole damn thing. We'll see Ellie gets her fair share and we can tell the lawyers to go straight to hell. How about it?"

Claire said uncomfortably, "You know that's out of the question, Thomas." She stood as she spoke, taking refuge in walking to the fridge. There was a pitcher of iced tea left over from the day before yesterday, probably strong enough to stand on. Nevertheless, Claire poured herself a glass.

As she set the pitcher on the counter, she heard the sound of a chair scraping. Turning quickly, she saw Thomas lumber to his feet then lurch toward her.

He muttered, "Damn it, Claire, get off that iceberg. You're not a little kid anymore, you're a *woman*."

She was virtually trapped, her back to the sink, and again he was so close Claire could smell his breath. It reeked of beer and whiskey, that combined stench making her feel sick. She tried to retreat and quickly realized she had no place to retreat to, feeling the sink's cool enamel through the thin fabric of her blouse.

"Please, Thomas..." she warned.

"'Please, Thomas!'" he mocked. "It was 'please Thomas' years ago, wasn't it, Claire? Except things were different then. You said you'd tell Lottie if I didn't leave you alone. Well, who are you going to tell now? Ellie?"

He flung the words in Claire's face, taunting her, daring her. Her mind raced. One false step and very likely she'd push this man over the edge. He was so much larger and stronger than she was he could easily take her by brute force. Her only hope was to reason with him, but could she possibly reason with a half-drunk paranoid?

That was a strong diagnosis, Claire admitted. Still, there'd always been something about Thomas Haskell that made her feel uneasy, something that went beyond his abortive lovemaking attempt years ago. Even then, she had sensed a streak of cruelty in him. A streak far more apparent to her now. He was a potential sadist... and God knows how he got his kicks from sex. Claire cringed and Thomas laughed in response, baring tobacco-stained teeth. She saw his tongue lick his upper lip. She felt his hands clutch her bare arms. "Thomas, please!" she implored.

His breath assaulting her face, he said, "I don't know what the hell excited me so much about you when you were sixteen, Claire, but something did. I wanted you, damn it! If it hadn't been that I knew damned well you'd tell Lottie, I would have had you. Every now and then, over the years, I've dreamed about you, Claire. Those eyes of yours, and the way you have of looking at people. That cool way of yours, the way you put a person down without even saying anything. I want to rip that coolness right out of you, Claire. I want to make you *feel*, damn it! I want *me* inside you. Do you understand what I'm saying?"

His grip was tightening as he spoke. He was getting redder in the face, and his breathing was heavier, coming faster. Suddenly it occurred to Claire he might be on the verge of a stroke or a coronary.

She twisted, trying to wrench herself out of his grasp. She tried to free one arm so she could reach the glass of iced tea behind her and fling it in his face. Then there would be a chance to escape, a chance to run for help. God, how she would run!

Thomas laughed again and growled, "You're only hurting yourself, Claire. Denying yourself, too." With this, he pushed her against the sink and, pressing his huge body against hers, he ground his mouth against her lips with bruising force.

Now Claire began to fight with every ounce of strength she had. She kicked his shins violently and when, momentarily diverted, he lifted his lips from hers, she bit him on the chin. Bit him so hard a line of blood marked the surface of his skin.

He swore loudly, his fingers like iron talons as he clutched her. And feeling the awful hardness of his arousal, Claire screamed.

From the doorway, a thunderous voice commanded, "Let her go, Haskell!"

Thomas and Claire were equally startled. Thomas turned toward the source of the voice, completely taken off guard and drunk enough to be equally befuddled.

Claire's eyes met King Faraday's scorching blue gaze and what she saw shocked her—an anger so intense it was terrifying.

King advanced menacingly, his eyes never leaving Thomas's face. "Get the hell out of here, Haskell," he threatened. "Get out now, and don't come back. Next time I'll put you in the hospital. And even I won't be able to help you!"

Claire didn't wait to see Thomas leave. She fled out the kitchen door, ran through the garden, thrust open the door to the dollhouse and flung herself into the little rocking chair, rocking back and forth with her arms clasped together while the tears streamed down her face.

King found her there. Found her huddled like a frightened child in this place he hadn't entered for fourteen years and had never intended to enter again. Looking at Claire, the past struck him full in the face. And he knew he'd been a fool to ever deny it, to shut out the irrefutable fact of its existence.

His memories were so vivid, so bitter, it was difficult to concentrate on the present, even though the present demanded his attention.

He crossed the tiny room, feeling like a giant who'd stumbled into a dwarf's quarters, and gently lifted Claire out of the rocking chair. He held her tenderly, letting her rest her head on his shoulder, letting her cry. Then, when her sobs began to subside, he gently smoothed away her tears, pausing to kiss her spiky, wet eyelashes.

"Don't cry anymore, Claire," he pleaded. "Please don't. He's not worth it."

"He's a monster," Claire sobbed. "A *monster*, King. If you hadn't come by, he would have raped me."

"Yes," King said. "Yes, I know." He also knew that in another second he would have been hard put to keep himself from killing Thomas Haskell.

He said, forcing calm, "He won't be back again, Claire. Not, at least, in that way."

"I know," she said, nodding. "I know. He's too much of a coward. But—" she raised tear-stained eyes to King's face "—if you hadn't happened by..."

"I didn't just happen by," King corrected. "I was on call until six o'clock this morning, so I have today off. I slept for a few hours after I got home, then remembered I'd said I'd get back over here to check out the rest of the china. Those cartons we were talking about? They must be around somewhere?"

"In the cellar, probably," Claire managed.

King suddenly felt the walls of the little room crushing him and asked, "Would you mind if we get out of here?"

Claire looked up at him, her eyes sympathetic. "You never did like the dollhouse, did you?"

He managed to grin. "It's not a question of liking or disliking it," he compromised, avoiding the truth. "I'm too big for this place, that's all."

Claire actually laughed, but her smile faded as she walked up the garden path with King beside her. At the kitchen door she hesitated and asked, "You don't think Thomas is still around, do you?"

"I guarantee he's taken refuge in the nearest bar."

"Yes, I suppose you're right. But even so, I...well, I don't especially want to stay around here just now.

Would you mind very much if we postpone looking for the china until another time?''

''I wouldn't mind at all,'' King assured her. ''Why don't we go for a drive and find a place where we can have some pie? I have a tremendous craving for home-made pie, all of a sudden.''

Claire had thought he was about to suggest going to Baskin's Beach for a swim, and wasn't sure how she'd respond to that invitation. Their last afternoon there was much too fresh in her mind. Not that history was apt to be repeated. But being there with King again would certainly lead to something.

Claire clipped her own thoughts. She said, ''That sounds much better. Just give me a minute to change.''

''You're fine as you are,'' King told her.

''No,'' Claire protested softly. ''I'd really like to put on another blouse.''

She didn't tell him why she wanted to change, but suspected he knew anyway. Thomas Haskell's clutching fingers had gripped the blouse she had on. And though it was one of her favorites, she knew she'd never wear it again.

## CHAPTER SIXTEEN

KING AND CLAIRE SPENT the next two hours driving around the countryside, but their excursion was not very relaxing. From the moment they got into King's car, Claire sensed a difference in him, a restraint. He spoke very little and seemed intensely preoccupied. Still shaken by her horrible experience with Thomas Haskell, she wondered if King's preoccupation had anything to do with her, or involved something, or someone, else.

King drove west out of town, avoiding the main highway and choosing back roads where they could enjoy a more leisurely pace. At one point, they drove along a side road that passed the picnic area at Pocomoonshine. Vivid memories flooded Claire and it was impossible not to recall how much in love they'd been that day King carried her halfway down the mountain. So long ago.

*An old love, a new love.* Could she ever become the new love in the life of this silent, serious man? As he had become in her life, Claire conceded, the concession bringing her a deep apprehension.

Did she *want* to become the new love in King Faraday's life? It seemed plain, there was no place for a woman in his scheme of existence. Even if there was, so many obstacles stood in their way: their shared past, their diverse careers, their homes so far apart.

They had proven the intensity of the physical passion that flared between them. Right now, Claire knew, she'd go wherever King wanted, do whatever King wanted. Just the thought of being with him as she'd been with him at Baskin's Beach was enough to set her afire.

But King, that afternoon, was making no suggestions.

They stopped in a small restaurant and ordered coffee and peach pie, peaches being in season. The pie was not homemade, though. The crust was soggy, the filling a sticky, gelatinous mess. Claire suspected the peaches were canned and was not surprised when King put down his fork, having eaten only half of his pie, and said disgustedly, "That's enough of that."

It was a small incident, but did nothing to improve their respective moods. By the time they got back to Lakeport the silence between them was as sticky as the pie filling had been.

King pulled up in front of the Parmeter house and Claire fully expected him to keep the motor running, let her slip out of the car by herself and exit with a quick goodbye.

He didn't, however. He turned the key in the ignition, then swerved around so he was facing Claire directly.

"I'm sorry," he said. "I've been rotten company."

"Not really."

King smiled ruefully. "Don't deny it," he said. "I know myself, and I get like this at times. Sometimes my coworkers complain that I'm moody, even for a surgeon! I guess I've just been going it alone for so long I forget to think about how I must seem to the people I'm with."

King was not speaking apologetically, he was speaking factually. He was telling her this was the way he was. He was indicating there wasn't much to be done about this facet of his personality. Or that he, at any rate, didn't intend to change.

Was this a veiled message? Claire wondered. Was he letting her know that basically he was a loner, and although he might regret how this struck others, he had no desire to behave differently?

Deciding she was making too much of what he was saying, she began, "King, you don't have to explain—"

"But I do," he corrected patiently. He reached out a long finger and gently touched her cheek.

The touch had an odd effect. Claire felt as if it had left a small yet indelible brand. King's brand. Would King want to brand her if he could? Would she want him to?

She was rehashing the same old thoughts, she warned herself. She was going around in mental circles.

King said, "I don't know what to do about us, Claire."

She held her breath, wordless.

"I can't get you out of my mind," he confessed. "I want you as I've never wanted another woman. As we were driving around, all I could think about was how I wished there was someplace we could go where we could be alone. I even thought about checking in at a motel. But that's so damned tacky."

He added wrly, "Ironic, isn't it? Two grown people with no place to go. At my place, there's my father. At your place, there's Ellie."

Claire didn't know what to say.

In the distance, lightning streaked across the dusky sky, then thunder rumbled. King said absently, "We can use a good storm. It might break this heat wave." His mouth tightened and after a moment, he said, "I keep thinking of Haskell. I keep thinking I should have beaten his brains in."

"It wouldn't have done any good, King."

"Perhaps not. But it occurs to me maybe you could use that miserable incident to your advantage."

"What do you mean?"

"Maybe you should tell Bill Edgerly about it. Then he could legally throw the fear of God into Haskell."

"Perhaps," Claire agreed.

It *was* hot. She'd been so aware of King she'd been unaware of the weather, but the breeze wafting in the window was so warm and humid she couldn't ignore it. She could feel her hair curling into damp tendrils around her face.

She said, "How about something cold to drink?" They both glanced toward the house as she spoke, and saw a light go on in the front parlor. Ellie was home.

"Sure I wouldn't be interfering with anything?" King asked.

"I'm sure."

Suddenly it started to rain, the thunder boomed closer, and the jagged lightning slashed the darkening sky with white-hot brilliance. Claire and King ran up the front walk side by side, then up the porch steps. But when Claire went to turn the doorknob King drew her aside, against the dark wall protected by the wide porch overhang. Tenderly, he encircled her with his arms and bent his head so their lips could touch.

His kiss became a new experience. There was not the unadulterated passion there'd been at Baskin's Beach. There was a great deal more. A poignancy combined with passion, with wanting, that wrenched Claire's heart and swamped her emotions.

The kiss deepened and, as Claire's love for him surfaced then overflowed, King clutched her desperately, wordlessly asking more of her as his urgency mounted. They moved together in an embrace where every gesture, every small nuance, was in itself an invitation to seduction. King, clasping her still closer, moaned softly. He whispered in her ear, "I don't know how much more of this I can take!"

Then his lips claimed hers again, and they swayed together, Claire possessed of her need for this man, her love for this man, her willingness to do anything that would show him how she felt.

King's lips moved away from her mouth and explored her face, brushing her forehead, her cheeks, the little hollow beneath her chin, while his hands roamed passionately over her body. Before Claire knew what was happening, he was lifting the sheer material of her blouse, unclasping the front fastener on her bra and cupping the fullness of her breasts. He was about to lower his head and drink of her sweetness when the front door suddenly banged open.

Ellie, silhouetted against the light from the hall, called out nervously, "Claire? King?"

Ellie, Claire remembered, had always been afraid of thunderstorms.

"Claire?" Ellie called again, her voice edged with fright.

King answered first. He'd been breathing hard but managed to gain control of himself while Claire did up her bra and blouse. "We're here, Ellie. On the way in."

Claire went first and King followed. Ellie was standing in the front hall, her dark eyes anxious. "This is going to be a bad one," she said. "I had the weather station on the radio. They said it's apt to spawn tornadoes..."

"Don't borrow trouble, Ellie," Claire advised lightly.

"I'm not," Ellie countered. "Aunt Lottie used to tell me all sorts of crazy things about storms. How it was the devil, setting out from hell to get you. The thunder was the echo of his chariot's wheels, the lightning was his sword, slashing through hell's fire."

"I never heard of such a thing," Claire protested. "Sometimes I wondered about Lottie. She tended to be flaky."

"Sometimes, maybe," Ellie conceded. "Come on, you two," she invited. "I'll make some cocoa."

"Ellie, it's too hot for cocoa," Claire reminded her.

"True. All right then, how about a rum and Coke?"

They were on their way to the kitchen, and it occurred to Claire that this was a routine pilgrimage, especially when they had visitors. She laughed and said, "I thought we drank all the rum."

"We did, but Bill was here about an hour ago and left us another bottle," Ellie replied. "He actually came to see you, Claire. He said he wanted to talk to you about Thomas Haskell. Maury Fletcher had just called him and said something about Thomas having some trouble with you and—"

"Thomas having trouble with *me*?" Claire echoed incredulously. "Now I've heard everything!" she added, her anger rising.

"Bill will be back a little later and he can explain," Ellie said. "He'd promised his sister he'd be home for dinner tonight. Anyway..." Ellie smiled up at King. "Would you know how to make a decent rum and Coke, King?"

"Oh, I think so," he answered.

When he'd passed their drinks around, Ellie observed, "We always seem to wind up in the kitchen. We don't have to sit out here."

"It's cozy," King told her.

"So it is, I suppose."

"Look, Ellie," King said, abruptly serious. "There's no point in beating around the bush about this. When you were out today Thomas Haskell came in here and was about to rape Claire when I walked in on them.''

"Oh, my God!'' Ellie moaned. "I knew I shouldn't have left you in this house alone, Claire. I knew it. I told you that.''

"I think Thomas would have caught up with me sooner or later,'' Claire said. "Evidently it was something he'd had in his system for a long time.''

"Thank God you came by, King.''

"I'll second that,'' he said. "You said Bill's coming over here?''

"After dinner, yes. And speaking of dinner,'' Ellie brightened, "Why don't I make us some cheese omelets?''

"Why don't I take you and Claire out?'' King countered. "We can call Bill and set a time to be back here. I've been thinking that you and Claire should capitalize on Claire's unfortunate experience with Haskell. Something must have shaken him if he called his attorney after he left here—''

King broke off because the telephone was ringing. Ellie said quickly, "I'll take that in the other room. It's probably Bill.''

Left alone in the kitchen, King turned swiftly to Claire. She was surprised at the tension suddenly evident on his face.

He said, his voice expressing the same strain, "We need to talk, Claire. I've been wrong—'' He stopped short when Ellie appeared in the doorway, her eyes wide with horror.

"My God, Ellie, what is it?'' Claire demanded, starting to her feet.

"There's been an explosion at the plastics plant. That was the hospital, calling for you, King. They didn't even let me ask any questions. They need you in the emergency room as fast as you can make it!''

King's face whitened. "Chris..." he said. "Did they say anything about Chris Talmadge?''

"No,'' Ellie stammered, tears beginning to cascade down her cheeks. "They didn't say anything about anything. Just that they tried your house, and your father said maybe you'd be here.''

Ellie stepped aside as King hurried toward the door. He was on the threshold when Claire rallied enough to call, "I'll come with you, King.''

He turned and she knew he was already miles away. Even so, his comment cut her to the quick.

"No!'' King ordered. "You'd only be in the way.''

THERE WAS AN OLD TELEVISION in the library off the Orchestra Room. The set had belonged to Ralph Parmeter, who had enjoyed watching TV, especially in the last months of his illness when he was too sick to do much of anything else.

Ellie rushed Claire into the library, turned on the local channel and simultaneously switched on a radio in the corner.

There was a game show on TV and the radio was playing rock and roll. Frustrated, Ellie said, "We've got to get some information. I'll call Bill.''

Bill Edgerly arrived at the house half an hour later. He was grim-faced as he walked into the library where the two women were still hoping to get a media report that would give them some clues about what had happened at Chris Talmadge's plastics plant.

The thunder and lightning had abated, but it was raining steadily. Bill's clothes were dripping wet. Ellie insisted on getting him a big bath towel, but he only dried himself perfunctorily then tossed the towel on a chair.

"As I understand it," he said, "Chris's place went up like a bomb. They've called in mutual aid from all the towns around here. Fire departments as well as rescue personnel. Lakeport General's better equipped than any other hospital in the area, so they'll be taking the casualties there." He grimaced. "King is going to have his hands full."

"How did you find this out, Bill?" Ellie asked nervously.

"I phoned the chief of police after you phoned me," Bill said. "John Brinkley, remember? He went to high school with us. You know him, Claire."

Claire nodded. She couldn't even remember what John Brinkley looked like and had far more serious concerns, anyway.

"Was Chris there when it happened?" she asked.

"I don't know," Bill said frankly. "I asked John, and he didn't know yet. They think the place was struck by lightning. An outbuilding, anyway. Whatever, it touched off a spark . . . and, as I've said, the plant went up like a bomb. There's been a hell of a fire in the wake of the explosion. John said . . . well, he said so far they know there are three people dead, and God knows how many injured."

Ellie sank down on the nearest chair. "I can't believe it," she murmured bleakly.

Claire slipped out of the room before either Bill or Ellie could ask where she was going and dialed the house next-door. She knew it was a futile hope, a futile prayer, but she would have given anything to hear Chris Talmadge's voice at the other end of the wire.

That wasn't to happen. The phone rang a dozen times before Claire hung up and dejectedly went back to the library. Along the short intervening distance, she made a decision.

"I'm going out there," she said.

"Claire, that's ridiculous," Ellie argued. "King was right," she began harshly, then finished more gently, "you would only be in the way, like it or not."

"There must be something we can do," Claire insisted. "Something helpful..." she muttered, half to herself.

"I've got an idea," Bill said suddenly. "There's a snack wagon, an old van actually, over in the ballpark. It's got a large coffee maker, and there's probably candy and who knows what left over from the Fourth. The Civic Club owns it and donates the profits to charity. Anyway—"

"We could set up a way station of sorts," Ellie cut in.

"Exactly!" Bill told her. "Let me call Joe Blake. He's the club president. Maybe we can get things moving."

Get things moving they did, but it was still an hour before the big concession wagon lumbered out to the plastics plant, with Claire, Ellie and Bill following in Bill's car.

Claire tried to prepare Ellie, as well as herself, for what they might see when they got to the explosion site. But neither of them were really ready for it. This was a scene from hell they were witnessing, Claire thought, as she stared at the smoldering remains of Chris Talmadge's business.

An occasional flame still darted skyward. Searchlights crisscrossed the darkening, cloud-filled sky, for workers trying to extricate the injured... and the dead.

Bill had worked with the food-wagon equipment before. He and Joe Blake made coffee, pot after pot, and put together sandwiches. Ellie and Claire served the drinks and sandwiches to the grimy, weary men, many of whom forced themselves to go on despite the fact they could have been diagnosed as having suffered smoke inhalation.

The media converged upon the scene and photographers even snapped pictures of the two cousins at work. Claire scowled at this and didn't give a damn about whether or not she emerged scowling on local front pages. This was no time to play heroine. She and Ellie were doing a job—and she was deeply thankful they had a job to do.

She kept thinking about King, about what he must be facing in the hospital's emergency room. Very possibly, by now, he had left the ER and was working in the operating room.

Claire tried desperately to find out if Chris Talmadge had been in the plant when the explosion occurred. If he had been hurt or, God forbid, worse.

Every now and then Bill or Joe would reconnoiter the area, but they always came back with negative information. Some of the fire fighters *had* been overcome with smoke inhalation at this point and were being rushed to the hospital in the overburdened ambulances that dotted the scene, coming and going in constant relays. Some of the rescue workers had been burned trying to sift through the debris and were being given first-aid treatment right in front of the snack wagon. The people most deeply involved with this scene had little time to answer questions. And they didn't know the answer to most of the questions, anyway. The death toll had risen to five, that much they knew. And three of the dead had been burned beyond recognition.

When she heard this, Claire literally swayed. She looked at Ellie and was afraid her cousin was going to faint. She saw Ellie bite her lip, then saw Ellie rally...and wanted to cheer, though there was very little to cheer about. Except that Ellie, when it got to the bottom line, was made of some pretty strong stuff, after all.

Hours went by and the rescue work continued. It was past midnight when Bill came back from one of his forays to say, finally, "Chris is alive, Claire. But badly hurt."

Claire moistened suddenly dry lips. "How badly, Bill?"

"I don't know. I just talked to Ray Devers, on the rescue squad. He said they got Chris out about an hour ago, and last trip he made to the hospital they told him Chris is undergoing emergency surgery. That's all he could tell me."

Claire looked around. Some of the Civic Club members had come out to the scene and Joe had conscripted them into helping with the food wagon. Ellie, meanwhile, looked as if she were about to drop on her feet.

"Take her home, Bill," Claire urged, pointing.

"I'm going to take you both home," Bill stated firmly.

"Not yet," Claire said. "I want you to drop me off at the hospital."

"There's no point in that," Bill protested wearily.

"Yes there is," Claire disagreed. "Very definitely, there is."

AFTER SITTING IN THE WAITING ROOM next to the ER for two hours, Claire began to think Bill had been right. Still, she had a lot of company. The waiting room was crowded with the families of the victims. For a moment, Claire felt like an intruder among them. But then she decided she belonged here as much as anyone else did.

She spied Dr. John Danforth a couple of times, the physician who had examined her before releasing her from the hospital when she had had food poisoning. She wished she could intercept him and ask him about Chris, but the portly physician looked more tense and worried than ever and glanced neither to the right nor the left in his excursions through the waiting room.

Tired, near exhaustion, Claire was only dimly aware of a woman standing in front of her. There were a lot of people around and it took a moment to realize this woman was looking down at her in a way that demanded attention.

Claire raised her eyes to a face that was very familiar...and yet strange. Memory came in waves and recognition dawned. This woman must be Rosalie Brenner's mother. She'd never met Mrs. Brenner, but the resemblance was uncanny. Then, with a shock, Claire knew she wasn't facing Rosalie's mother at all. This was Rosalie herself.

Time had not been kind to Rosalie. She had gained weight and looked puffy and overstuffed, older than she should have looked, even after the passage of fourteen years. She was overdressed, overly made-up. The affect was garish...and, somehow, pathetic.

Rosalie said dully, "They just told me, my Aunt Theresa's dead."

Dimly, Claire remembered Chris telling her that an aunt of Rosalie Brenner's worked in his factory. She stared up at Rosalie, honestly horrified. "I'm very sorry," she said, her voice choking because all of this was coming much too close to home. "I really am."

Rosalie nodded then asked without preamble, "Who are you waiting to hear about?"

"Chris Talmadge," Claire said. "All I know is that he was badly injured."

"He's still in the OR," Rosalie told her. "King Faraday's operating on him. One of the OR nurses came down a while ago. I know her, and she told me." Rosalie added, "I'm a nurse myself, or I was. I haven't practiced nursing for years. I should have offered to help, but . . . I couldn't."

Rosalie's face was getting paler each second and, watching her, Claire realized that in another moment she was going to pass out. Jumping to her feet, she said abruptly, "Come on, let's see if the cafeteria's open."

"What?" Rosalie asked dully.

"Come on, Rosalie. You need some coffee. You need something fast."

She took Rosalie firmly by the arm and steered her out of the waiting room and down the corridor. The cafeteria had reopened for business, given the unusual circumstances of this night, but there weren't as many people there as Claire would have expected. People with injured loved ones probably wanted to stay closer to the source of information, she realized.

She chose a corner table, left Rosalie there and went in search of coffee. At the last minute, she decided to make it iced coffee. The hospital air conditioning seemed to be functioning at a low ebb, possibly because of the heat wave, and iced coffee might be more stimulating.

Rosalie sipped the beverage Claire handed her and, after a moment, said dully, "This is decent of you."

When Claire didn't immediately respond, she added, "There's no reason why you should do a thing for me,

Claire. Very much the contrary. I . . . I ruined your life
fourteen years ago. I know that.''

Claire found herself looking into those stormy dark
eyes she would never forget. Rosalie said, ''Matter of
fact, I wasn't pregnant at all, which makes it even worse.
I drummed that up because I was making a last bid for
King's sympathy. King and I never slept together once he
met you. I used to try to get him to fool around with me.
A couple of times he gave in a little. But not enough,
Claire. I used every trick in the book, and I knew a lot of
tricks. But that wasn't enough, either. He loved you, and
I couldn't handle that. I couldn't face up to a life with-
out King. So I took the last resort, and lied. . . .''

Hearing this was an incredible shock, and Claire
couldn't cope with it right now. Instinctively, she took
refuge in an idle remark. ''You do have children, I understand, Rosalie.''

''Yes, three of them. But they came later, and they've
been a handful, all of them.'' Rosalie finished her coffee
and stood up. ''I have things to do,'' she said awkwardly. ''Aunt Theresa . . .''

There was an odd helplessness in her attitude and
Claire came close to feeling sorry for her, but not close
enough. After Rosalie left the cafeteria, the full impact
of what she'd said struck home. With it came remorse
and guilt and bitterness. And the knowledge of how
deeply, irretrievably, she had wounded King Faraday
fourteen years ago.

She'd never even given the man she loved the chance
to tell her the truth.

## CHAPTER SEVENTEEN

KING CAME UPON CLAIRE still seated at the corner table in the hospital cafeteria. Slumped in her chair, she was staring dully at her half-empty cup of iced coffee, her face eloquently mirroring her fatigue.

He was still wearing his operating-room greens and a surgical mask dangled from his neck. He was weary to the bone, drained from his long hours at the operating table and so preoccupied with his own concerns for Chris Talmadge—his terrible fears for Chris's life—that Claire's problems at this moment were almost more than he could handle.

Briefly, he wished she wasn't there. Then he remembered what people had been telling him, through the night, about the way Claire and Ellie were doling out coffee to the rescue workers at the explosion site, about how much a cup of coffee could mean at a time like that. King looked at Claire again and he saw something he hadn't seen before. The Claire of his memory was a beautiful, wonderful, somewhat petulant and definitely possessive girl. This Claire, this woman, was different in so many ways. The girl he had once loved, yes. But... more than that.

He pulled out a chair, sat down next to her and asked softly, "Just what do you think you're doing here?"

She raised her eyes slowly. "I suppose," she said, the weariness of her voice matching that etched on her face, "I'm waiting for you."

King hadn't expected that and he stared at her, taken aback. But before he could accept her comment as concern solely for him, she added, "How's Chris?"

King rallied, unconsciously becoming professional because he was used to wearing his professional mask when he answered such questions, "His condition is critical," he said, "but we hope that by morning—"

Claire cut across his words impatiently. "Speak to me as his friend, not as a doctor," she commanded. "How *is* Chris, King?"

He looked at her bleakly. "There's a chance he's not going to make it," he admitted. "I wish there had been an orthopedic surgeon around to approve what I was doing. I could have used an internist and a neurologist and a few other specialists, too. As it was, we were so short staffed and they were bringing in so many injured people I had to go ahead pretty much by myself. Relying on my own judgment, that is."

King drew a long breath. "No one should ever be called upon to perform crucial surgery—or any surgery—on his best friend," he stated.

"Maybe so," Claire granted, "but in this case it's lucky Chris's best friend was a surgeon." She reached out a slender hand and touched King's wrist.

Weary as he was, her touch had an instant effect. Even now, he needed her, he wanted her. He would not have believed himself capable of being sexually aroused after a night like the one he'd just been through. But desire twisted, making its demands....

He turned to Claire and said brokenly, "Right now, I need you so much."

She rose slowly. "We'll go back to the house," she told him.

"We can't."

"Then we'll go to your house."

"We can't do that, either. Dad will probably be waiting up even at this hour."

They stared at each other helplessly and after a moment King laughed, but it was a mirthless laugh.

"No place for us, is there, Claire?" he commented, then answered his own question. "No place for us at all." He shrugged, and got to his feet wearily. "Come on," he invited. "I'll drive you home."

By the time they reached the Parmeter house, Claire, exhausted, was nestled asleep in her corner of the front seat. King shut off the engine and watched her, watched the curve of her breast rising and falling evenly. A nearby streetlight cast enough glow so he could see the smooth white column of Claire's neck. Her hair looked almost black in this light, tumbled around her shoulders. And sleep gave her an aura of innocence, made her look like a child.

It took willpower not to draw her into his arms, not to vent some of the sexual tension playing havoc within him. King felt as taut as a steel cable and refrained only because he knew it would be even worse if he started something he couldn't finish.

Quietly he got out of the car, then went around and opened the door on Claire's side. He reached for her and she came into his arms, sleepily murmuring something he couldn't decipher. He carried her up the walk, up the front steps, and inevitably remembered that other time when he'd carried her halfway down a mountain. She was lighter now than she had been then.

Ellie had left the light on in the front hall. Beyond it, the house stretched dark and silent. King strode through the Orchestra Room and into the small library adjoining it.

Lights and shadows played through the windows and along the walls. King lowered Claire on to a studio couch and saw a silvery radiance brush her hair and caress her features. As he wanted, incredibly so, to caress her himself.

He dropped to his knees by the couch, conflicting emotions warring inside him. Then he gently removed Claire's shoes and placed them on the floor beside the couch, doing this carefully, noiselessly, so he wouldn't awaken her abruptly.

Her legs were bare, the flowery cotton skirt she was wearing hitched up over one knee. Her blouse was low-necked, buttoning down the front. King, thirsty for her beyond belief, lost control of his hands, but was gentle as he unbuttoned her blouse, freed her breasts and buried his face between their twin peaks of softness.

He felt her stir, felt her hands touch him, tentatively, heard her murmur, "King?" and the walls he'd kept intact for so long crumbled, the dam burst.

"Oh, my darling, my darling," King groaned, and in another instant moved onto the couch with her.

He was a starved man brought to a banquet and told to feast freely as he began making love to Claire. Perhaps because he was tired, nearly exhausted, perhaps because he had lived through hell as he worked over Chris Talmadge in the OR, everything appeared now in a different perspective. He felt no need for haste, even though the forces straining within him threatened to burst out of control. And once his passion was unleashed, it would be bent solely on conquest, he knew.

He slipped Claire's clothes free of her body with loving tenderness…and, with far less attention to detail, sent
his surgical greens after them. He lay at Claire's side and,
while she was still on her back, more asleep than awake,
he began exploring every inch of her silken body, pausing to linger, with his fingers and his lips, on those areas
that evoked breathless responses from her.

And tonight, her responses were primal. She was
yielding to him, King knew, in a different fashion…
stripped of conditioned behavior patterns, entirely herself, the essence of Claire.

There were small spots that emanated their own erotic
signals when caressed, King discovered. The little hollow beneath her earlobe. That smooth area in the curve
of her arm. King, exploring, came to know all of Claire's
places and exulted in her responses as he touched them,
made her ready for him, until finally there was no further holding back and he entered her.

Moments later, their passion ebbed peacefully as King
held Claire within the circle of his arm. She pillowed his
head on her chest and murmured something sleepily.
Again, he couldn't translate her sounds. But he smiled
into the silvery darkness anyway, for at this moment they
were in heaven.

Very shortly, the tenor of her breathing changed and
King's smile deepened. She had fallen asleep in his arms
and, closing his eyes, he let sleep claim him, as well.

CLAIRE WOKE to face the soft light of dawn and an eerie
stillness in the house. She lifted her head slowly and
looked around, momentarily disoriented. For a topsy-
turvy moment, she wasn't sure where she was.

She discovered she was covered by an old crocheted
afghan. Beneath the afghan, she was naked. Struggling

to a sitting position, she glanced around the room and saw her clothes folded neatly on a nearby chair.

She had no idea what time it was, no idea what she was doing here, no idea how she'd gotten here . . . until memory filtered back.

King had made love to her during the last lost hours of the night. He'd carried her into an entirely different dimension of lovemaking, had taken her so completely that they had merged in every way, two individuals become one.

Or . . . that's what she thought had happened. In retrospect, their lovemaking seemed half dream, half reality.

Claire quickly slipped on her blouse and skirt and, holding her underthings and her shoes, tiptoed back through the Orchestra Room and into the hall. Then she stood irresolutely at the foot of the stairs and strained her ears. She still didn't hear anything, but as if to answer her unspoken question, as if to prove there was still sound in the world, the grandfather clock in the front parlor suddenly chimed. Claire counted the booming notes that followed the chimes. Six. It was six o'clock in the morning!

Years ago, Claire had known which of the stair treads creaked and carefully avoided them when coming home late from a date. Nothing aroused Grandfather Parmeter's ire more than failure to abide by his curfew. Now, Claire forgot which steps were solid and which weren't, and almost immediately heard wood creak beneath her feet.

But the sound didn't wake Ellie, and Claire made it all the way to her room without incident. She tossed off her clothes, put on a thin cotton nightgown and climbed into bed. But she couldn't sleep.

Images of the explosion site returned to haunt her. Her conversation with Rosalie Brenner echoed, tormenting her. Then, in the hospital cafeteria, King had been professionally wary in his comments about Chris. She'd forced an admission from him, the fact that Chris might not make it. Thinking this, she froze. *Had* Chris made it? The predawn hours seemed the time when life's threads were the thinnest and broke most easily. Had Chris made it through the night?

Claire found it impossible to doze off. The thunderstorms and torrential rains of the previous evening had cooled things down, but the air was still humid. Glancing out the window, Claire saw that the sky was totally overcast, with no glimpse of a sunrise this morning.

She got up, went downstairs and brewed a pot of coffee. The silence of the house struck her with renewed force. It seemed strange to have this house so quiet. She'd always associated it with the sound of music. Off-key sounds, sometimes, she thought wryly, remembering the many struggling pupils trying to evoke music from violins and cellos, flutes and clarinets. But music, still.

It occurred to her that Ellie never played anymore. Yet Ellie had studied cello with her father, piccolo with Aunt Lottie and piano with Aunt Delia. And she was knowledgeable enough to assume the task of conducting the symphony orchestra and do a good job. So why had Ellie shut music out of her life insofar as playing was concerned?

Pouring herself a cup of coffee, Claire thought of a number of reasons. For one, rebellion, perhaps unconscious, against Grandfather Parmeter. He'd been such a tyrant in inflicting his will on everyone in the family. As a result of this, maybe Ellie just became totally fed up with music in general. Maybe...

As if hearing these silent questions, Ellie loomed in the kitchen doorway.

The two cousins stared at each other in mutual astonishment. Then Claire realized Ellie was fully dressed, wearing the same clothes she'd been wearing last night. And she had not come down from upstairs. She had come in from outside!

Ellie had been out all night! It was almost too much to believe.

Before she had a chance to say anything, Claire saw her cousin's face flush. Then Ellie said, "I guess you must have wondered..."

"I just got up, actually," Claire said. She glanced at the kitchen clock. It was not yet seven.

"I thought you'd sleep later," Ellie murmured, her message obvious. She had hoped to get back to the house and up to her room without Claire being any the wiser.

Claire couldn't decide whether this was funny or sad. A bit of both, perhaps. Ellie, a woman in her midthirties, was looking absolutely frightened, and terribly guilty.

The words came involuntarily. "Grandfather died a long time ago, you know," Claire said gently.

Ellie started. She looked perplexed, but only briefly. Then she met Claire's eyes directly, her chin held high. She said, "You're right, Claire. Grandfather *did* die a long time ago. It's his influence that has lived on. I'm only just beginning to realize how much he influenced me."

"He was a good person," Claire found herself saying, to her surprise. "He meant well for all of us. He was born in an age of male autocrats, Ellie. And no one could have fit more perfectly into the mold than he did. But you can't entirely blame him."

"No," Ellie said. "I suppose, when you put it like that, you can't blame him too much at all. We . . . we have to force some people, though, to see the fault of their ways. No one ever got close to Grandfather in that respect." She managed a smile. "If you'd stayed around longer, you might have."

"I doubt it," Claire said sadly. "I doubt if I would have had the nerve to try." Claire knew that wasn't entirely true, but this wasn't the time to play up her strength and Ellie's weakness. She asked, "Would you like a cup of coffee?"

Ellie took refuge in this escape. "Yes," she said. She sat down at the kitchen table, accepted the coffee Claire gave her and stirred sugar into it. "I guess you expected when Bill and I left you at the hospital last night that we'd come back here."

"Well . . . yes," Claire admitted.

Ellie shook her head. "We went to his house. Bill said he had something he wanted to tell me."

Hearing this, Claire remembered that King had indicated there were things the two of *them* must talk over.

"Stella baby-sits sometimes for her friends who go away," Ellie said. "Stella's good with small children. She was sitting last night, in fact. That's why Bill took me to his house. Yesterday, Stella told him she wants to move away."

Stella Edgerly was a shadowy figure to Claire. Older than the rest of them, she'd always kept pretty much to herself. Claire remembered someone saying once that Stella had always wanted to be a nun . . . and would have, had she been born a Catholic.

"A college classmate of Stella's moved to Arizona a few years ago," Ellie went on. "She was widowed recently, and she's been asking Stella to come out and live with her. Stella has arthritis, and the winters here don't do her any good. So she's been tempted. Bill says the only reason she hasn't packed up and bought her plane ticket is because of him.''

"Really?"

Ellie nodded. "In a lot of ways, Bill's more like a son to her than a brother," she confided. "She's older, of course, though not that much older. But their mother died when Bill was pretty young, and Stella sort of took over. Then Bill went off to college and law school and got married. He and his wife had their own home here, on Pine Street. But when she died, Bill sold the place and moved back to the family house with Stella. That's easy to understand, really.''

Ellie paused. "When you're used to looking after people, it's hard to stop," she admitted. "Stella had her father to look after, just as I had mine. Mr. Edgerly died, oh, seven or eight years ago. Anyway, when Bill came home again, it was natural for Stella to take over, to act as his housekeeper. She needs a chance to live her own life, Claire.''

Claire nodded, wondering where this was leading.

"So," Ellie said, "last night Bill took me back to his house to tell me all that, and—" she hesitated "—to talk about *us*," she said finally.

Claire waited, both curious and hopeful.

"There was something else, too. Yesterday, at dinnertime, Maury Fletcher called Bill. Bill didn't tell us last night, for obvious reasons, but . . . Thomas is withdrawing any claim to a second will.''

Claire stared at her cousin. Thomas Haskell and the will had been looming larger than anything else in Ellie's life. Claire had come back to Lakeport because of this. And now Ellie was saying that Thomas was giving up as calmly as she might predict the sun was likely to shine, if not today, tomorrow.

"What brought that decision about?" Claire asked carefully.

"Bill told Maury he was advising you to prefer an attempted rape charge against Thomas," Ellie said succinctly.

*"What?"*

"Calm down, Claire," Ellie said hastily. "Bill knows you'd never have gone through with it, and I think Maury Fletcher does, too. But Thomas doesn't. He was scared through, Bill says. He told his lawyer if anything like that came out it would ruin him in Lakeport forever. He said if you could be persuaded to drop action, he'd go along with whatever the two of us want."

"Amazing," Claire said dryly, feeling partially vindicated. "Was there really a second will?"

Ellie nodded. "Bill saw it, and Lottie signed it, all right. It was even witnessed by a couple of builders working out on the point. Bill thinks Thomas probably called them over and paid them a few dollars for signing their names. But Bill also says that Lottie must have been out of it when she signed the will herself. He thinks he could have proved that in court, so it's doubtful the will would have held up. But this way...we're spared so much hassle, Claire."

Claire said slowly, "Yes. I know how much you dreaded going to court, Ellie. So...you and Thomas own this property jointly, but what about the contents?"

"Thomas is signing papers today renouncing any claims. Everything here is to be divided between you and me."

It was pointless to say, again, that she didn't want anything, Claire decided. She poured herself a second cup of coffee and sipped it as she walked over to the window. The scent of roses wafted toward her, the flowers still in bloom. She stared out at the garden and the dollhouse. She remembered, again, that terrible day when she'd left. But she was remembering it differently this time.

Regardless of what King felt about reopening the past, she had to tell him how wrong she'd been!

Behind her, Ellie said shyly, "Claire..."

Claire turned and Ellie was smiling. She said, "I know you didn't notice last night, with all the excitement, but I did. Bill isn't wearing his wedding ring any longer."

"No, I didn't notice," Claire admitted.

"It was the one thing holding me back," Ellie confessed. "Ever since Bill and I started meeting over this mess concerning Thomas, I...I've liked him more and more."

Claire smiled. "You certainly hid it well."

"I've worn my heart on my sleeve too often," Ellie said softly. "Or maybe hidden it when I shouldn't have. This time, I guess maybe I hid it too long. At least, Bill was unsure of where he stood with me. And I was so sure he was still in love with his wife."

"And I was so sure you were wrong about that," Claire said gently. "Bill's feelings for you have been written all over him, Ellie. I read them the first time I saw him here with you."

"Well," Ellie said, "last night..."

Claire saw that her cousin was blushing. She said hastily, "Ellie, you don't have to tell me anything you don't want to."

"I do want to tell you," Ellie said. "Last night...we did. And I'm glad we did." She managed a lopsided grin. "I'd say it was high time, wouldn't you?"

Claire was between laughter and tears as she went to her cousin, threw her arms around her and held her tight. "Oh, Ellie," she said, "indeed I'd say it was high time! Past high time!"

CHRIS TALMADGE HOVERED between life and death for the next three days. King spent every moment he could at his friend's bedside, checking and rechecking his injuries, making sure his vital signs were stable. Considering that the two people standing nearest him in the plant had been killed, Chris was extremely lucky to be alive. He'd been pinned under a heavy steel rafter and had suffered a broken leg, a broken hip and a ruptured spleen, which King removed in surgery. Miraculously, his burns were relatively minor, but he'd lost a lot of blood, this complicated by the smoke damage to his lungs.

When King was away from Chris's room, his time was totally taken up with other patients. The hospital was full to capacity in the wake of the tragedy. Most of the people injured in the explosion had been admitted, most were still on the patient list, some still remained in serious condition. And to add to this, there seemed to be a minor epidemic of car crashes, appendectomies and other emergencies that demanded King's attention.

Dedicated though he was, King was nearing the edge of his sanity. He wanted to see Claire, needed to talk to her. He knew there were things that desperately needed clearing up before either of them could be totally free. King thought he'd escaped the chains of the past, but now knew he hadn't. He knew, too, that whatever the future might hold for Claire and himself, they deserved, first, to let the truth be told.

He had managed to call Claire a few times, but always something would interrupt their conversation, adding to his frustration.

On day four, Chris was finally out of the woods and strong enough to have a visitor. Claire was the lucky person. She'd been clamoring to see him, and Chris admitted to King that she would be a treat for his tired eyes.

She edged into his room, apprehensive. King had explained over the phone how Chris had been pinned in the burning building by a section of rafter that had struck his left side and leg. His burns, mostly on the arms and shoulders, were remarkably superficial, though extremely painful. The long hours in surgery had been spent removing Chris's spleen, then setting his leg which was broken in several places. Still, King's terrible fear, Claire knew, was that there might be nerve damage and partial paralysis.

Claire was wearing a pale-yellow dress, accented by chunky white jewelry. She'd twisted her hair into a coil on top of her head and looked cool, lovely and far more sure of herself than she felt.

Chris grinned up at her and she marveled that he could grin at all. She bent and kissed his cheek. "Cheers," she said. "They've finally let me in here."

"I'm the one who's cheering about that," Chris told her. "You smell wonderful."

"Joy," Claire said.

"What?"

"Patou's Joy."

"You would pick the expensive stuff," Chris teased.

"It takes an experienced man to know the price of perfume," Claire teased back.

Chris held out a hand and she took it gently. His arms were bandaged and a bulky cast covered his left leg, suspended in traction. His eyes were shadowed with pain, his face very pale. But he was alive and was going to make it—because of King.

Thinking this, Claire suddenly felt as if King was in an entirely different world from hers. It was easy to see why, in some people's minds, great doctors, great surgeons, were nothing less than human gods.

She saw Chris wince and said quickly, "Hey, am I tiring you?"

"Hell, no," he assured her. "You're the best thing that's happened in recent memory...though that's not much of a compliment, considering," he allowed. "So let's rephrase it. You're the best thing that could possibly happen right now. Especially since I can share some news with you."

"What news?"

"I wiggled my toes this morning," he told her. "Not much, mind you, but King says not to be so damned impatient."

*No paralysis,* Claire thought thankfully. Her eyes filled with tears. "That is...so wonderful," she murmured brokenly.

"So's that guy of yours," Chris said unexpectedly.

Her voice quavered. "Unfortunately," she said, "King's not my guy. I presume you were speaking of King?"

"I am speaking of King," Chris corrected. "And I think you're mistaken, Claire."

It was not the time to get into even a casual debate with Chris, so Claire sidestepped by saying, "Look, right now I'm concentrating on you."

Chris laughed. "So concentrate away," he advised.

After only ten minutes a nurse came in to tell Claire her time was up. Again she kissed Chris on the cheek and murmured that she'd be back to visit him as soon as she was allowed.

On her way out of the hospital, Claire glanced around, hoping she'd see King. She wanted to tell him how thrilled she was with the news Chris had given her. Still, it hurt to think that King hadn't seen fit to tell her himself. He knew how deeply she shared his concern about Chris.

There were no storm clouds on the horizon and it would be a perfect day to go out to Baskin's Beach for a swim or let King give her a Windsurfing lesson. He'd been suggesting this. But Chris told her how King had been working around the clock, finishing, with a shake of his head, "I don't see how the guy does it." It was most unlikely that King would have a few hours off, even for sleep, Claire decided.

Ellie came out the front door the instant Claire pulled up the driveway. Ellie's face had always mirrored her feelings, and it did now. As Claire climbed the steps to the porch, she knew something had happened and guessed Ellie had been watching for her from the front-parlor windows.

Her apprehensions were confirmed when Ellie said, "Your secretary at the gallery has been calling. Something dreadful has happened to Mr. Underwood."

"Brent?" Claire gasped, grabbing Ellie's shoulder for support.

"He's in the hospital. He's had a heart attack. I guess it's pretty serious, Claire," Ellie babbled, following Claire into the house. "Your secretary sounded so upset I couldn't make sense of what she was saying. She's at the gallery...."

"Okay, okay," Claire told her, heading for the phone. Half an hour later, she had packed her bags, having made a reservation on the first plane out of Lakeport. An hour and a half later, she was in the air, flying toward New York.

Two hours after Claire left, King phoned the Parmeter house. The situation at the hospital had stabilized to the point that he actually could take the rest of the afternoon off for himself. It was a perfect summer day, an ideal time to take Claire out to Baskin's Beach and give her a Windsurfing lesson. Not only did he have enough time for this, he yearned to get out on the lake himself. Then maybe they could finally discuss the many things he knew they had to confront.

When Ellie told him Claire was on her way to New York, King did not believe what he was hearing. Ellie blurted something about someone in the art gallery having suddenly taken sick, but this made no sense, either.

The only thing that made sense to King was that Claire had known damned well the moment was at hand when they had to face up to the past—and to the present and future, too. And, with that moment of truth at hand, she had once again walked out on him.

King slammed down the receiver after a muttered, "Thanks, Ellie. Goodbye." He faced a choice, he knew: go back to the hospital and plunge himself into work or get thoroughly, totally, drunk.

A bitterness King hadn't felt for many years crept through him insidiously as he made his decision in favor of the hospital.

# CHAPTER EIGHTEEN

BRENT SAID FIRMLY, "It was just a warning. Nothing more."

He was lying on a couch in his Beekman Place apartment overlooking the East River, wearing a paisley satin dressing gown, into the front of which he'd tucked the ends of a flowing yellow ascot. Claire decided he looked like a Shakespearean actor, resting after having given the most successful performance of his career.

Not that Brent's heart attack had been a performance. At first, it had been frighteningly real and very ominous. But Brent was right. In actuality it had been a relatively small incident, a warning.

"Not even any restrictions," Brent said. "Perhaps to cut down a bit on my Scotch consumption," he added wryly. "To tell you the truth, I'm wondering if it wasn't food poisoning. I'd been at a luncheon given by one of our eminent art critics. He served an elaborate shrimp concoction so camouflaged with sherry and various herbs and spices one couldn't even taste the shrimp!"

"Brent," Claire said, "don't be ridiculous. It makes common sense to accept the fact that you're going to have to take life easier."

"I couldn't," Brent murmured.

"What's that supposed to mean?"

"It means my life is more than easy enough as it is," he said. "My family left me independently wealthy. I've never *had* to work." He smiled faintly. "I've given my all to Bailey Galleries because I wanted to. I love art, I love acquiring wonderful things. Oh, what the hell, Claire," he finished impatiently. "You know what I'm saying."

"Yes, I know what you're saying," she agreed. "And no one's suggesting that you should retire—"

"Retire?" Brent interrupted, aghast. "My God, that's a word that should be stricken from the language!"

"Some people spend lifetimes working so they can look forward to retirement," Claire pointed out.

"Well, bully for them," Brent retorted. "Perhaps I've never worked enough. Whatever—"

"Brent, why don't you go down to Siesta Key and get away from everything for a few weeks?" Claire suggested.

"Florida in July?" Brent was properly horrified. "My dear, I would broil."

"The beach house is air conditioned."

"Even so..."

"You never want to leave Manhattan, do you, Brent?"

"Not really," he admitted. He pointed over Claire's shoulder to the river view visible through a wide picture window. A tugboat was pulling a caravan of barges against the current. Brent said, "This is my city. I know all her evils and all her virtues. I love her in all her many guises. I like the faces she wears. I love the hype, too, Claire."

"So do I," she said. "But not, I realize, as you do."

Brent's gaze was speculative. "You could live happily away from New York, couldn't you?" he asked.

"Perhaps. It would depend on so many things."

"That man is still in your system, Claire."

She sighed. "You're right, of course." There was no point in hedging with Brent about King. King was very much in her system.

At first she had intended to telephone King and explain what had happened to take her away from Lakeport so precipitately. But, as each day passed and—in Brent's absence—she was called upon to handle so many details involving gallery business, it had become more and more difficult to make that phone call.

She started a letter to King at least a dozen times. But when it came to putting her heart on paper words failed her.

She knew that only a face-to-face confrontation would do. She and King needed some time and space in which to tell each other everything.

But the days went by, and they were busy days. With Brent convalescing, Claire spent long hours at the gallery, but King was never far from her thoughts. And with the passage of time Claire became increasingly convinced that King's total lack of communication proved he had no room for her in his life.

Alone in her apartment at night, her hand strayed toward the phone more than once in the course of each evening. But she never dialed his number. For one thing, chances were his father would answer the phone, not King.

Claire did call Ellie regularly. And Ellie always had a lot to report, but hardly a word involved King. At the most, King was mentioned in passing. Ellie was very busy with her own affairs, and they centered primarily around Bill. She even told Claire, ecstatically, that she and Bill were setting their wedding date.

"Right after Labor Day, I think," she said one night. "It's going to be a very small wedding in the Episcopal

Church chapel. Afterward, we're going back to Bill's house for a little buffet. Stella's going to arrange that. She'll be taking off for Arizona a few days after the wedding. Bill and I are going up to Montreal for a brief honeymoon, because I have to get back and finish getting things ready for the auction.''

They had agreed, after tossing the subject back and forth, that the sensible course was to get an auctioneer and dispose of the house contents at one giant sale. ''Except for the things we both want to keep for ourselves,'' Ellie had added.

Strangely, there was only one object Claire could think of that she wanted for her own, and it was not a family heirloom. It was her redheaded doll, Jewel, who for so long had presided in the little house at the end of the garden. Claire couldn't have said exactly why she wanted Jewel. She knew only it was for intensely personal reasons. In fact, she was afraid Ellie would laugh when she told her she wanted the doll. But Ellie didn't.

''Most of what I really want is for my own sentimental reasons,'' Ellie said. ''Aunt Delia's piano. I *would* like to have that. I'd like to get back to music, one of these days. To play, for once in my life, just because I'd like to play.'' Ellie paused, then added, ''We're going to divide the proceeds, Claire.''

''Absolutely not,'' Claire insisted. ''The proceeds from the auction will be a wedding gift to you.''

Ellie began to protest, but Claire had the last word. ''For once I'm going to settle a family matter my way.''

When the wedding date was set, finally, for the Saturday after Labor Day, Ellie called one night and asked Claire to be her matron of honor.

''I can't get married without you,'' she said simply.

By this time, Brent had returned to work at the gallery, with his doctor's approval. For the first time since she arrived in Manhattan, Claire felt free to leave New York for a few days. Nevertheless, she felt very awkward about going back to Lakeport. If King had only gotten in touch with her, it would have been different. It had been up to her, in a sense, to get in touch with him first, but he knew better than anyone how difficult he could be to reach when he was following an especially busy schedule, as he evidently had been, ever since the explosion at Chris's plant.

August passed, and Claire flew to Lakeport the day before the wedding. Ellie and Bill met her at the airport, and Claire would not have believed her cousin could look so radiant.

That night, friends of Bill's entertained the wedding couple and Claire at a small dinner. Claire realized that Bill and King evidently didn't travel in the same circles, but she had half hoped, half expected he would be included on this occasion. He wasn't present, though. And her letdown, once she realized he was not going to appear, was tremendous.

Ellie had asked Claire to select her wedding outfit in New York and Claire had agreed eagerly, insisting this be a wedding present. Ellie hadn't wanted to wear white, so Claire had chosen a simple dress in a luscious coffee-and-cream shade. A designer she knew had whipped up a matching headdress for Ellie, combining velvet flowers, bits of lace and wisps of veil into an astonishingly lovely creation. The only thing Claire hadn't bought for Ellie's wedding outfit was her shoes. Ellie, laughingly, agreed she should handle that on her own, and had bought slim, medium-heeled satin sandals, dyed to match her gown from a swatch of fabric Claire had sent her.

Claire chose a pale amethyst dress for herself, with matching accessories. As the two cousins dressed, the morning of the wedding, Claire couldn't help but recall that long-ago day when, had she not strayed down to the dollhouse at the end of the garden, she would have been standing in this same room, slipping on the beautiful gown that had belonged to their great-grandmother. There was no way Ellie could have worn that gown. She had admitted freely that if she starved for a year she still wouldn't be able to get into it.

The wedding was simple and lovely. Stella had out-done herself at the reception that followed. The bride and groom could not have been happier. And Claire was happy for them, but a deep ache remained in her heart. An ache that refused to go away.

She knew, now, why King wasn't at the wedding, and wouldn't be at the reception. She had asked Ellie about King the night before, as they were getting ready for bed. And Ellie had looked at her in genuine surprise and answered, "Didn't you know? King's off in Europe some-where."

Claire had stood stock-still, trying to digest this. Ellie, frowning, said, "I think it's Stockholm, or maybe Oslo. Some sort of international convention for surgeons, anyway. King was asked to attend and decided to go for it. As his father pointed out, it's been years since King's had any sort of vacation, and this was a good chance to combine business and pleasure."

Ellie added thoughtfully, "I can't believe he went off without telling you he was going."

Claire said hastily, "He probably meant to, and didn't have time. We . . . we've been kind of out of touch lately, Ellie."

That was the understatement of the year. And Claire knew very well that it would not have satisfied her cousin had she not been so preoccupied with her own much happier affairs.

There was no chance to talk about King the morning of Ellie's wedding. Certainly no chance to talk about him at the reception. Then Ellie and Bill rode away from the Edgerly house in a car bedecked with white ribbons and a Just Married sign and trailing tin cans, while their friends pelted them with rice. As they turned the corner Claire looked away, feeling strangely cold and forlorn, happy though she was for her cousin.

Shortly afterward she took her leave, but didn't go directly home. She drove to the hospital, having learned from a mutual acquaintance at the reception that Chris Talmadge was still a patient.

She found Chris in a solarium on the second floor, sitting in a wheelchair, his leg propped in front of him. Though he looked a thousand times better than he had the last time she'd seen him, Claire observed that his face was very thin and shadows of pain still etched his eyes.

He was so happy to see her, though, that Claire was glad she'd yielded to the impulse to pay him a visit. They discussed his health and though he assured her he was doing very well, he said he still had a long hospital stay ahead. He was somewhat depressed about his business affairs: there was still insurance to be settled, and he had no idea what the future might hold. Then, though Claire had intended to concentrate solely on Chris, he switched the subject to King.

"What the hell did you do to him, Claire?" he asked simply.

Claire had no answer and her face mirrored her bewilderment. "That's exactly it," she confessed. "I didn't do anything to him, Chris."

"Well, King changed from one day to the next," Chris insisted. "He'd come a long way out of his shell, but I actually watched him withdraw back into it, retreating further than ever. Every time I asked him about you, he changed the subject. Ellie came out to see me—she's been great, incidentally, both she and Bill. I only wish I could have gotten to their wedding. Anyway, Ellie came out to see me and I asked her about you. She told me about your associate having a coronary, and how you had to go back to New York on the spur of the moment...." Chris paused, frowning. "Certainly she must have told King the same thing?"

"I don't know," Claire admitted. "I honestly don't know."

It was crazy to think that the last time she'd seen King she had been suspended somewhere between sleep and wakefulness, dreamily aware that he had taken her on a voyage to paradise. After that predawn encounter, they had spoken on the phone a few times, but each time they had been interrupted by King's insistent beeper. He'd had to tear himself away, promising he'd call back as soon as he could.

At first, she'd waited by the phone for a return call. Then she realized she was being foolish, because there were few emergencies in King's field that could be dealt with swiftly. Finally, she'd gone to see Chris, hoping she'd meet King face-to-face in the hospital. When that hadn't happened, she gone home to find Ellie waiting for her with the bad news about Brent.

Claire had not intended to inflict any of this upon Chris. But she began telling him about it, and then about the night of the explosion when Rosalie Brenner had approached her in the emergency room waiting area.

When she finished, the last of the words she needed so desperately to get out of her system tumbling forth, Chris shook his head. Then his mouth turned up in a smile.

"You and King are my two favorite people," he confessed. "But, Lord, you're both blockheads!"

Then he added, "Can't you see, Claire? King must have thought you walked out on him, just as you did fourteen years ago."

It was unthinkable. "How could he possibly believe such a thing?" Claire demanded.

Chris's smile was bittersweet. "People don't always think straight when they're in love," he told her. "They do stupid things, make ghastly mistakes."

Claire shook her head. "If King's faith in me is so fragile, there's no chance for us," she said.

"Come on, Claire," Chris protested. "You don't know what you're saying."

"Yes, I do. Love's fine, passion's fine, but there also has to be faith and trust. King's a doctor. He'd know better than most people how everything just leaves your mind when someone close suffers something like a heart attack. You're caught up in their welfare, concerned about nothing else."

Chris held up an imploring hand. "Look," he urged. "Don't judge King too harshly. At least give him another chance."

Claire surveyed him sadly. "What other chance is there to give him?"

LIKE BRENT UNDERWOOD, Claire did not consider Florida the best place to visit other than during the winter or early spring. But in mid-October, it became imperative for her to fly to Sarasota, to deal with some matters at the gallery on Siesta Key.

Claire rented a car at the airport and drove directly to the beach cottage she owned off Midnight Pass Road. The house fronted a magnificent white beach on the Gulf of Mexico. Behind it, stretching to the road, was a thickly tangled grove of palms and other lush tropical trees and bushes. The place was a sanctuary for Claire, an oasis. And as she unlocked the door, stepped inside and quickly switched on the air conditioner, she felt she'd never needed a retreat more than she did right now.

She'd left Lakeport the day after her conversation with Chris. Since, she'd been on the phone frequently with Ellie, who was imploring her, primarily, to come back for the auction.

"I don't want to let them sell anything you might want," Ellie insisted.

Claire, on the verge of telling her cousin yet again that she wanted nothing at all, bit her tongue. She said, compromising, "You know my taste, Ellie. Just pick out a few things you'd like me to have and let the rest go."

"King's been around and he bought the rest of the pewter," Ellie said suddenly.

Claire's heart flipped, hearing this. She'd imagined King wouldn't be paying any more visits to the Parmeter house, wouldn't want to, for any reason.

"We've had an excellent offer for the house," Ellie continued. "The realtor called this morning, and Bill's going to get in touch with Thomas. I don't think Thomas is going to hold out. I think he's as anxious to get things settled as I am. Claire, I really want to get on with my own life with Bill. There are so many things we both want to do. I want to fix up his house, for one. Not much has been done there for years, and he's giving me a free hand..."

Ellie babbled on happily and Claire listened patiently. But when the conversation was over, she dwelled only on the fact that King Faraday had gotten back from his Scandinavian safari and still had not bothered to get in touch with her.

On her first afternoon in Siesta Key, Claire postponed her visit to the gallery and gave herself time to take a swim in the gulf. The water was warm and wonderfully soothing. She felt considerably more relaxed by the time she returned to the house, slipped on a cool dress and then drove over to the gallery, located in tiny Siesta Village.

The gallery was managed by Eleanor Whittington, a charming, middle-aged woman who had been an art critic for an area newspaper for years and had published several books on the subject. Eleanor's value, Claire had long conceded, was beyond measure. And, like Brent, Eleanor worked not because she needed to, but because she loved what she was doing.

They conferred, that night, in a Spanish restaurant that offered casual seclusion and excellent food. Eleanor's concerns involved acquisitions, primarily. She had the chance to acquire some paintings she thought would be excellent values, but she wanted to be sure Claire was willing to extend the gallery budget far enough to cover her purchases.

Some of the paintings she was interested in came from private collections, but most were the work of promising local artists. There was one young man, in particular, in whom Eleanor had great faith.

"I think he's going to go places, just as Paul Hayes did in Provincetown not so long ago," Eleanor opined, sipping an after-dinner liqueur. "I have a Hayes original I bought at an art show three summers ago—I could sell it today for ten times what I paid. That's what happens when an artist is really good." Eleanor smiled apologetically. "Claire, why am I telling you things you already know?"

"Eleanor, I love your enthusiasm," Claire said quickly. She didn't add that Eleanor could have discussed this with her over the phone and saved her the off-season trip to Florida. She had implicit faith in Eleanor's judgment and would have okayed the budget increase on her recommendation alone.

"Look," she continued, "if you have faith in this young man, go for it." She finished her cappuccino and said, "Now, if you'll excuse me for tonight, I think I'm going to go home and get some sleep. Maybe it's the climate that's relaxing me, or maybe it's jet lag...though I've never heard of anyone getting jet lag on a trip from New York to Florida," she admitted, smiling.

She was bone-tired though, and was glad the drive from Siesta Village to her beach house took only a few minutes. She swung into her driveway, her headlights shining on the yellow hibiscus flowers that bordered each side. Then the lights touched something else. Metal glinted, and she realized there was a car parked to one side of her front door.

Claire did not frighten easily. Nevertheless, very few people knew of this oasis of hers, so the thought occurred that maybe someone—knowing the owner was absent most of the time—had been taking advantage of that fact, and using her premises.

She dismissed this notion as quickly as it came to her, remembering that there'd been no sign of any recent occupation in the house when she'd arrived that afternoon.

Eleanor had come over early and turned on the fridge, then stocked it with milk and orange juice. And she'd left a few other essentials on the kitchen counter. The air conditioner she'd left off, because she'd not known exactly when Claire would arrive, but the beds had been freshly made by the girl Eleanor hired for occasional day work when Claire was in residence.

Maybe the cleaning girl had forgotten something? Maybe she'd come back because of that? At ten o'clock at night? Claire got out of her car and advanced toward the front door, wishing she'd thought to bring a flashlight.

She passed close to the strange car and, glancing inside, saw it was empty. At that moment, the moon edged out from behind a cloud, splashing the scene with pale silver. There was no one around the house that Claire could see. No lurking strangers. No one hiding behind the bushes.

Puzzled, she let herself in the front door and, though she couldn't have defined why, she didn't turn on any lights. Instead, she moved over to the big front window that looked out on the gulf... and saw the silhouette of a man, etched by the moonlight, walking slowly along the water's edge.

Claire didn't have to be told who that man was. She knew instinctively. And, knowing, she went completely weak.

Invisible wings became attached to her feet and she flew out the side door. Then, guided by the glimmering moonlit gulf, she ran down the narrow path to the beach and sped across the sand.

King turned to face her and, even from this distance, Claire could sense his wariness. His posture was tense as he stood, statuelike, his arms stiff at his sides. But that didn't matter, either. She flung her arms around his neck and, after a moment so intense she thought she would burst, he reached to enfold her in his embrace.

They kissed, their mouths parched with desire. They were two people dying of thirst for each other, seeking love's sustenance. The moonlight turned King's gold hair to silver and colored his face with surreal pale light. By contrast, his eyes were as dark as the distant gulf waters...and almost as remote, Claire feared, until she looked into them more deeply.

Slowly, disbelievingly, she said, "You followed me! You found out where I was and you followed me."

"Yes," King told her, his voice husky. "You're damned right I found out where you were and followed you. About time...wouldn't you say?"

Claire couldn't answer, because she was starting to cry. The sobs wracked her body, her shoulders shook, and King drew her closer. "Dearest, lovely Claire," he whispered tenderly. "There aren't going to be any more mistakes between us. No more foolish misunderstandings." He paused and, with a loving finger, brushed the tears from her moistened cheeks. Cradling her head gently in his strong hands, he added softly, "We both have to grow up now and stop torturing each other."

Claire's sobs subsided and, reaching up and touching his face, she said shakily, "I can't believe you're really here."

"I'm here," King said. "And I'm staying until we've said everything, until we've covered every fact and every feeling."

"And then?"

"And then we'll face whatever comes next," King temporized.

He nudged her closer against him and, with his arm around her shoulders, they began to walk along the beach. After a moment he said, "I want to take my shoes off. I want to feel the sand."

"Me, too," Claire breathed, feeling more relaxed with every passing second.

King took their shoes and tossed them high above the tidemark, and Claire giggled. "You're quite good at getting rid of surplus clothes on beaches, you know."

"I should have been better," King mused sadly. "I should have gotten rid of many superfluous things a long time ago, Claire. Chris was right—"

"Right?"

"I know he told you about my thinking you'd left me again when you went back to New York, and...I did think that. Somehow our signals got mixed up. I was so damned busy, worried sick about Chris, caught up with a number of other patients, as well. Wrapped up in myself, my career. Too wrapped up..."

"Surgeons have to be wrapped up in their careers," Claire said gently. "You're dealing with life and death. You have no choice."

"I agree," King said, "but only to a point. My problem was compounded by the fact that, a long time ago, I conditioned myself to always put my career and myself first. I really believed I had to, just to survive. Because, a long time ago, I'd been willing to live my life for someone else..."

"And she deserted you," Claire finished softly.

"Yes. And now I know why she deserted me. Chris told me about Rosalie...about your learning, finally, that she was not carrying my child. Not carrying any man's child, at that point."

King paused and looked down at Claire, his face bathed in shadows. He murmured, "It hurt like hell . . . hearing that from Chris. It hurt like hell to think you left me on our wedding day because you thought I'd been sleeping with another girl and had gotten her pregnant. Even after all these years, that hurt so damned much that I—"

He broke off and sighed heavily. "Finally I convinced myself I was a fool," King said. "I told you, remember, that we should close the door to the past and lock it, once and for all. Then slowly I realized I couldn't do that, not until I knew the answer to the question that had been haunting me, plaguing me, all these years. *Why?*"

The word echoed between them and King shook his head. "I'd learned to live without knowing why, Claire. But when you'd come back into my life, I recognized the question for the obstacle it would always be between us. And then...unexpectedly, actually...Chris answered it. And I wished he'd left me ignorant.

"I was an idiot, Claire. You were only twenty, for God's sake, a very inexperienced twenty. And though I'd done my share of playing around when you get down to the essentials I was pretty naive myself. What happened fourteen years ago happened to a couple of kids. The same people, but two different people. Do you know what I mean?"

"Yes," Claire managed, her voice a husky whisper. "Yes, I know what you mean."

King laughed softly and Claire knew he was laughing at himself.

"I was going to invent a couple of stories to tell you when I got down here," he admitted. "I was going to tell you Dad wanted me to come down and check out a condo he's interested in buying over on Longboat Key, which is not entirely untrue. A couple of his old colleagues have purchased homes there, and the prospect of Florida winters are beginning to look pretty good to Dad. So I was going to use that as my excuse for being here, until I told myself my real reason was so much more valid. I had to see you, Claire. I had to face you. I needed you to help burn our bridges, so we can go on from here.''

King shook his head. ''I'm saying all this very badly. Am I making any sense at all?''

Claire said unsteadily, ''I've never heard anyone make better sense.''

For a moment they walked on in silence. Then King released his embrace and turned to face her. ''There's something else,'' he said. ''The Parmeter house.''

''What about the house?''

''I'm the person who's made the bid Ellie told you about,'' King confessed.

''You!'' Claire blurted, shocked. ''But Ellie never said—''

''Ellie didn't know,'' King said patiently. ''I asked the realtor to keep my name a secret until we got down to specifics. It's a beautiful house, Claire. We could make it more of a mansion that it ever was. Dad, I know, is going to want to sell our place if he opts for a condo down here....''

*Had King said "we"?* Claire asked silently, her emotions whirling.

''Claire, I know there are all sorts of things to work out. You have your career, and God knows I have mine. I can't give my work up, and I'm not asking you to give up yours. I suppose I'm asking for a compromise. Believe me when I say I'm willing to meet you more than halfway, because...I love you, Claire. I love you so much more than ever before.''

Claire trembled wonderfully, joyfully, the ecstasy of King's words overwhelming her with emotion. She'd wanted to hear those words so badly, yearned so desperately for King to tell her he loved her.

He stared down at her, his eyes caressing hers. "You've been letting me do all the talking, darling," he said shakily, his own emotions surfacing. "Aren't you going to say a thing?"

Claire moved against his chest and pulled him close. "Once I start talking," she whispered, "I may very well talk all night." She hesitated because there was still such an unreality to saying these things to King. Still the lovely unreality of his even being here, in her arms.

"I've been lost from the moment I met you again," she told him. "And now you've found me, and I'm not about to let you go." She kissed King passionately and felt his instant response.

"We will work things out, my love, because we must," Claire went on. "I...I can be flexible. We know what we want, above all else. We want each other."

They kissed again, their tensions and emotions released like cascading snow water in spring. For a time they were absorbed only in each other. Then Claire said, "You've boggled my mind with your idea about buying my family homestead. Yet when I think about making the house as beautiful as it once was, I admit it's a challenge. Quite a lovely challenge, actually. And..."

"Yes?" King urged.

"Well, except for mountain climbing, I've always loved a good challenge."

"Really?" King queried, beginning to breathe normally again. He looked out at the moon sprinkled gulf water and said, "I dare you!"

Claire ran past him, splashing through the shallows. And as King caught up with her they fell into the gentle waves, tasting the warm salt as they kissed. King's hands fumbled with Claire's clothing, and this time she helped him. Handing King the dripping garments, she teased, "Another famous toss, Dr. Faraday?"

King shook his head. "I can replace these later," he told her. "So . . . let the tide take over. My mind's on the rest of you."

They rocked together, tumbling through the waves, touching in every intimate way then being forced apart until, in the wet warm gulf, their bodies meshed feverishly as they began yet another sensuous voyage toward the ultimate. As her passion mounted to match King's, Claire moaned breathlessly, "My old love, my new love. My forever promise."

"What?" King asked, then sealed her mouth with his before she could repeat those words. But there would be time enough to tell him later, Claire knew. Time enough to tell him that long ago they'd made a promise. A promise as forever as their love.

## AND, ON CHRISTMAS EVE...

THE HOSPITAL CHAPEL WAS FILLED with red poinsettias. The beautiful flowers also decorated the small conference room nearby, a room usually reserved for meetings of Lakeport General Hospital's board of trustees.

Christopher Talmadge carefully navigated the distance between the chapel—where he'd just acted as King Faraday's best man—and the boardroom where the wedding reception was being held. Spying a chair, Chris gratefully lowered himself onto it and set his crutches aside.

Claire frowned as she watched him and whispered anxiously to her new husband, "King, I'm worried about Chris. He looks exhausted."

"I'm sure he is exhausted," King agreed. He gave his best man a quick, professional scrutiny then continued, "But it's a positive exhaustion. Chris has a way to go, but thank God he's on his way. He's going to an orthopedic rehab center for a few weeks to get used to handling that bad leg, then I think he should take a long holiday someplace where it's warm. After that..." King paused. "Speaking of holidays and warm places," he murmured, "we do have a plane to catch if we're going to make it to Martinique for Christmas. How about cutting that wedding cake so we can get out of here?"

Claire smiled. She was as eager as he was to slip away, to start the honeymoon that would guarantee them ten golden days away from the sounds of telephones and hospital beepers. Ten days when they could get to know each other all over again. They didn't *need* to get to know each other all over again, but it was a lovely thought.

Claire teased, "You sound ... anxious, darling."

"I'm anxious as hell," King growled in her ear. "And if you don't oblige me soon, woman, I'm going to carry you off to one of those cubicles staff members use for napping ... and ravish you!"

"Exploratory surgery?" Claire asked archly.

"You'd better believe it!" King threatened, then burst out laughing.

The sound of his laughter made bells ring for Claire ... bells even sweeter than the wedding bells ringing in her head ever since she and Ellie and Bill Edgerly had left the Edgerly house to meet King here at the hospital. Wedding bells, of course, couldn't ring out in a hospital. But it had been far more important to be married in a place where Chris Talmadge could be involved in the ceremony than to traipse down a traditional aisle.

Chris was one of two people who had mentioned that long, long delay in Claire and King's wedding plans. "I've waited fourteen and a half years for this," he told Claire.

The other person who mentioned the fateful time gap—an interlude no one would have guessed could have such an incredibly happy ending—was King's father, Dr. George Faraday.

Just before the ceremony began, Dr. Faraday found the chance to take Claire aside. His eyes were glowing as he said, "May I be trite, Claire, and say I think this is the happiest day of my life?" There was a touch of moisture in those blue eyes as he continued, "I've waited a long time for you to be my daughter-in-law. But it's been worth it, Claire. There never could be anyone else for King.''

At that point, Claire's happiness was so intense she was giddy from the wonder of it. She threw her arms around King's father and kissed him soundly, just before the strain of the wedding march—played on a portable stereo someone had borrowed for the occasion—began to peal through the little chapel.

Now Claire felt King's hand on her elbow. He nudged her forward and she said, ''I get the message, doctor.'' She moved toward the table where a tiered wedding cake, ornamented with miniature poinsettias, beckoned.

This was a Christmas Eve wedding. A marriage at a time of ultimate joy. Claire, who had shied away from a traditional all-white ceremony, had asked for this splash of color on her cake.

She was wearing ivory satin, her satin shoes were piped with red and the roses in her corsage almost exactly matched the poinsettias. She was a beautiful bride, unconscious of just how lovely she was as she picked up the long silver knife, tied with a garland of red and white ribbons.

She plunged the knife into the cake and fed a morsel of the first slice to King. Then she placed a piece of cake on a paper plate and took it to Chris. Standing over him, she ordered, ''Open your mouth.''

There was a shaky edge to Chris's smile, but he complied. Claire wedged a crumbling bit of cake into his mouth, then bent down, gave him a hug and kissed his cheek. She said, close to his ear, ''Next time we have one of these affairs, King's going to be your best man!''

Chris didn't answer and Claire briefly wished she could bite the words back. Of late, King had spent a lot of time with his best friend and had relayed Chris's discouragement because, though the rest of his injuries had healed very well, there were still problems with his left leg—and probably always would be.

"It's hard to think of Chris being crippled," King had admitted to Claire gloomily, casting aside his usual habit of being clinical about medical conditions.

"Chris will make out," Claire had insisted, and was sure he would.

Still her comment now had not been the most tactful one in the world. She gave Chris another hug. There was a smudge of icing on his mouth as he smiled. He said, in a voice so low that only Claire could hear him, "I don't know how I can ever thank you guys. Who else would get married in a hospital for the sake of someone else?"

"We got married here just as much for ourselves as for you," Claire told him. "I'd say it's pretty symbolic, wouldn't you, seeing that the hospital plays such an important role in King's life? Anyway, you had to be at our wedding, Chris." Tears misted her eyes and she turned away before she embarrassed Chris by becoming too emotional.

Almost at once, she saw Ellie waving to her frantically. Puzzled, she turned the balance of the cake cutting over to Eleanor Whittington—who had come up from the Siesta Key gallery for the wedding—and went quickly to Ellie's side.

Ellie was already making for the side door. Over her shoulder, she whispered urgently, "I think I'm going to be sick, Claire. Please . . . come to the ladies' room with me."

Ellie did look pale. Pale, but lovely. She hadn't lost any weight since her marriage to Bill Edgerly, but she was paying much more attention to her grooming, makeup and clothes.

"What is it?" Claire asked anxiously.

Ellie stopped short, drew a long breath then laughed shakily. "I think I'm okay... for now, anyway," she decided.

"Ellie, what's the matter with you?"

A bit of color crept back into Ellie's cheeks and her eyes became radiant. "I'm pregnant," she announced jubilantly.

"You're *what*?"

"Pregnant, Claire," Ellie bubbled. "You know...with child. Isn't it terrific? Bill and I didn't want to wait. I'm not exactly young anymore...."

Claire laughed. "You're young enough, obviously." The thought crossed her mind that she, too, was young enough. Even so, she couldn't see children in her and King's future. Not yet, anyway. Not until they'd given each other some special months to adjust to their life as a married couple.

She knew she was the one making most of the adjustments, but as she'd told King on the beach at Siesta Key, it was possible for her to be flexible, more so than it was for him. This meant allotting more responsibility for the galleries to Eleanor and Brent, and she'd already put that concept into effect, making them both partners in her business. This was definitely a step in the right direction, she knew, even if she and King hadn't decided to get married.

Claire would remain at the helm, as far as the business was concerned. This would mean spending every other week in New York—except during the summer months when business was slow—and occasional peak-season winter weeks on Siesta Key. King already had agreed that he would—somehow, someway—take time off from his

work at the hospital for one or two of those Florida so-
journs.

Slowly, they were adjusting to the demands of their
respective careers. To each other, they'd adjusted perfectly.

Children? Maybe, Claire thought. Maybe, later on . . .

Meantime, she hugged her cousin. "Ellie, that's wonderful," she said, her voice choked with emotion. After
so many prime years of giving up her life to others, Ellie
Parmeter Edgerly was finally coming into her own.

As the two cousins walked back together toward the
room where the reception was being held, Ellie confessed, "I do get these little spells of queasiness every so
often."

Claire laughed. "As I understand it, that's par for the
course for most women."

"I guess it is."

Just inside the door, Brent intercepted Claire.

"May I steal you for a moment?" he pleaded. "Before King puts you on his white horse and vaults up into
the clouds?"

Brent was wearing a black velvet jacket, black and gray
pinstriped slacks, and had a red carnation in his button-
hole. As usual, he looked resplendent, elegant and ultra-
sophisticated.

Claire couldn't help smiling. Should Brent decide to
take a stroll down Lakeport's Main Street, he'd really
stand out!

Drawing her away from the party and into the corridor again, Brent said, "Darling, there's something I must
say to you."

"Oh?"

"Your husband is terrific," Brent stated. "Being with
the two of you at dinner last night effected my conver-

sion to his side. Then, when I saw the way he was looking at you while you were taking your wedding vows, I
came closer to blubbering than I have in many a year. The
man's insane about you, Claire.''

"I hope so," Claire managed.

"I know so," Brent told her, summoning all of the
considerable authority with which he could make a pro-
nouncement. "By the way, have you wondered about
your wedding present from me?"

This was the last thing on Claire's mind, and she
looked at Brent quizzically.

"I'm giving you one of the Monets, darling," he said,
breathlessly excited himself.

*"What?"*

"I thought you might want to postpone the delivery
until you've finished with your renovations," Brent
continued airily. "It occurred to me you'd probably prefer having it here in Lakeport rather than in your New
York apartment. You will, of course, have to find the
exactly perfect place for it to hang."

Claire was staring at him and shaking her head deter-
minedly. "No way, Brent," she urged. "You can't give
us a wedding gift like that. A Monet, for God's sake?"

"Who could enjoy such a painting better than you?"
Brent asked affectionately. "And your husband. While
we were chatting last night he confided to me that Monet's his favorite artist, too." Brent took a deep breath,
then quipped, "Anyway, it's yours . . . or I quit!"

Claire was at a complete loss for words. Finally, she
managed, "You told King about this?"

"No, no," Brent said quickly. "I was sure he'd protest, just as you are. It's up to you to convince him, darling, that I'm not bankrupting myself by giving you both
something I want to give you. Far from it, as you know.

Now...do you suppose we could have a glass of champagne together before you go off?''

Claire and King sipped champagne with their well-wishers and joked and laughed as best they could. But they were both getting increasingly edgy. Finally King announced, "This is *it*, Mrs. Faraday," and grabbing her arm he literally pulled her toward the door. Luckily, everyone was ready for their escape and doused them with rice as they ran down the hospital corridor.

Two nurses were waiting at the hospital entrance with their coats, which King and Claire donned quickly. As they climbed into the waiting taxi before heading to the airport, King said, "I doubt Lakeport General's ever seen anything like this before, or ever will again."

"Oh, I don't know," Claire answered. "I should think it's a perfect place for a doctor's wedding. If someone needs you, the page could put out a call, your beeper would buzz and..."

King clutched her shoulders, and swung Claire around to face him. "That for your bright ideas," he said, kissing one cheek. "And that for beepers," he added, kissing the other.

Before Claire could respond, King silenced her with a passionate kiss full on the mouth. A kiss that went on and on and on...until the taxi driver, sneaking a glance in his rearview mirror, wondered how two people could possibly hold their breaths so long.

# *Harlequin Superromance*

## COMING NEXT MONTH

**#238 TEMPTING FATE • Risa Kirk**
Reya Merrill thought that handling public relations
for the controversial Geneticon account would cinch
her promotion. But when Colin Hughes, owner of
the genetic research laboratories, defies her every
move, she loses her job...and her heart.

**#239 A DISTANT PROMISE • Debbie Bedford**
Advertising copywriter Emily Lattrell seemed to have
it all until she met handsome real-estate magnate
Philip Manning. Almost overnight she quit her job,
moved to a northern Texan farm and became
adopted mom to Philip's nephew and two nieces.
Now she'd truly have it all...if she could learn to
accept Philip's love.

**#240 SEASON OF MIRACLES • Emilie Richards**
Schoolteacher Elise Ramsey had chosen duty over
love once. Then, in the middle of her life, she was
offered another opportunity to find joy in the strong
arms of Sloane Tyson. Her first lover. The boy was
gone forever, replaced by a man impossible to deny.

**#241 GYPSY FIRE • Sara Orwig**
After star witnesses Jake and Molly escape the
watchful eye of the Detriot police, they find
themselves holed up together in the Ozarks. Molly
can't bear Jake's workaholic lists and thirst for
success. But Jake discovers he can't bear to take his
eyes off Molly....

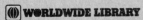

# ATTRACTIVE, SPACE SAVING BOOK RACK

Display your most prized novels on this handsome and sturdy book rack. The hand-rubbed walnut finish will blend into your library decor with quiet elegance, providing a practical organizer for your favorite hard-or soft-covered books.

**Only $9.95**

**Approximately 16" x 8" when assembled**

**Assembles in seconds!**

--------------------------------------------------

To order, rush your name, address and zip code, along with a check or money order for $10.70 ($9.95 plus 75¢ postage and handling) (New York residents add appropriate sales tax), payable to *Harlequin Reader Service* to:

In the U.S.

Harlequin Reader Service
Book Rack Offer
901 Fuhrmann Blvd.
P.O. Box 1325
Buffalo, NY 14269-1325

*Offer not available in Canada.*

BKR-1

# *Can you keep a secret?*

## You can keep this one plus 4 free novels

Don't miss a single title from this great collection. The first eight titles have already been published. Complete and mail this coupon today to order books you may have missed.

**Harlequin Reader Service**

*In U.S.A.*
901 Fuhrmann Blvd.
P.O. Box 1397
Buffalo, N.Y. 14140

*In Canada*
P.O. Box 2800
Postal Station A
5170 Yonge Street
Willowdale, Ont. M2N 6J3

Please send me the following titles from the Janet Dailey Americana Collection. I am enclosing a check or money order for $2.75 for each book ordered, plus 75¢ for postage and handling.

| | | |
|---|---|---|
| _____ | ALABAMA | Dangerous Masquerade |
| _____ | ALASKA | Northern Magic |
| _____ | ARIZONA | Sonora Sundown |
| _____ | ARKANSAS | Valley of the Vapours |
| _____ | CALIFORNIA | Fire and Ice |
| _____ | COLORADO | After the Storm |
| _____ | CONNECTICUT | Difficult Decision |
| _____ | DELAWARE | The Matchmakers |

Number of titles checked @ $2.75 each =          $_____

N.Y. RESIDENTS ADD
  APPROPRIATE SALES TAX                          $_____

Postage and Handling                            $\_\_\_.75\_\_\_

                              TOTAL             $_____

I enclose _____

(Please send check or money order. We cannot be responsible for cash sent through the mail.)

PLEASE PRINT

NAME _____

ADDRESS _____

CITY _____

STATE/PROV. _____